*For every student who missed their school
library during the pandemic*

# CHAPTER 1

I've never been stared at this much in my whole life.

That's not completely true – there was a time before this. But still, right now a substantial proportion of the students in the canteen seem to think it's OK to openly gawk at the new girl.

We find a table with three spare seats. I'm with a tall, serious-looking girl called Georgia, who's been assigned to show me round today because we have the same form tutor and timetable, and her friend Amber.

"Just so you know, Ruby," says Georgia, as she places her tray down. "You have a banned hair colour. That's why they're staring."

Dove-grey covers my natural blonde. "How's *grey* a banned colour?"

"When it looks too … noticeable," Georgia says. Her own long hair is dyed auburn at the ends. She's attractive in a big-eyed, fragile-featured way, and her black blazer looks as brand new as mine. She stops churning her kung pao chicken into the rice, holds her fork up and fixes me with an intense gaze. "How come you joined late, and in your GCSE year? It's a really rubbish time to move schools."

Like I don't know that. Everyone else started the school year at Robinson Academy two weeks ago, and it sucks. I snap my KitKat in two and eat one half. I brought a random selection of food with me from home today, in case my lunch card wasn't ready. The satsuma in front of me has greenish peel on one side. "House move," I say. "It was supposed to happen in the holidays."

Georgia nods. She's trying to work me out, and I bet the most likely options in her head are *attention seeker*, *awkward loser*, or *loner*. In each class there's been a seating plan. I've been put at the back of the class on my own, clearly a holding measure until the teachers can work out what sort of student I am and where I can be suitably placed in their ecosystem.

Being at the back of the classroom suits me fine. I like to observe people.

"Where've you moved from?" asks Amber. She's petite with short hair and dark eye make-up. The sleeves of her blazer are rolled up to just below the elbow.

"Out of the area," I say. Her narrow eyebrows stay raised. She wants more. I name a town not far from my old one. "My mum got a new job and she had to take it," I add. I eat a bite of KitKat, suddenly hungry. It's pretty much the truth. Mum's new job is far better paid than her last one and I'm pleased for her, but I hope she can manage it.

Amber nods. "So you don't know anyone in Barchester?"

I shake my head. She doesn't know what a relief that is. Georgia finishes her mouthful of chicken and says, "Amber and I have known each other since we were at the same preschool. Like, *years*." She looks at Amber expectantly.

Amber doesn't quite run with it. She nods, and says, "What d'you think of Robinson so far then, Ruby?"

I look around the noisy canteen. There's a slice of pizza sliding down a wall, rubbish under the tables, a couple of students having a fight in the lunch queue and the supervising member of staff is on her phone. "A bit crap, to be honest."

"Seriously?" says Amber with a faint air of surprise, as if she can't see what I can.

"It is," says Georgia. "But you get used to it, don't you, Amber?"

I eat my remaining KitKat. "It's pretty similar to my old school."

"Most people in our year are all right," Amber says. "There are different groups, like anywhere – we've got

3

the Sporty Lot, the Theatricals, the Weirdos, the Absolute Neeks and the Glossies —" She nods her head towards a table of girls laughing. "The Head Glossy is Naz. She's minted and thinks she's better than everyone else." I immediately work out who Naz is — tall and haughty with glossy black hair and enviable cheekbones.

"Then there are the Linesmen," continues Amber. She points to a noisy crowd at a table near us. Good-looking, with a lot more edge than the Glossies and the Sporty crew.

"Linesmen?" I repeat.

"Because it's Isaac Linesman's group," says Amber. "They're a sub-branch of the Sporty Lot. Some people find them amusing, but they're best avoided. That's Isaac," says Amber, as a tall, broad boy stands up with his tray. The other three get to their feet immediately. "And he has an on-off thing with Monique, the girl with the hoops."

I identify Monique, a girl with big earrings and blonde-brown hair piled on top of her head in a messy bun.

"We hate Monique," says Georgia. "She's vicious."

I watch as Isaac makes his way to the tray station. He walks slowly, as if he owns the canteen. The others follow, chatting, laughing. Walking past us, he turns to Monique and says loudly, "Who's that with the granny hair?"

"I don't know, but she should sue her hairdresser," she says. The whole bunch crack up.

Georgia shrinks and occupies herself with her phone,

and Amber carries on eating her panini.

My hand curls over my satsuma. I need to get my head down and pass my exams in this school. Otherwise, I might have thrown it at either Isaac or Monique.

Amber is looking at my hand, clenched around the fruit. "Ignore them. Your hair's kinda cool," she says. "Not my vibe, but it suits you."

"Thanks," I say. I take my planner out of my bag. Next period is English. I was warned before I came that I'd be studying different set texts to my old school. Three brand-new books are at the bottom of my bag, making it heavy. My phone is lit up with a message. A Snapchat from Luffy, telling me his brother has a court date.

I feel a pang of nostalgia. I miss Luffy. We would hang out behind the maintenance shed at my last school and he would share his endless political theories, which only worked on the premise that everyone in the world was as free-spirited and pacifist as him. I tell him to make sure his brother ditches the joggers for court. Then I take a sneaky selfie showing the Robinson logo on my school blazer: the initial R, a lion and the words *Together We Can*.

He replies with *Together we can what?* and I send back *Get mauled by a lion?*

As Georgia, Amber and I leave the canteen, we're stopped by a plump, thin-haired boy with a neon-green backpack. I have no problem picturing him in ten or twenty years' time.

"Time to buy your tickets for the Halloween disco,

raising money for performing arts." He looks me up and down, then holds out his hand. "I'm Scott. We haven't met. You're gorgeous!"

"Oh. Thanks?" I shake his hand. I've never heard the word *gorgeous* used in relation to me. "I'm Ruby Marshall."

Amber shakes her head slowly. She doesn't need to. I know he's hamming it up.

"Disco ticket, Ruby?" Mr Self-Confident holds up a wad of badly photocopied tickets. "Dressing up is compulsory."

"I'll pass, sorry," I say. "I'm not a fan of dressing up."

Scott gasps dramatically, recovers himself quickly and says, "It's *the* event of term. You'll want to be seen there. Amber will be covering it for the school newspaper."

School newspaper? That sounds cool. We didn't have one at my last school.

"Yeah, about that," says Amber. "I shouldn't have to pay for my ticket if I'm there as a reporter for the *Robinson Record*."

"Watch out!" says Georgia, as a crowd of raucous younger students comes careering towards us. She pulls Amber out of the way, leaving me standing there.

I don't move quickly enough and one of them, a short, muscly kid, slams hard into my shoulder. I use both hands to push him off me, and he ricochets into the opposite wall.

"Hey!" he yells. "What's your problem?"

"Haven't you heard of social distancing?" I shout. My

6

shoulder really hurts.

"Freak," mutters the boy. They move off down the corridor.

"You nearly sent him through the wall," says Amber. I can't tell if she's impressed or horrified.

"Weasels," says Scott, and I smile at that. "Anyway, if you change your mind, Ruby, come and find me in the performing arts office. I'm there most lunchtimes."

"Did you get my piece about Recycling Week?" asks Amber.

"Yeah, not gonna lie, I think it's one for the back page. We need a big story. Sorry. Better luck next time." He speed-walks off.

Amber makes a huffing sound. "He thinks he's editing a tabloid."

I shift my heavy bag on to my other shoulder. Georgia glances at her watch. "Come on, Ruby. We'll be late for English." She looks genuinely worried by the thought and sets off at speed. I have to jog a couple of paces to catch up with her.

"So that's Scott," she says, not breaking stride. "He's a massive gossip. Don't tell him anything." She glances at me. "Seriously."

English goes OK, until I'm asked to read out loud from *A Christmas Carol*. I stumble over the words. In my head they flow and make total sense, but out loud they become obstacles waiting to trip me up. Monique keeps up a low-voiced commentary with her neighbour about me, which the teacher either can't hear or ignores. I'm asked to stop before I finish the page. I keep my head low after that, distracted only by the light from Isaac Linesman's phone screen, which is propped up against his book. He's watching a film on mute.

After English, it's the end of the school day.

"The first buses can be crowded," Georgia tells me. "Better to wait a few minutes. I need to go. Maths tutor."

I watch her disappear, checking her phone as she walks purposefully, clutching her bag like a briefcase, as if she's off to a business meeting.

The crowds start to disperse. I need to head to my locker and get my coat. As I walk, I feel my phone vibrate with a call. It's my sister. I reject the call and realize I'm going in the wrong direction to the lockers. The school looks different when it's virtually empty. There are just a few people still in the corridor, making their way to clubs or waiting for friends.

When I reach my locker area, I see that there is something attached to one of the lockers. A piece of white paper.

It's my locker.

I move more quickly. I tug the paper free. There are five words written in capital letters in black felt-tip pen.

*I KNOW YOU DID IT.*

# CHAPTER 2

I slam the note on the kitchen counter in front of Mum.

"What's this?" she asks, halfway through taking off her coat. Her eye make-up is smudged as if she's rubbed her eyes at some point in the day.

"It was on my locker at the end of the day." Surely she understands the awful significance of the words. "Someone knows about me," I say.

Mum sits down on a chair, holding her coat on her lap, as if she's in a waiting room, and not in her own tiny kitchen-dining room after a day at her new job. She picks up the note and examines it. It still has the remains of Blu-Tack on the back where it was stuck to the metal of my locker.

"Ruby, someone's just trying their luck. It's a joke. You're ... what's the word? Catastrophizing." She had counselling a while back. She uses words like that now. "You need to put this in the bin and move on." She crumples up the note. "Now. Tell me about the rest of your day. Were there *some* good bits?"

"Not really, no," I say. I've been home forty-five minutes and done nothing more than sit in a deckchair in the living room. My grandparents are bringing over a second-hand sofa and chairs at the weekend to replace the ones my dad walked off with before we moved. Walked off with as in parked up outside the house with a man and a van and loaded up all the things he hadn't taken before, when he decided he wanted to pursue his music career without the distraction of his family. Our piano was picked up by specialist movers the same day. When I messaged him to ask why he'd turned our house into a freaking shell of a building, he replied, *Don't worry, Rubes. I've paid your mum her fifty per cent and your grandparents have spare furniture. When I make enough money from my music, you're getting your own piano.*

As if that's likely to happen.

"Well, it's only day one. It'll get better from here, I promise. You want a tea?" asks Mum. She's left her coat on the chair and is filling up the kettle. The note is still lying on the table, waiting for me to bin it.

I hate it when she makes ridiculous promises about things that are out of her control. And I don't believe the note is a joke. "Mum, what if someone at school really has found out?"

"They haven't. How could they?"

"But what if they have?"

Mum gives me her stern look. "Then we deal with it. It's behind you. It doesn't define you. Right, you need some tea." She reaches for two mugs, then pauses a moment. "You were four years old, for goodness' sake. *Four*, Ruby."

*Old enough to know what she was doing.* That's what Grandma said.

While she waits for the kettle to boil, Mum finds teabags and unscrews the lid of the milk, giving it a quick sniff. Always off-putting. I watch her, her shoulders slumped all of a sudden. The upside of having to move for her new job, even though the timing sucks, was I'd have a chance to escape being that person who everyone knows killed a girl.

It's been nearly twelve years. I can remember everything clearly because my brain's been over it so many times there's got to be a deep groove in my hippocampus, or wherever memory is stored.

The play park was less than ten minutes' walk from our house, hardly any distance, even for a four-year-old. What Happened took place on the big slide. It was a busy day, and there was a girl who refused to wait her turn. Her name was Hannah.

"You don't want to talk about the rest of your day?" Mum's voice cuts in. She's handing me a mug. It's one

11

Alice and I gave Dad a few birthdays ago. He chose to leave it behind.

"No, it was very average."

We don't mention Hannah by name when we talk about What Happened. But I remember. Whenever anyone calls out "Hannah" in the street, or I see it written down, I have a stomach-punch moment. It's as if she is reminding me she existed, and that I have no right to forget her for more than short stretches of time.

"First days are always difficult," says Mum. "There's so much to take in." Her own first day at her new office was on Friday, and she'd come back exhausted. "And I really think it's nothing. But just in case, I think we should keep that note." She reaches for it on the table, unscrunches it and smooths it out, then folds it in half, to cover up the words again.

"So it's not nothing?"

Mum frowns as she puts it in her pocket. "I should speak to the school about it."

"That's not a good idea," I say.

While signing the Robinson admission form before we moved, Mum had said, "Is there anything I should add in the additional comments box?" I'd shaken my head vigorously. I didn't want them to know anything about me, though I guessed maybe a school report might follow, summarizing all the ways in which I'd been labelled a difficult student. It seemed I rubbed people up the wrong way just for being myself.

"I want your head of year to know things haven't been easy for you," says Mum. "It would make me feel better." She looks at me. "Please, Ruby?"

"If you have to," I say. When she says please like that, it's hard to refuse. "I'll take my tea upstairs," I say now, carefully lifting my bag from the floor while still holding my mug.

My room has a bedsheet up at the window because there are no curtains yet. Unpacked boxes and several black bin liners of clothes crouch in one corner. My chest of drawers is too small now that I don't have a fitted cupboard or shelves like I did in our old house. The leap from how I'd like my bedroom to be and the state it's in now feels overwhelming.

I take a couple of gulps of tea then place the mug on top of the chest of drawers, in amongst stationery, make-up and the knick-knacks that made it through the pre-move cull, and get into bed with my school bag. The house is cold. It'll have to become arctic for Mum to contemplate switching on the heating.

My bag vibrates against my leg, and I reach in for my phone. My sister doesn't give up. She's video-calling me.

I answer. "What's up, Alice?" I say, as soon as I see her round face with her new silver nose ring. She's in the lounge area of the kitchen-diner of her shared house. Her second year of uni is about to start and she had to sort out that house rather than ours. I hear the loud metal click of a toaster popping up, and the thump-thump of drum and bass. "Why do you keep calling me?"

"Because you won't answer my messages," says Alice, irritatingly perky.

"I don't have anything to say."

"I want to know about the new house and how it's all going."

"I've already given you the virtual tour."

"That was a couple of days ago. What's new? How are things?"

A boy – not one of her housemates, who are all girls – pops up in the background with a bottle of beer in his hand. "Who are you talking to?" he asks.

"My sister," says Alice, grinning.

The boy waves his beer at me. "Hey! Your big sister is an adorable pumpkin."

Why isn't she calling me from somewhere more private? And how does she manage to find so many boys who think she's adorable?

"Nothing's changed in the last two days," I say. "Except the door fell off the bathroom cupboard."

When Alice comes home at Christmas, the two of us will have to share this bedroom. It's a deeply depressing thought.

"How's Mum doing?" she asks. "She seemed tired when I spoke to her yesterday."

"She's OK," I say.

"You're sure?" She leans in. "How was your first day?"

"Bad."

Alice wasn't there the day it happened. It was just me and Dad, and Hannah and her grandparents. Alice would never have done what I did. She was always the sweet, well-behaved one.

The boy slides into the shot and presses his face against Alice's. "Hello there, Alice's little sister. I want the dirt. Give me a deep, dark secret from her past." He laughs.

I press the end-call button.

# CHAPTER 3

Mum's left for work the next morning before I wake up, but she's set my alarm clock and WhatsApped me to say she'll be emailing school. My stomach lurches as I remember the note, and I pull up the duvet so it's half over my head. The alarm clock is positioned outside my bedroom door so I have to get out of bed to turn it off. That was a suggestion from the head of year at my last school, since I was always late in. Even so, most times, I'd turn it off and go back to bed.

The actual reasons I couldn't get out of bed often weren't clear, even to me. Some days my limbs and brain were just too heavy.

"You're such a bright girl," my old head said when

things had escalated. "But you repeatedly let yourself down." The way he said it reminded me of a joke Alice once told me about an inflatable school, an inflatable head teacher and an inflatable boy with a pin. The punchline was something about the boy letting himself, the head, and the whole school down. It made me smile that time in the head's office, and I was told smirking would get me nowhere.

Hannah hadn't come from our town. She'd only been staying the weekend with her grandparents. After her death, her grandmother raised money for a memorial garden in a fenced-off part of the rec, in sight of the play park. Dogs weren't allowed in it. I didn't feel welcome either, although I'd never been told that. I wished I could lift it up and drop it somewhere far away, in a place where no one knew why it had been made, and the plants were just plants, unburdened with meaning.

Even age four, I was aware of the murmurs around me. Hannah's family tried to sue the council in charge of the play park. But regardless of the equipment, my grandmother wasn't the only one who thought I was old enough not to have behaved with such spite and anger; so did Hannah's, who according to Mum and Dad "accidentally" leaked my name to the local newspaper when the memorial garden was vandalized years later.

The newspaper had to issue an apology for naming me, but the damage was done. For weeks after the article was printed, I was stared at and whispered about. Stared at so much, I could feel my skin harden and my muscles tighten. Nobody said anything to me directly, not even Luffy, who watched while I gouged rotting-wood chunks out of the back of the maintenance shed with a knife from the canteen.

Now, I get up, dress, double lock the door, and walk up the road towards the bus stop for my second day at Robinson. According to my travel app, it's the last bus I can get before being late for school. There's a crowd of school kids at the bus stop, and I hold back, which means when the bus arrives I'm one of the last ones on and have to stand. The boy in a seat near me is highlighting chunks of *A Christmas Carol* with a blue highlighter. Must be the same year as me, but I don't think he was in my English class. He's doodling zigzag lines up the side of a page now. He looks up and we make eye contact. He smiles. Cute. His messy hair reminds me of the type of dog that needs clipping so they can see out properly.

I look away. He's the laid-back type with idiot friends and an easy life. There were plenty of them at my last school too. I busy myself untangling my earphones.

As the bus arrives at Robinson – a large, sprawling group of buildings, some of them blackened with polluted neglect – I move back to let everyone else off first. The anxiety about that note on my locker resurfaces. Those words drum in my brain: *I know you did it.* Who was messing with me?

As soon as I step off the bus, a face looms close to

mine. It's Monique, the Linesman with the bun and hoop earrings. She's swinging her silver water bottle in her hand.

"I've got something to say to you, new girl. You hurt my brother, so now you've got me to worry about."

I step back, my heart racing. "What are you on about?" I say. I try and sound bored.

"You pushed him into a wall in the corridor yesterday. He's got a massive bruise on his arm."

*That* boy. I've still got a sore shoulder but I'm not going to whine about it. I can see by the set of her mouth and the hardness of her eyes that nothing I say is going to help, and an apology will make me seem weak.

I ignore her and walk past, jamming in my earphones to drown out the sound of her swearing after me. I have a clearer idea of the school layout now, and walk in through the student entrance nearest to my locker.

"You!"

I pull out an earbud.

A man who's old enough to be my grandpa, with a grey beard, is standing in front of me, holding out his hand. "Give me those."

I frown. "Sorry?"

"Are you new?" He carries on without giving me a chance to answer. "I'm Mr Pompley. Headphones, earphones, AirPods, whatever, aren't to be used on school premises. Put them away or they'll get confiscated." He nods approvingly as I tuck them into my jacket pocket, then frowns. "The hair. You'll need to fix that."

"It's very similar to your hair colour, though?" I say.

He blinks. "I'm sorry?" His tone suggests he's not sorry about anything. "Young lady, I advise you to tread very carefully in this school." He looks me up and down, perhaps going for a third strike, but can't seem to find anything else to object to. "Off you go. Don't be late to class."

I scoot off towards my locker, which is one of a large bank of lockers against the yellow wall in the DT corridor. There are big windows looking out over the sports field, and in between the windows hang huge photos of Robinson student life. I recognize Georgia in one of them, taken when she was further down the school. She's wearing huge goggles and a pristine white lab coat, and holding a tiny object over a Bunsen burner flame with pincers. Amber is next to her, half out of shot, writing something down.

I approach my locker warily. But there is no note.

Scott is perched against one of the window sills, his neon-green backpack at his feet. He's typing really fast on his phone. "Hey!" he says, looking up. "How's it going?"

"Fine," I say.

"You sure?" he says, standing up. "You look kind of tense."

"Being new is tiring," I say, as I open my locker and shove my coat inside. "You know. Sussing everyone out."

"You need to join my private Insta account, Robinson Reveals." He grins. He's obviously desperate for me to ask him all about it.

"Right." I turn the key in my locker and count in my head to see how long it takes him to crack. One … two … three … four…

"It's a gossip site, but so much more," Scott says. "Everyone loves it. Anonymous crushes, confessions and bitchy observations, plus a touch of hard-hitting journalism slipped in."

I nod. "I'll check it out."

Scott's face falls slightly. "You can't right now. It's been disabled. Someone couldn't take a joke. But that's only temporary, we'll be up and running in no time. Let me know if you ever want to share anything. My DMs are always open." He winks at me. "Nothing ever stays secret for long around here."

# CHAPTER 4

Georgia is sitting at a desk on her own in our form room when I walk in. She sees me and pats the seat next to her. There's an open history revision guide in front of her. Amber is at a table with a group at the back of the class. She's copying something out from another person's exercise book.

I would have preferred sitting at a desk by myself. I'm wary of being friends with other girls; I've been stung in the past. They can change without me understanding why, and I don't give enough of myself to them, the way I see other people do. My only enduring friendship has been with Luffy. Still, I feel bad ignoring Georgia.

"Amber won't mind. Tolla's helping her with her

Spanish homework," says Georgia as I sit down. "It's due next lesson," she adds with what sounds like a note of disapproval. "I'd have helped her, but I don't do Spanish."

"I know. We have the same timetable, remember?" Perhaps it comes out too harsh because she blinks.

"I really wanted to do Spanish," continues Georgia. "I couldn't take all the subjects I wanted to, though. I might take it as an extra subject next year…" She picks up a history revision book. "I should have told you, we have a test on Elizabethan politics next period."

"We have a test?"

Just then our tutor, Mr Baldini, comes bouncing in. He calls for quiet, and rattles off the register. He's young, like just-out-of-uni young, and his face is self-tan orange. Not Trump-level, but hardly subtle. He reads a message from his laptop reminding students that nail varnish isn't allowed. "Got that, girls?" he says. I note he needs to work on his self-tan application, particularly the knuckles.

"And boys," I say.

"What's that, Ruby?" he says, cupping his hand to his ear.

I hesitate. I had spoken without thinking, but I also don't want to be the student who says, "Nothing," whenever they're challenged by a member of staff.

"And boys," I say, a little louder.

"Err, yes," he says. "Thanks. And boys, too."

Around the class, people make groaning noises,

and mutter that I think I'm so woke. Georgia looks embarrassed for me, but I hear Amber say, "She's right."

On our way to history, we pass the Linesmen, coming in the opposite direction. Isaac and Monique first, followed at a distance by the other two, another boy and girl. The girl has an asymmetrical haircut, half shaved and half flopping over her face. How is that allowed and my hair colour isn't? The boy has a diamond ear stud and swagger.

Monique turns back and calls, "Hey, Dani! Jay!" and they speed up. Clearly these two are the minions.

"It's Little Miss Perfect and her granny," Isaac says, as he sees me and Georgia. "How's it going?"

"Not bad, thanks for asking," I say.

Monique repeats my words in a squeaky voice, then says, "She hurt my brother yesterday. Straight up slammed him against the wall because he was in her way."

"You're joking?" says Isaac. "That's out of order."

"Well out of order," says Jay.

Dani nods. "She better watch herself."

Monique makes a move towards me and I jerk back. She laughs, "Scared ya!"

I give her the finger.

Isaac taps Georgia hard on her head with an exercise book as he saunters by.

Georgia recoils, holding her hand to her head. "That hurt," she says after they've gone.

"You should have hit him back," I say. If he'd done

that to me, I wouldn't have hesitated. But I'm not going to fight Georgia's battles for her.

"It's best to ignore them," she says. Her jaw is clenched.

In history, we sit the test, and I remember everything I learned from Georgia's revision book during tutor time. I have a good memory, and if I work hard, I can do OK this year. I want to be a journalist, and going to uni would be an advantage. I also need to write more articles, try and get something published. The only ones I've written are in a notebook, not even typed up, too basic to show anyone.

We peer-mark. I'm happy with my score of ten out of fifteen. Georgia gets fourteen and when she's handed her paper back, she double-rings the question she got wrong with a red biro.

Mr Roderick sits on his desk and tells us we have to do a group assignment, a five-minute talk in two weeks' time on one aspect of Elizabethan life. He puts us into groups of three by using the most unpopular method ever: numbering our class of thirty from one to ten, so friendship groups are obliterated. I'm an eight. The other eights are a boy called Khalid and a girl called Claudia, and our topic is "the theatre", which seems to be one of the easier ones. We have the rest of the lesson to plan, and then we can use the computer room next lesson to put together PowerPoints which we can then work on as homework.

"Right," says Mr Roderick. "Get going!"

Claudia immediately turns her back on me and Khalid and leans back in her chair to talk to the girl in the group next to us.

Khalid raises his eyebrows. "Looks like it's just you and me."

I notice Khalid has a metal badge with the words *Head Prefect* on it, and he certainly seems keen. He and I decide on an annotated diagram of the Globe Theatre, followed by a couple of slides with key features explained and one about the fire that destroyed it.

"Sorted!" says Khalid. "I'm glad we're doing the theatre."

I'm doing a rough sketch of what our PowerPoint slides will look like. "Yeah? Are you doing drama?"

"I'm doing an improv drama course out of school," says Khalid. "I want to do stand-up."

I look at him afresh. He's slight with beautiful skin and an earnest expression. "That's brave."

He says, "It's terrifying. My routine is based around coming out to my parents."

"Sounds cool," I say, adding some red felt-tip flames to the roof of my Globe Theatre.

"Can I ask you a personal question?" he says, playing with the chunky gold watch round his skinny wrist.

"No. Unless it's about my hair. Questions about my hair are always welcome. This colour is called Dove Grey."

One side of his mouth lifts into a smile, and I decide I like him.

Claudia lands the front legs of her chair back on to the floor with a thump. "Are we done planning yet?" she says.

God, I hate group work. "Yes," say Khalid and I at the same time.

It's as we're leaving the classroom that Khalid slips in his question. "Was that your locker with a note on it yesterday?"

My heart does a massive thud. "I don't know what you're talking about," I say. So people *did* see it. I expect photos were taken and shared. "I didn't see a note," I lie.

"My bad," says Khalid. "Must have been someone else's locker. Or maybe it was removed before you could see it."

"What did it say?" I stop and look him in the eye, fronting it out. Georgia is coming towards us.

"I can't remember," says Khalid, looking flustered. "I'm sure it was nothing. Students here can be very immature."

He pulls a beat-up, vibrating phone out from inside his blazer. "Got to go," he says quickly, turning away from me. I watch him as he disappears into the crowded corridor, messaging as he goes.

# CHAPTER 5

"There's a rumour going round about you, Ruby," says Amber, three hours later.

"Oh really?" I say, keeping my tone neutral.

"Yeah. That you were expelled from your last school."

I make a what-the-hell face. It's lunchtime and I'm sitting with Amber, Georgia, and a couple of girls from Amber's Spanish class. I've just listened to five solid minutes of moaning about the insane amount of homework they get from Spanish.

"Who did you hear that from?" asks Georgia.

"Scott says it's doing the rounds," says Amber. "And he should know."

"You don't believe everything that comes out of that

boy's mouth, do you?" asks Tolla, the loudest one. "He's desperate to stay relevant because his stupid Robinson Reveals account is down. He'll come out with anything right now just to get people talking."

"Of course I don't believe everything he says," says Amber, annoyed. "I'm warning Ruby, that's all. Like, if it's true, sometimes it's better to come out with it rather than have Scott expose it. He can smell blood a mile off."

"Gross," says Tolla. She stabs a piece of pasta with her fork. "But is it true, Ruby?"

"No," I say. "It's not. So, do you – did you – all follow Robinson Reveals?" Each one of them nods. "You've got to keep up with the drama," says Amber. "Especially me, working for the paper. It helps give us ideas for features."

"It can be funny, though, right?" says Tolla. "I'm sorry, Georgia, but that post about you fancying Isaac Linesman was funny."

Georgia stops chewing her mouthful of sandwich and rolls her eyes. I think I see her flush though. "It stayed up way too long." She shoots a look at Amber. "You could have talked Scott into taking it down."

"Come on, Georgia," says Amber. She runs her hand through her short hair. "Robinson Reveals is nothing to do with me. That's Scott's side hustle. He doesn't take any notice of me."

"Did you actually fancy Isaac, Georgia?" asks the other girl. "I get he's fit and has chat, but he's a bully."

"She had a crush on him when she was eleven," says

Amber. "We all had lapses of judgement in year seven."

Georgia glares at her. "Amber!"

"That's one awkward lapse," says Tolla.

Everyone laughs, except for Georgia. "OK, OK. Give me a break. It was a long time ago!"

"Isaac and Monique deserve each other," says Tolla.

"Ugh, they so do," says Amber.

I'm left out of the conversation after that, not that I expect it to be otherwise. Tolla teases Amber about some shoes Amber's thinking of buying that Tolla thinks are ugly, and Georgia complains about being told off in a class when she was only trying to help the person sitting next to her. I was there; it was hardly a telling-off. Just a pointed reminder she shouldn't be talking. Something tells me that Georgia has thin skin.

They talk about a homeless person being attacked in Barchester the previous week. Grim. I say I need to go to the drama office to pick up a copy of *Blood Brothers,* which everyone else was issued with at the start of the term. It could wait until my lesson tomorrow, but I'd like some space. The others wave without looking up.

The music and performing arts block is single storey and more modern than the main school. From the outside it looks a bit like a reception building at a holiday resort, with two trees in pots by the entrance, and a big porch. At closer range, I see one of the trees is forty per cent dead leaves, and the porch has huge cobwebs hanging underneath it, one dangling dangerously low.

In the lobby area there are kids hanging out, posters advertising auditions for an upcoming production of *Grease*, and a noticeboard with schedules for music lessons and orchestra practice. I wander through the building, reading the blue signs on the doors, until I come to the drama office. I look through the little square of glass and see the room is empty. I try the door anyway, and it's locked. I lean against it, feeling conspicuous in front of everyone sitting in huddles on the hairy carpet tiles.

Khalid's words float in my head: *Was that your locker with a note on it yesterday?*

A girl comes out of a music practice room, leaving the door open, and I run forward to catch it before it closes and requires a PIN. It's a tiny cubicle with a piano taking up almost one side of it, a couple of violins in cases propped in the corner, and music stands in various stages of decline.

I sit on the worn velvet-cushioned piano stool and dig out my phone. My stomach aches as I type in *accident rosemead park*. It's not a healthy thing to do, reading about What Happened, but I want to be sure there's no new information about me online that might have led to that note.

There's the initial local news story: how the family of a four-year-old girl are being comforted by relatives and friends following the tragic accident which took place in Rosemead Play Park when she fell from a slide. The girl was taken to hospital but was pronounced dead on arrival. A spokesperson for the police said they were "investigating the circumstances surrounding the death of a four-year-old child on Saturday".

My name isn't mentioned. I'm not named in any of the official reports online because I was a child myself.

I search the other articles. I know them all by heart now. The story was picked up by a small newspaper in Scotland, and another in Canada. There's a short follow-up article to the original, reporting a verdict of accidental death. Then there are features about child safety in play parks, referring to Hannah Cole in passing, and a few around the time the memorial garden was built and opened, and plenty around the time it was vandalized. The article which originally had my name in it was edited so it no longer does.

Some articles are accompanied by a photo of Hannah. She has big round eyes that are the sort of blue that could never be mistaken for any other colour. Neatly brushed hair hangs to just under her chin, and her expression is cheerful and happy.

It's not quite the Hannah from my memory – her hair was much longer, her eyes narrower, and her expression determined.

I do a search of my name and my Insta comes up. It's private though, and I stopped posting a couple of years ago. I trawl through forums for families local to where I used to live, search back until I find the discussions about Hannah. Someone says, "I heard from the grandmother that another child went for her, attacked her, but they couldn't prosecute." The phrase "true evil" is used. Another says, "Imagine if it was your kid who'd done it – so awful." A few people say things like, "They were only children, it was a tragic accident, a scuffle, it could have happened to anyone."

There are years of quiet and then when I've only been at secondary school a few months, the garden is vandalized and it starts up again. Coffeemum42 says, "I hear the girl who pushed Hannah is a nightmare at school," and JacksDad says, "You don't think she was behind the trouble in the garden, do you?" CoffeeMum42 replies, "Who knows? It's possible. Disgusting behaviour."

My stomach hurts. I put my phone down. To distract myself, I place my fingers on the piano keys in front of me. I slowly pick out a tune I've known for ever. It's one of Dad's compositions, called "Ladders" because it moves up the keyboard in steps. "Ladders" used to be the code word Alice and I used for something bad, because it annoyed us so much. Before Dad disappeared with the piano, I'd come home and thump it out when I'd had a really terrible day.

I stop. Instead I attempt a fast-rippling number from back when I had piano lessons, in the days when I didn't mind being told what to do, before Mum got ill and before Dad left, and when we had more money.

The door swings open. "So, the thing is, I've booked this room," a voice says. I take my hands off the keys and look up. It's the cute boy from the bus.

I stand up. "Sorry. I was just hiding out."

He hesitates. "Oh, well, if you need to stay I'm—"

"It's OK," I say, moving closer to the door. "I snuck in as someone was coming out. I don't even know the code." Then, not quite ready to face wandering around until the bell goes, I say, "What do you play?"

"Guess," he says.

"Tambourine?" I hope it's the violin; I have a thing against keyboard players.

He laughs. "Flute," he says, swinging his backpack round and pulling out a case.

I'm surprised. It seems too delicate an instrument for him.

He lowers the backpack to the ground and balances the case on top of it. "You're new in our year, aren't you? Who are you hiding from?"

"It's complicated," I say, even though it really isn't. I open the door and say, "Happy flute practice."

"Thanks. And welcome to Robinson. Wait." He moves to the door. "I'm Euan. If you need to escape again, the code's 3141."

"Pi," I say, and I'm gone, smiling because it sounded like bye. I glance back through the glass and catch him smiling too.

I walk away slowly from the music practice room. I'm wondering where else I can hide out to kill time when I catch sight of a flash of neon green through a door window: Scott's backpack by an office desk. He's sitting in front of a large computer monitor.

The image of him waiting near my locker this morning comes back to me. He was obviously hoping I'd open up to him about the note and satisfy his horrible curiosity. And now he's been spreading rumours about me. I walk in without knocking.

Scott turns, his mouth slack-jawed. "Ruby?" His screen has loads of tabs open and I glimpse what looks like a news site. "Nice to see you. Had a rethink on the Halloween tickets?"

"Screw the Halloween tickets," I say. "I hear you're spreading a rumour about me having been expelled. What's going on?"

He looks taken aback but recovers quickly. "Ah. I must have been misinformed. Rumours fly around when someone new arrives after the start of term, particularly in year eleven. And then there was that crass note on your locker... I have a nose for a story, and I get the impression you have ... *history*."

I roll my eyes. The word *crass* makes him sound as if he should be wearing a cravat. "Well, I wasn't expelled. For all I know, you put that note there yourself to stir up drama. Just leave me alone, OK?"

"You're the one who's flounced in," says Scott calmly. "Believe it or not, I have better things to do than attach phishing notes on lockers. I've got a newspaper deadline."

A printout on the desk in front of him catches my eye. It's a newspaper-style layout but with nonsense words in the columns and two squares with crosses through them where photos might go. The heavy type at the top says: *The Robinson Record*. He follows where I'm looking. "That's a mock-up of the front page."

"What are you running with?" I ask, using a term I've

heard on TV. "'New girl suspected of being expelled from last school'?"

"Nice. That might get us a few new readers," says Scott. "Unfortunately we get a lot of censorship here, so it wouldn't be allowed on the grounds that it's not in keeping with the school's core values. Nope, I have a bigger story than you. Want to see it?"

I'd love to, but I don't want him to know that. "Fine," I say. "It's not like I have anything better to do."

I sit on the seat next to the desk, and he pulls up a page with a photo of an old bloke with scraggly hair and purple bruises on his face, and another of a black-and-white CCTV image. I lean closer and squint at it. I can make out two figures and the arm and shoulder of a third just out of shot. The headline screams *Despicable Attack!*

"Three people assaulted a homeless man in Barchester last weekend," he says. "A CCTV image has just been released." He turns to me and makes sure I'm properly paying attention before he says, "I've given the piece a Robinson twist."

"Which is?" I ask.

"The police say the man thinks the attackers were teenagers. Probably local. So we're asking if anyone in Robinson knows them," says Scott. "Basically we're encouraging people to snitch."

"Right." I look more closely at the grainy image. "There's not a lot to go on. Two of them have hoods up and their backs to the camera. You can't see the third one."

"There's a shoulder and an arm. Denim jacket. But, yes. It's a challenge."

I look again. One of the figures is kicking something at the bottom of the picture. The something is a person, and he's lying in the doorway of a shop.

"They chucked urine over him too," says Scott. "From a bottle. It looks like they planned it."

"Poor guy," I say. I turn my gaze to the photo of him staring into the camera. He appears startled, still in shock. I feel anger build. What a cowardly, cruel thing to do.

Scott nods. "I know. We're launching a campaign. We haven't had one of those for a while. We're going to fundraise and get the guy a new sleeping bag. A bit of cash." He scrolls further down the article. "Jim. That's his name. Jim Mason."

"Justice for Jim," I murmur.

Scott jots it down on a Post-it. "That works. In fact, that's spot on. Want to help us with this potentially award-winning campaign?" He raises his eyebrows. "You could put it down on your college application form."

I hesitate. Part of me really does. Not only does the campaign sound worthwhile, I would get to do some actual journalism. But it feels too risky. If there's one thing I've learned from school, it's to keep my head down.

"No thanks," I say as the bell goes, and I pick up my bag and leave the room.

"Think about it," calls Scott after me. "I could use someone like you."

# CHAPTER 6

Mum asks me to be up by nine a.m. for Grandma and Grandpa's visit on Saturday to help with the furniture they're bringing over. Also, although she doesn't voice it, she probably wants the backup around her mother. Grandma can be obnoxious.

We're being gifted the sofa and two armchairs from their conservatory. It has bamboo frames and bold floral cushions, and is gross. Grandma and Grandpa are buying themselves a new set.

As usual, Grandma honks her car horn to announce her arrival instead of ringing the doorbell, expecting us to rush out to greet her. I haven't had time for a shower, but I'm up and dressed in joggers and a sweatshirt, and I've hastily pulled my hair up into a ponytail so it looks less like it needs a wash. I stand on the doorstep in bare feet, while Mum grabs her coat and goes out.

Grandma steps out of her shiny red car, with its bumper sticker saying, *If you can read this you're too close. Back off!* "Where's Grandpa and the furniture?" I call.

"He's coming in a van with Ron. I didn't want to be squeezed in with them," says Grandma. It takes me a moment to remember that Ron is their next-door neighbour. She turns to Mum. "No hugs, please. Your dad and I don't want any viruses. We explained your difficult situation to dear Ron and he kindly agreed to give us a hand."

"That's nice," says Mum. "But he didn't need to. Ruby and I are capable of moving furniture."

Grandma ignores Mum and turns her attention to me. "I hope you're being helpful to your poor mum, Ruby. Are you allowed to have your hair that colour at your new school?"

She moves on into the house without waiting for an answer. I mime trying not to explode, and Mum makes a calming motion.

"Not a bad-sized living room," Grandma calls. "There's a lot you can do to liven this place up. Goodness, have you not finished unpacking yet?"

"We'll get there," says Mum.

Grandma moves into the kitchen, lifts up the kettle and takes it to the sink to refill. "How's Alice doing?" she asks.

She opens a cupboard and frowns. "Where do you keep your teabags? They should be in here, next to the kettle. That would be the obvious place." She peers out of the kitchen window. "The last people left a mess out there with all that broken furniture, didn't they?" She tuts.

The doorbell rings, and I open the door to Grandpa and Ron. I smile awkwardly at Ron, and fall into Grandpa's outstretched arms. He rests his head on top of mine. The only good memory I have around the time of Hannah's death is sitting for hours scrunched up close to him as he watched football. Mum once told me Grandpa had been spotted by a football scout when he was a teenager, but Grandpa'd broken his ankle tripping over a bottle in the road and it had all come to nothing.

"No hugging, remember," calls Grandma from the kitchen. Grandpa grins at me.

I lead the two of them into the hall, and Ron pokes his head into the living room.

"Furniture to be situated in here, then?" says Ron, and I'm tempted to give him a slow handclap for working out that this room – empty apart from two deckchairs and a coffee table – is indeed where the hideous sofa and chairs are to be situated.

While Grandma makes tea, which involves rewashing mugs to her satisfaction, the rest of us bring in the furniture. I find a blanket from a half-unpacked box of bedding and throw it over the sofa to make it marginally less of an eyesore. Mum gives me a look which I interpret as, *Couldn't you wait until they'd gone?* but I don't feel like playing grateful.

Grandma brings in the tray and sits down.

"You heard from your dad recently, Ruby?" she asks. I'm perched on one of the deckchairs because I don't fancy being wedged in between Mum and Ron on the sofa. I see Mum stiffen at Grandma's question, and Ron looks down at his brown lace-ups, which resemble burnt Cornish pasties.

"Nope," I say. "You?" The idea that Dad would have been in touch with them is laughable.

"Not a word," says Grandma. "I still can't get over what he's done to you all."

Mum and I sit absolutely still. If we don't react, this conversation might go away.

"I mean, what chance does he have with a music career at his age?" Grandma asks the room. "None. Talk about a midlife crisis."

Grandpa takes a Jaffa Cake from the plate and says, "My favourites." He says that about whatever biscuits are placed in front of him.

"He's had a lot to put up with over the years, of course," says Grandma. She seems, inexplicably, to be on Dad's side now. "He had to take that miserable job because of your *episodes*, didn't he, dear?" That is how she refers to Mum's chronic fatigue syndrome. "It's a shame he kept being overlooked for promotion. And of course, there was that business with the girl in the play park…"

41

The twist of my gut is immediate.

Mum moves to the edge of the sofa. "When are you going to let that go?" she says softly.

Grandma doesn't miss a beat. "I'm not going to pretend it didn't happen! Some of us live in the real world."

I stand up quickly and slosh hot tea on to my hand. "I've got homework to do. I'll see you all later."

"I hope you're not letting her get away with too much," I hear Grandma say as I step into the hall. "You shouldn't encourage her odd behaviour."

I dump my mug in the kitchen and go upstairs. I climb into bed and click on a bookmarked music site. I check I'm logged into one of my anonymous accounts and write another quick review trashing Dad's latest track, which dropped a few weeks ago. God knows why, but a few of his tracks have been used for corporate videos, which doesn't exactly go with his hippy persona, repairing bicycles when he's not doing music. He's good at self-promotion though, I'll give him that, getting his music on to various platforms, and seems to have got himself a tiny fanbase of people with no taste. I've been working through synonyms of *abysmal* and I'm looking forward to using *Execrable* for my title. I press publish, and wait for the buzz of seeing it appear.

It's hard to do homework when I'm feeling like this, so I get out of bed and empty one of the bin liners on to the floor. I fold clothes and put them in four piles: tops, sweaters, bottoms and socks/underwear.

Alice video-calls as I'm scrunching up the bin liner. She's in the shared kitchen again, sitting at the table, which is littered with books, used plates and mugs.

"Grandma and Grandpa are here," I say. "I'm in my bedroom keeping out of the way."

"Smart move," says Alice.

"Grandma said she didn't blame Dad for leaving," I say.

"What?" Alice moves even closer to the screen. Her gold bracelet hits the edge of an abandoned mug. "How did she come to that conclusion? The woman is delusional."

I've often wondered if Grandma has always preferred Alice, or if she loved us equally before *that business with the girl in the play park*.

"It was probably my fault," I say, and Alice laughs even though I'm not joking.

"Did they find us a sofa and chairs?" she asks.

"Sort of. They've given us the bamboo furniture from their conservatory."

"You're joking."

I shake my head. "Nope. It's as hideous as you remember."

Alice face-palms. "At least you never invite friends back home," she says, when she lifts her head. "Silver linings."

# CHAPTER 7

On Monday morning, first thing, I have a meeting with Mum and my head of year, Miss Starling. After Mum sent her email about the note on my locker, it was suggested we come in for "a little chat".

"Lovely to meet you again, Ruby! Now, let's discuss how you're settling in," beams Miss Starling. She's quite young, with a round body and skinny legs, wearing a dress with birds printed on it, which seems apt given her name. "How would you say it was going?"

"OK, yeah," I say.

"I know you've been shadowing Georgia... She's a very reliable student. I hope she's helped you find your feet?"

I return Miss Starling's professional smile and nod. She

draws her mouth downwards, signalling things are going to get serious. "I gather there was a note on your locker which caused you upset."

"It was disturbing," says Mum. "Especially given what I mentioned in my email to you."

"How do *you* feel about it, Ruby?" asks Miss Starling, pointedly ignoring Mum, who flushes. I can tell Mum feels embarrassed for coming across like a parent who doesn't give her kid a chance to talk, and I wish I could say to Miss Starling I don't mind she did that. I like how she stands up for me.

I chew on the inside of my mouth, by the corner near my cheek. I feel the fibres of that pink flesh separate. They make a noise in my head, like faint bubble wrap pops. For the billionth time, I try to imagine what it must be like to live without regret. I asked Luffy once, but I didn't phrase it quite right, and he thought I was asking if he regretted anything in his life. He said there were plenty of things, including watching videos that he could never unsee.

"It wasn't nice, on my first day," I say. As though it would have been fine on any other day.

"Mm-hmm," says Miss Starling. "I can imagine that it was a shock, given … your experience. I'm definitely going to look into it." On her desk is a framed photo of a smiley little girl in a yellow sundress holding a rabbit. She's about four years old. My eyes keep being drawn back to it. "You must come and talk to me, Ruby, if there's anything else that upsets or unsettles you. This is a fresh start and we

45

want to support you." She pauses, and the correct response is to nod, so I do.

"Ruby wasn't always treated fairly," Mum says. "At her last school."

"Oh?" says Miss Starling warily. She thinks Mum might be one of those parents who are always complaining, as well as someone who likes to talk for her child.

Mum doesn't elaborate. If she had, she would have told Miss Starling that it was all Mrs Lipperton's fault.

Mrs Lipperton in the school office had short white hair and a sour face. She was friends with Hannah's grandmother, but maybe she'd have hated me anyway. From day one, she set out to make my life difficult. I would see her whispering to staff and looking in my direction. If she ever saw me do anything out of order, no matter how small, she'd report me. Every day brought some new barely-veiled reference to me being a troublemaker. And soon, everyone believed it. Even me.

Mum made a complaint, but Mrs Lipperton swore blind that she was only doing her job, and said I had a nasty vendetta against her. There wasn't anything concrete I could point to. Just dirty looks and whispers behind my back.

Miss Starling leans forward and blocks my view of the smiling four-year-old. "It's not that long until the summer and your exams," she says gently. "It's not the ideal time to start a new school. We all have to pull together to get you where you need to be…"

Miss Starling launches into the importance of sticking to good routines, and to my horror Mum asks if I can do homework at school because my laptop is temperamental and I won't be getting a new one until Christmas. Miss Starling's face lights up. "Of course!" she says. "We have a homework club in the library. And I don't know if you've seen the gym yet, Ruby? It's open any day after school to your year and the one below. Completely refurbished last year." She smiles warmly. "How about you make the most of everything Robinson has to offer while you're here?"

The birds on her dress look as if they're hovering, waiting for my answer.

"Sure," I say, and I've said it mostly for Mum, to see her shoulders relax a little.

I head to homework club at the end of the day. It's not like I have anywhere else to be.

A skinny boy with a few hairs of moustache and an orange metal librarian badge asks me to sign in.

"You're the new girl," he says, like I don't know. He tells me the librarian was made redundant the previous year, so he's in charge. Then he lowers his voice. "What was that note on your locker all about?"

Oh great. "Wasn't my locker," I lie. He starts to ask me which one is my locker, but I walk away.

I select a laptop from the trolley and find a seat in a quiet area, among the non-fiction books. Within five minutes, a couple sit down at the table next to me. I recognize them as the lesser Linesmen, Dani and Jay. They prop a phone against a pile of books. Not long afterwards, Isaac walks in, glances at what they're watching for a moment, then finds a music video and ramps up the volume. The three of them sing along loudly.

"Please can you turn that off?" asks the student librarian.

"You what, mate?" says Isaac, acting as if he can't hear.

They laugh at the librarian, mocking the way he's standing. He asks them to leave and Jay pelts him with Hula-Hoops, his ear stud glittering as he puts some energy into his throws. I glare at them but I don't want to get involved. Bad things will happen if I do.

The library door swings open and bangs against the wall as Mr Baldini, my form tutor, struggles in with a clear plastic crate of exercise books.

"There should be quiet in here," he shouts. "Turn that music off. I have a headache." He positions himself at the main desk to mark books, and I sink down on one elbow to read how a reflex works.

The library fills up and occasionally Mr Baldini bellows at people. Most are using it as a hang-out rather than a study space. The Linesmen have pulled library books from the shelves to use as bats to shove a pencil sharpener between themselves. Midway through the ten-mark question I'm answering under very loosely timed conditions, I look up to see Euan from the music room come past my table. He acknowledges me with a dip of the head and I shoot him a tentative smile. He sits near the display of out-of-date *National Geographic* magazines, and when I look round he has his head on the table and his eyes closed.

I go back to my ten-marker, blocking everything out until I hear Isaac Linesman's voice say, "Hey, guys! I learned some very interesting facts about our friend Granny over there. Want to hear them?"

I could move to the other end of the library, but they'd love that. I pretend I haven't heard.

"Go on," says Jay.

"She held a compass at the throat of a boy at her old school," says Isaac.

My cheeks flame. How does he know that? The library is completely silent for the first time since I arrived. Out of the corner of my eye I'm aware of Euan raising his head off his table. I flick my eyes towards the main desk. Mr Baldini isn't there, although his stack of marking is. He must have stepped outside for a moment. The student librarian looks worried.

"And she pushed someone's head into hot gravy in their canteen," he says into the silence, and laughs. "Not bad, Granny. Not bad at all."

*Who told him?* "Stop spreading lies about me," I say.

"But they're not lies, Granny, are they? It's fact, innit? And I got one more for today. You flashed your tits at a teacher." He's grinning so much his cheeks are pushing up into his eye sockets, making his eyes smaller, but just as mean.

49

That one isn't true. Rage begins to fizz inside me like a lit firework.

"Is that what the note was on about?" asks Dani, eyes round. "On her locker?"

Isaac ignores her. He stage-whispers to me, "You want to know who told me?" His face is smug and cruel.

*Don't fall for it.*

I sigh and shake my head to show I think he's pathetic.

"Well, when you're ready to find out, just let me know," says Isaac. He smirks. "And don't bother flashing anyone here. Flat as a pancake, aren't you?"

Before I know what I'm doing, I've thrown my pencil case at him. He catches it easily in one hand, and I'm furious with myself for rising to his bait.

"Whoa, that might have hurt me bad, Granny. You need to watch that temper." He unzips the pencil case and makes a big deal of inspecting what's inside. He pulls out a compass and mimes stabbing himself in the neck to the sycophantic sniggers of the other two. When he gets to the pen that Luffy found on the street and gave to me because it had musical notes on it, I lose it.

Before Isaac can register, I'm practically on top of him, trying to grab the pen from him. He doesn't let go, and we're caught in a tussle, me screaming at him that he's such a jerk and him yelling that I'm a psycho.

Mr Baldini is suddenly between us. "What's going on?" We step apart, glaring at each other. "Ruby, stop shouting. Isaac, if that pen's hers, give it back."

Isaac chucks my pen on to the table I was sitting at. It rolls to the edge but doesn't fall off. He makes an amused snort.

"You're year elevens, for goodness' sake," says Mr Baldini. "The library's closing in ten minutes. Use your time wisely."

Isaac goes back to his seat, but I return my laptop and pack up my things. Tears sting behind my eyes, but I keep my face calm. I walk out slowly, my head at its natural height, neither too low nor too high. It's something I've had practice at.

Outside the library, my breath falters, and I quickly make my way to my locker to get my coat. When I reach it, my key won't fit into the lock. Somebody's pushed chewing gum into it. I slam my palms against the locker and let the tears fall.

"Ruby!"

I straighten immediately and wipe my eyes. It's Euan, fully awake. His hair is kind of tufty. He's wearing his coat and has his backpack over one shoulder.

He comes a bit closer, his expression concerned. "Isaac will say anything for attention. Don't let him get to you."

"It's not that." Although it mostly is. I work hard not to let my voice judder with more sobs. "I can't get to my coat because the lock on my locker is stuffed with gum..." I take a deep breath, imagining it sucking up the sobs.

"Not again." Euan shakes his head in sympathy. "People went round doing that at the start of term. The premises manager will help you, but you might have to leave it until tomorrow."

I nod. "OK, thanks."

Euan crouches to examine the lock. I want to tell him that I'm scared because Isaac knew those things about me, things Mum and I haven't told anyone at this school. Both the compass incident and the time I dunked a girl's head in her plate in the canteen I was defending Luffy from disgusting things being said about his mum, because he didn't believe in fighting back. I went too far each time.

The third thing – flashing my boobs – would have been laughable if any of the Linesmen truly knew me and how self-conscious I am about my small chest. But how did he find out about the rest?

Euan straightens up. "Nope. You're not going to get that out yourself. Is your bus pass in there?"

I shake my head with relief. "It's in my bag."

"That's good. And at least it's not that cold," says Euan. "You going out this way?" He nods towards the exit. "Let's go before my brother makes us tidy the library."

"Who's your brother?"

Euan's wince takes over his whole face. "Ah. You don't know... Mr Baldini. Frazer." He watches closely for my reaction.

"You're ... Euan *Baldini*?"

Euan nods. "Yes. But I was here before him. Three years before him." He sounds indignant. "The day he told me he'd got a job here was pretty much the worst day of my life."

I laugh. But if that's honestly the worst day he's had, I was right about his easy life when I first saw him on the bus.

"He gets called Baldy," says Euan. "That's standard, right, with a surname like ours. My dad's Italian and my mum's Scottish – that's why we've got Scottish first names. But Frazer also gets called the Satsuma." I look blank and he sighs. "The self-tan?"

"Ah."

"It's embarrassing, sometimes. A lot of the time. *All* the time." He takes a few steps towards the car park, then turns. "It must be hard, starting late in the year. I bet you miss your old school?"

"Yeah," I say, giving him a brief wave goodbye.

I should have sounded more convincing.

# CHAPTER 8

At break the next day, outside in the windy quad, there's a cake sale for #JusticeForJim. Scott and his team clearly don't mess around.

Attached to the table, fluttering noisily, is a big poster with the same photo of Jim that was in the *Robinson Record*. It turns out the newspaper is hot off the press. Mr Baldini told us in tutor time there are a few paper copies around the school, and the online version is available on the homework portal.

I don't like that photo of Jim, I decide. I don't think he was ready for it to be taken. He's been attacked, and he looks old and weary. No one asked him if it was OK to have it plastered all over the place. It's as if he's been taken advantage of all over again.

I look away, and eye up the cakes. There are a surprising number. Pastries, doughnuts, traybakes, one large Costco red velvet cake cut into slices, and some cupcakes iced with "#J4J". There's also a stack of thin white napkins, the sort which are pulled out of metal containers in fast-food places. Scott and Amber are standing behind the table, taking the money.

Euan is hovering nearby with Khalid from my history class. The two of them are eating flapjacks that ooze with stickiness.

"Hey, Ruby, you sorted your locker?" Euan calls, and I nod briefly, trying to communicate that I don't want to attract any more attention than I already have. I'd tracked down the premises manager, who had moaned a lot and said he had a list of jobs up to his armpit, but at least he'd blasted out the chewing gum with a small can of something he had in the top pocket of his shirt.

"You mean that note?"

I turn to see Naz, chief Glossy, with another couple of girls by her side. Her perfume is gorgeous, and her uniform fits so well, she must have had it altered.

"Everyone's been wondering about that," she says, and her friends nod. "Have you got a stalker, Ruby?"

"I've no idea what it was about," I say, as if it's of no relevance to my life whatsoever.

Khalid jumps in. "Great to see so many people buying cakes," he says.

Naz gives a light laugh. "Well, we're here to support

55

Scott," she says brightly, and Khalid says, "Nice one." The three girls head off towards the stall.

Khalid breaks into my thoughts. "You going to buy something?" He chucks the remainder of his flapjack in a bin. "You'll end up in Robinson Reveals if you don't."

"Is it back up?" I say.

"Not yet, but it will be soon with Scott on the case," says Khalid. "Nothing slows him down."

Euan laughs. "You should know that Scott and Khalid are Robinson's power couple, Ruby. You don't want to get the wrong side of either of them." He nods at the stalls, laden with cakes and buzzing with students. "This isn't your average bake sale. They've pulled in a load of favours."

So Khalid and Scott are a couple. The head prefect and the social media entrepreneur. One tall with dark, good looks, the other short, fair and round.

"Guess I'd better buy something, then," I say.

Khalid laughs and watches me scrabble in my bag. "No money?"

"I'll get you something," says Euan. "Monty's, the café where I work, donated a ton of nice stuff. Danish? Doughnut? You'd better decide quickly. The crowds are moving in – you'll be left with one of Amber's dried-out cupcakes."

More classes have been let out, and word's got round that there are cakes. The quad is filling up rapidly. A teacher calls for students to queue properly.

"Danish, please," I say.

"Hold this," Euan says, handing me the remains of his flapjack in a napkin. He heads to the queue.

"I heard about your … altercation with Isaac in the library," says Khalid.

"Altercation?" I say. "That's a big word for something so minor." I barely slept last night thinking about the things Isaac said, wondering which person at my old school could have fed him the information. Two truths and one lie.

"You're one of those people who like to be noticed, aren't you?" says Khalid. He's looking at my hair. In my French class earlier, I coloured some of the tips at the front with pink Sharpie. I did it absent-mindedly in a throwback to primary school. I used to find it hard to sit and do nothing.

"I don't mind standing out," I say eventually. "I'd say you're someone who likes to go under the radar."

"Interesting," he says. He holds his phone up. It's the latest iPhone, very different to the beat-up one he was messaging on last week. "I said I'd take some photos for Scott. Pretend you're about to take a big bite of Euan's flapjack."

A few metres away, Euan waves a cinnamon swirl at me. "Last one!" he says. "Lucky!"

I glance away and lower my head. The fewer photos of me online, the better. I don't want any of the haters at my old school knowing where I am. "Take one of Euan instead," I say. "This flapjack is a mess."

Khalid turns to Euan. "Say cheese!"

I look up enough to see Euan posing obligingly. I like the way he's so quick to smile, that he doesn't fret about how he looks. He walks over, hands me the cinnamon swirl, and takes back the flapjack. It would be nice to have him as a friend, but I'm just here to pass my exams and move on. Better to keep things simple.

Throughout the day, a strange nervous energy builds inside me. I feel constantly alert.

At the end of my last lesson, I go to my locker and stand and stare at my PE kit. Inside the black drawstring bag is a pristine, never-worn-before, compulsory Robinson green polo shirt, some black shorts, green socks, and a pair of ugly trainers that were cheap on ASOS. Mum refused to shell out on trainers that were going to live most of their life in a school locker. The Robinson-branded shorts are too big; my size was sold out. I'd put them and the too-wide trainers out of my mind, but now I had to confront them.

What had I said to Khalid? *I don't mind standing out.* Sure. Time to walk the talk at Robinson's gym.

The changing room is empty apart from a couple of girls sitting in regular clothes gossiping. I change quickly into my ugly shorts and try to act as if I know the routine. The lockers work on a PIN code system and it takes me a couple of attempts to work it out. I stand by the mirror to tie up my hair, psyching myself up. It's been a while since I did any exercise.

I occasionally used to go to the gym where Luffy's mum worked as a cleaner and could get free passes. Luffy never had the stamina to keep exercising for as long as I could. He'd lie on the mats or walk on the treadmill next to the one I was running on and talk to me about capitalism or global conspiracies.

The gym at school may have been recently refurbished, but one of the exercise machines has an *Out of Order* notice taped to it, and the CCTV camera, which is high up in a corner, has a dangling cable. A member of PE staff is cleaning the mirrors, there are two girls timing a third on the rowing machine, and Georgia is doing stretches on a mat. Her hair is tied back into a high ponytail with a green, velvety scrunchie.

"Hey," she says. "First time in the gym?"

"Yeah." She's a bit intense, but I'm grateful to see a friendly face.

"You need to bring a towel with you to wipe down the equipment," she says. "If you've forgotten one, there's a lost property box over there."

"So I should wipe down the equipment with a towel that lives in lost property and never gets washed? Eww," I say, walking over to select the cleanest-looking one, which has *Arsenal FC* on it.

Georgia doesn't hear me. She's rubbing her temples with the tips of her fingers.

"Are you all right?" I ask.

"Headache," she says. "I've got athletics club in a

minute, but ... well, Isaac's there, and ... I'll wait until a teacher turns up."

I want to tell her she needs to stick up for herself, but it's none of my business. I peer out of the window, which overlooks the running track. There's a group of people in PE kit chatting, some doing stretches. I can't see Isaac, but I spot Amber. She's in school uniform, standing over by the fence, talking intently to a girl holding a silver water bottle. Monique. "Are those two friends?" I ask Georgia, who has come to stand next to me.

She shakes her head, frowning. "That's weird. Amber hates Monique. We both do."

I glance at Amber and Monique again. Their body language doesn't seem confrontational.

We watch a teacher jog out of the sports building on to the field and blow a whistle. "See you later," says Georgia. "You should come and watch. We're competing in houses. Come and cheer for Avon!"

She heads off. And after running 5k on the treadmill, I leave the gym with no intention of going anywhere near the house competition. There are a couple of revolting shower cubicles off the changing room, which clearly missed the refurbishment. I can't imagine anyone ever having a shower here. Walking past the sports field on my way to the gates, I hear someone call my name. It's Georgia again, waving me over.

"Ruby! Come on! We need you."

I sigh. The houses in Robinson are named after rivers,

and all I know is I'm in the same one as Georgia. To be honest, I couldn't care less.

"You're in Avon?" The girl next to Georgia looks delighted. I don't recognize her from our year. She must be a year ten. "I'm Mara, and this is Charlotte and Stevie. We'll teach you the Avon cheer!"

"I'm going to run the 400-metres now," says Georgia. She's pale and nervous, as if this is the defining race of her athletic career. Her perfectionism must be exhausting.

"You'll smash it," says Mara. "You always do." The girls teach me a cheer that we start shouting as soon as Georgia goes to stand near the start line. Georgia doesn't smash it. She comes second, and I can tell by her dejected body language that she's upset, but Mara keeps us cheering anyway. *Avon are winners, we can't be beat! We've got the power, to knock you off your FEET!* I get a kick out of shouting into the open space and the grass-scented air, letting myself go for the first time in ages, unexpectedly breaking into laughter.

# CHAPTER 9

Mum gives me a lift to school the next morning because she doesn't have to be in until later. She hums along to the music on the radio. The cloudy sky is an intense pink, like strawberry ice-cream layered within yellow vanilla, and the air is still and cold, in rehearsal for winter.

"I'm proud of you," says Mum suddenly, as she swerves into a space another car has just left. "I can see you're trying hard at Robinson."

She says this because after the cheerleading I came home and worked on an English essay all evening, and maybe because I emptied the dishwasher this morning without being asked. Her bar for feeling proud is low, but I'm pleased she's happy.

I'm in a more buoyant mood this morning too. Getting a lift in is a good start to the day. I'm proud of the essay I'm about to hand in this morning, and I'm planning to go to the gym again later.

"Thanks," I say, releasing my seat belt. "I'll see you later, OK?"

Georgia and Amber are sitting on the window seat near my block of lockers.

When they hear me, they look up, and immediately I know from their apprehensive faces something is wrong. My heart flaps like a cornered bird.

They both stand up. "Is it true you killed someone?" asks Amber. She blurts it out, as if she didn't want to ask but somebody had to.

I go cold and force my face to remain impassive, to remember the mantras Mum taught me. *It's behind me. It's not who I am.*

There's expanding silence. I can ask them how they know, or I can deny it. Or I can say nothing.

That's the one I go for.

I push past them to my locker and get my books, then walk away, leaving them staring after me.

When I walk into the form room, I know it's me everyone is whispering about. I sit on my own at the back and wonder if the information came via Isaac, from the unknown source.

Mr Baldini speeds through the register. Everyone is quiet, but there's a buzz in the room, an excitement, and I can tell he knows something is up. My stomach churns slowly like a washing machine at the beginning of a cycle.

"Everyone OK?" Mr Baldini says, his eyes searching the room. "Just a few small announcements," he continues. "The following people need to return their overdue books to the library…"

Georgia is waiting for me to walk to history. I carry on straight past her, but she doesn't take the hint.

"Maybe Amber could have worded it better," she says, walking alongside me. "We only wanted to know the truth. Isaac posted it on a couple of group chats last night. No one knew whether to believe it… He says an anonymous number messaged him with the information and he was just putting it out there to see what everyone thought."

My mouth goes dry. I was right. Was Isaac behind the note on my locker too?

"It was an accident on a slide," I say. "I was four. *Four*. Happy now?"

Georgia's eyes widen. "Was it awful?" she asks softly.

When anyone tries to talk to me about What Happened, they expect me to be sad about what happened to Hannah. The disgusting truth is I often still hate Hannah as much as I hate myself.

"Leave me alone," I say, walking ahead of her. My head is pounding.

Mr Roderick isn't in the classroom yet, but when I walk

in, the noisy room goes silent. All eyes swivel towards me. My stomach sinks. I'm aware of the heat in my cheeks but I make sure to return the stares until everyone looks away, uncomfortable. Naz is the last to look away, eyeing me up and down as if she can't believe I have the cheek to be here.

We're taken to a computer room to make our PowerPoint presentations, and we split off into our groups. Claudia is suddenly much more interested than she was the other day. I feel her staring at me while I insert a photo of the Globe Theatre on to a slide.

"I don't mean to be rude or anything, but everyone is talking about it," she says. "What's your side of the story?"

Beside her, Khalid goes still.

"What story?" I ask, frowning as though puzzled. Let her spell it out.

Claudia reddens. "You know. That you, um, killed someone."

I look at her. "Oh, thaaat," I say sweetly. "Screw you."

"God, no need to be nasty," says Claudia. "I thought you might want to give your version. Given what everyone's been saying." She gets up and heads straight over to her friends, presumably to report the conversation to them.

There is a brief silence.

"So that note on your locker *was* meant for you," Khalid says. "*I know you did it.* That's what it said, right?"

65

He's studying my face in a way I've been looked at many times. Like I'm something scary but fascinating. I don't answer.

At lunch I head to the music block, punch in the pi code that Euan told me and sit on the floor in the music practice room, to one side of the door, so no one can see me in there. I message Luffy: *Hey – what's new?* He doesn't reply. He's crap with his phone and with communication in general. I stare at my phone screen until it goes dark.

*Not much – what's new with you?* That's what he'd say if he were sitting next to me, leaning against this wall. And I'd tell him about everything that has happened, because although he wasn't what most people would think of as a fully functional friend, he never made me feel like a freak. He told me he'd write me a letter, old-school style, but it hasn't materialized. I lean my head back against the wall and sigh. I can't make him be the sort of friend I need him to be, that's not how it works.

I worry that Euan will come into the practice room, but he doesn't. Nobody does. I write a nasty one-line review of Dad's music on a website, but instead of bringing relief, it pricks me with the thought that I deserve everything I get.

When there are only a few minutes until the bell rings, I go to the toilets in the main building. As I'm washing my hands, I become aware that Monique is next to me. Dani stands near the door, in front of the hand dryer, ready to block my exit.

66

"Heard some interesting stuff about you from Isaac," Monique says. "So. How long did you get for murder?"

"You what?" I say.

"She's not old enough for prison, Mon," says Dani.

"Shut up, Dani. Young offenders or whatever," Monique says, annoyed. Close up I see her smooth skin and eyelash extensions. Her eyes are like hard grey rocks.

"It was an accident," I say stiffly. "I was four. It was a long time ago. Sorry to disappoint you."

I've washed my hands for a long time now. Since Monique is in front of the hand dryer, I shake them instead. Some droplets land on her.

Her hand is suddenly, shockingly, around my neck. "Don't disrespect me."

There were other people in the toilets, but they have melted away. Only Dani remains, watching expressionless. Someone opens the door, sees something's kicking off, and lets it bang closed again. There's a terrible silence. Burning with panic and rage, I sink my nails deep into Monique's arms.

She screams and lets go, and I bolt while she examines her arms, wailing to Dani to come and see. I sprint past the grey-bearded teacher Mr Pompley, who booms, "No running in the corridor," and out of an exit into a blast of fresh air. I can't walk out of the school grounds because the front gates are locked.

Isaac is suddenly alongside me. "Bad day, Granny?"

I wheel round. "Tell me how you know."

His face is full of exaggerated bewilderment, laughable in other circumstances. "Straight up, can't tell you. Don't know who it was who sent me the message. So don't even think about getting me into trouble. I was only passing on what I'd heard." He gives me a nasty smile.

"You put that note on my locker too, didn't you?"

He looks confused. "The note? Nah, that wasn't me. Don't go pinning that on me. You're the evil one."

I push him away and he laughs. As the bell goes for fifth period, I walk quickly into the performing arts building and back into the practice room, where I sit up against the radiator and cry.

# CHAPTER 10

"What's up?" asks Mum, as I sit at the dinner table. There's a bowl of vegetable curry and rice in front of me. When she came in from work earlier I yelled that I had homework and stayed upstairs in my room. I thought if I avoided her she might not notice that anything was the matter – but Mum always notices.

She narrows her eyes. "Ruby? Come on, I can tell something is wrong."

"Everyone knows what happened," I say. "Isaac, a boy in my year, put it on a group chat."

Her face changes in an instant. "What?"

"Yeah. Everyone's talking about it, asking me about it." I don't tell her I have an after-school detention tomorrow for missing maths this afternoon, when I was hiding out in the practice room. "It's all started up again. Someone – I've no idea who – messaged Isaac knowing he'd blab to everyone…"

"I'm so sorry, Ruby," she says, her face clouded with concern.

My voice cracks. "I can't believe I've got to go through this all again."

"We'll sort it," Mum says. She pushes her fork into her curry and leaves it there. "I'll phone Miss Starling tomorrow and get to the bottom of it. She'll want to know what this Isaac's done, and deal with him appropriately."

"Please don't," I say. "I want to handle it myself." I don't want Mum and Miss Starling to make things worse.

"Ruby," begins Mum, "I don't think that's a good—"

"Let me try. Please?" I say. Mum has tried and failed to put a stop to this before, at my old school. In the end, all it does is upset both of us. Nothing changes. I just have to avoid Isaac and keep my head down.

We sit in silence.

"I suppose at the end of the day it's just silly gossip," Mum says at last. "You're older now, Ruby. You have coping strategies. Shrug off the comments and get on with making friends. Your studies."

It sounds so easy when she says it like that, but I know how hard it will be.

"They'll forget all about it soon. Let's plan something

nice," says Mum. "Something to look forward to. A proper shopping trip at half-term. We could visit Alice at uni one weekend?"

"Alice would hate that," I say. "She's always busy."

"Course she wouldn't hate it," says Mum. "It could be a little city break for us."

Once upon a time, we were a family who went away every summer for two weeks. We'd drive to somewhere hot in Europe and camp, and there would be trips to markets and beaches, and Alice would always say she felt carsick so she could travel in the front passenger seat. Dad used to make us take turns listening to each other's music choices. His choices were always terrible. Old bands or female vocalists with too much vibrato. We used to tease him about it and he didn't mind, and then slowly his music taste changed. It became marginally less tragic, more wannabe cool, and he minded when we teased him.

"We need to explore Barchester, too," says Mum. "We haven't even walked down the high street. Shall we do that on Saturday?" She squeezes my upper arm playfully. "Hot chocolate and cake will be involved."

"Sure," I say, and offer up a smile, even though we're bound to see people from Robinson and I'd rather be hiding at home.

When the bell goes at the end of form, Mr Baldini asks me to stay behind. Everyone stares at me as I stay seated, my stomach sinking.

71

He comes and sits on the desk in front of me, his expression serious. "Ruby, thanks for staying behind. Thought we should have a little chat."

I freeze. Did Mum say something even though she promised she wouldn't?

"I … er… I gather things have been somewhat difficult recently." His ears are red and they clash with his self-tan. "How are you doing?"

*Somewhat difficult?* This is muscle-tensingly awkward. He's so bad at it. "I'm all right," I say, dredging up a fake smile for the situation.

"Good. That's good," he says. "Are you making friends here?"

I shrug.

"It takes time," he says reassuringly. "I understand you had some trouble at your old school. Let's try and make this a fresh start, though." He sounds like Miss Starling. She must have asked him to speak to me. "I want you to come to me if you need to talk about anything, so problems can be ironed out before they grow. That's what I'm here for."

I can't imagine wanting to open up to him about anything, but I say, "OK, thanks. Can I go now?" Being late for my first lesson is going to draw even more attention.

"Erm, sure," says Mr Baldini. "And, Ruby? Keep calm and carry on."

I manage not to roll my eyes until I've turned away towards the door.

On my way to the music practice room at lunchtime, I realize I forgot to bring a drink so go to the canteen to buy one. After I've paid for a carton of apple juice, Amber beckons me over to the table she's at with Georgia.

"Don't ask her," says Georgia as I reach them, placing her hand over Amber's mouth.

Amber wriggles backwards, pushing Georgia's hand away. "Georgia's been doing this zoning-out thing where she forgets where she is. She should get that checked out by a doctor, shouldn't she?"

I look at her, then Georgia, who's now mashing baked beans into her potato with a fork and rolling her eyes. "It was one time, Amber."

Amber raises an eyebrow.

"Er…" I feel stuck between the two of them. "If it continues, yeah, see a doctor, I suppose," I say.

"I just have trouble concentrating sometimes, that's all," says Georgia. There's barely a pause before she adds, "Ruby, what did Mr Baldini want to talk to you about this morning … the rumour?"

"It's not a rumour," I say and watch her squirm at my directness. "It happened. He asked how I was doing."

Both of them are studying me with undisguised curiosity now. "Have a seat. What did you tell him? Did you say it was Isaac's fault?" asks Amber.

I shake my head as I sit. "I told him how much I love being stared at and overhearing people talk about me wherever I go."

The two of them look at each other, unsure.

"I'm joking," I say. I push the straw out of its plastic wrapping and jab it into the foiled carton opening. "Obviously. I just said I was OK and escaped as soon as I could."

Amber says, "Mr Baldini means well though, doesn't he?" She stands up. "I've got to catch Tolla about our Spanish homework before period five. I'll see you both later." She's gone to sit at a nearby table before it sinks in that I can't leave for the music practice room until Georgia's finished her lunch. At least, I could, but it doesn't seem very kind.

"Do you really have trouble concentrating?" I ask, willing her to stop playing with her food and eat it. "You always look as if you're working really hard."

"I get days when I can't stop worrying," says Georgia, staring at the orangey potato mess on her plate. "I've got high predicted grades. I want to make my parents happy. Reach my potential."

"You're doing your best," I say, aware I'm parroting Mum. "Can't do more than that." She doesn't say anything, and before I'm fully aware of them, the Linesmen are standing in front of our table.

"Granny, I hoped I'd see you here," Isaac says. "You interest me. You interest me very much."

Georgia stands up, her chair scraping backwards, more loudly than she wanted it to because she flinches at the sound. Isaac's eyes flick to her. "Are you scuttling off,

74

Little Miss Perfect?" he says. "You scared of us?" He finds that amusing. His teeth are very white – I wonder if he's had them whitened. He's well groomed, I'll give him that. "You should be more scared of Granny!"

"I've got to go for a prefects' meeting," Georgia says, picking up her tray.

"I find her hilarious," Isaac says, as Georgia almost runs to the tray trolley. I get up to follow her, but Isaac, Monique, Jay and Dani sit down at the table, Monique next to me. "You're not going anywhere," she says as Georgia leaves the canteen without looking back. So much for solidarity.

Fear prickles my armpits, and my throat tightens. I take a quick sip of my apple juice.

"Show her, Mon," says Isaac.

Monique shakes off her blazer and lifts the short sleeve of her shirt to reveal a painful red mark at the top of her arm. "You did that, Granny," she says.

I remember the feeling as I sank my nails into her arms. "Apologize," says Dani.

I glance round, unsure how this is going to go. There's a member of staff at the far end of the canteen, but she's not looking this way. One of my legs is bouncing up and down under the table, and my heart is at double-speed.

"Sorry," I say, making a big effort to keep my head up and not mumble.

"Get on your knees and say that," says Isaac.

"Now," says Dani.

I look at their faces and see that they aren't joking. "Er, no," I say. I stand up. My hands are shaking, which I hate.

Monique flies at me, bringing her knee up to my stomach. I drop my apple juice and double over in pain.

"Stop!" shouts someone, and for an instant I think it's me. But then I lift my head and see that Amber is dragging Monique off me, even though she's much smaller.

Monique pulls away from Amber, without even looking at her or saying anything, and spits at me. It lands on my cheek. She says to the others, "C'mon."

They move off slowly, Dani saying in a loud voice, "I think she might have wet herself."

The volume level in the hall returns to normal, with chattering and laughing resumed. I wipe my cheek with the sleeve of my blazer. I need to wash my face. "Thanks," I call to Amber, who's already back in her seat. She lifts her head in the briefest of acknowledgements.

"For the record, I haven't wet myself," I say, but her attention has returned to what Tolla is saying.

# CHAPTER 11

My after-school detention is in a classroom in the humanities corridor. I message Mum to say I'm staying after school to work in the library and she sends me a heart emoji back, which makes me feel guilty.

When I arrive at the classroom, Mr Pompley is outside, talking to another member of staff, a younger woman in a navy trouser suit. It looks as if she's having to listen to him, rather than have a two-way conversation. As I go to open the door, he holds his arm out. He has a walkie-talkie in his hand.

"Hold up there, Ruby."

He knows my name. Not a good sign.

"I'm told there was an incident with you and Monique

yesterday. Very nasty marks on her arms as a result. Hmm?"

The other teacher stares at me. I can almost hear her thinking to herself, *So* this *is Ruby Marshall.*

"She had her hands round my neck, sir," I say. "It was self-defence."

He narrows his eyes. "I see. There is no excuse for violence, Ruby. I hope you reflect on some of your choices during the next hour."

I nod and head inside. The classroom is full. Robinson must dish out detentions on the regular. I sign in, and look around for an empty table to sit at, but there aren't any. There's a low murmur of chat because Mr Pompley is still outside the room.

"Oi!" I look round and see Euan. "Sit next to me if you want," he hisses.

I drop into the seat beside him. "Thanks," I say. He's not someone I'd expect to see here. He seems like the ideal student.

"What did you do?" he asks.

"Skipped period five yesterday," I murmur. "You?"

"Forgot to do my maths homework," says Euan.

"They gave you an after-school for that?"

"I got a day's extension," says Euan. "And forgot *that.*" He grins. "Too busy with social activism."

That's a phrase I haven't heard since I was sitting behind the maintenance shed with Luffy. "What sort of social activism?"

"Scott called a meeting for his Justice for Jim campaign, so I was round at his."

As I consider this, my stomach rumbles, and I clutch it. He pretends to look alarmed. "I've got a pain au chocolat somewhere," he whispers. "Hang on." He brings out a brown paper bag and hands it to me. Inside, between a folded napkin, is the pastry. "It's yesterday's, I'm afraid. Quick, before the teacher comes in."

I lunge at the pastry as if my mouth is taking a running jump at it, and take the biggest bite I can.

"Silence, please," says the teacher in the navy trouser suit as she walks into the class. "Turn to the front and sit still."

I try to swallow in a hurry and spray flakes of pastry. Euan snorts.

"Euan, what's so funny?"

"Nothing, miss."

"Ruby? Got any questions about what you're supposed to be doing?"

I shake my head, jaw frozen.

"Right, then." She sits, eyeing me warily. "Don't push your luck, people. Heads down."

An hour later, we're dismissed and everyone bundles out of the room. Euan and I head out together.

He looks round to check no one's listening and says, "I'm sorry that Isaac's continuing to be a—"

"You two. Take these to my car, would you?" We turn

to see Mr Baldini walking down the corridor towards me and Euan, carrying an enormous pile of exercise books.

"Can't believe you got another after-school detention, you muppet," he says to Euan as he tips half the books into his arms. "Ruby, you don't mind helping, do you? I've got to go back and fetch more of the wretched things."

In that teacherly way of assuming a student is going to say yes, Mr Baldini dumps the rest on to me, drops the keys into Euan's blazer pocket, and heads back to the staff room. I don't mind.

"Apologies for this," says Euan as we go downstairs – super-carefully because it's hard to see where we're going over the piles of books. "Frazer is an arse."

"It's OK," I say. I consider telling him that his brother tried to have a deep chat with me this morning about being at the centre of Robinson gossip, but I don't want to embarrass Euan any further, or talk about Isaac. Instead, I say, "Tell me about the social activism."

"Oh, that." Euan laughs and looks as if he regrets saying that to me. We make our way towards the exit for the car park. "Once Scott gets an idea into his head, he has to run with it until he can't go any further," he says. "He asked his mates to come up with a load of ideas for Justice for Jim campaign."

"To raise money?"

Euan holds open one of the double doors into the next corridor for me with his foot. "Money, awareness, information about the people who might have done the attack."

"Who was there doing all of this activism?" I don't know why I'm pushing, but I can sense something on his part – a reluctance, maybe.

For some reason, Euan hesitates. Then he says, "There were five of us. Scott, Khalid, Amber, me, Naz. Why?"

"Just wondered," I say, and now I'm wondering even more. The five of them definitely aren't a friendship group – I've only been here a short time, but I know that much. Naz is Miss Popular, Euan the easy-going nice guy, Khalid a golden-boy head prefect, Scott thinks he's running a global newsroom and Amber is the long-suffering reporter who doesn't give much away. I suddenly feel like I don't know the first thing about Robinson.

"We came up with some good stuff," Euan says. "Scott is running a social media campaign, I'll do some busking with Amber, Khalid's going to try to get corporate sponsorship for a comedy gig, and Naz is getting together clothes from her friends to sell on Depop."

"Cool," I say. It's hard to imagine Naz selling clothes for charity out of the kindness of her heart.

We step out on to the path that leads to the car park. There's the noise of some kind of match going on – shouts, and a whistle being blown from time to time.

"Hang on a moment," Euan says when we reach the car park. "Need to get the keys." He slides the books in the crook of one arm, and attempts to reach into his pocket. A book falls off his pile.

"Wait," I say. "I'll get them." I step closer, suddenly aware of my proximity to him. His blazer smells of pizza but the rest of him smells of something citrusy. Lemon meringue pie, or a zingy deodorant. I notice that he has dimples in his cheeks. I slide my hand into his pocket and get the keys.

Smiling, I wave the keys in his face, then press the unlock button. A small black car flashes its lights and makes an electronic noise.

I drop the keys back in his pocket and pick up the book for him. "There you go."

"Thanks."

"Scott's lucky he's got you lot to help," I say as Euan opens the car boot and chucks in the books.

Euan shrugs. "We owe him," he says absently.

"What d'you mean?" I ask as I place my pile of books in more carefully.

"Oh…" says Euan. "You know. He's helped us out." He slams the boot shut and doesn't make eye contact. "Where's Frazer got to?" He wanders towards a bench just beyond the car park, and I follow.

I prod him again. "Tell me why you all owe Scott," I say as I sit down.

"He's good at helping people," he says finally. "And if he helps you, you help him."

I wait.

"He helps people with their image, sometimes. He's really into social media and how it can be manipulated. Like, everyone thought Khalid was really uncool and a nerdy try-hard, but Scott turned that round by letting people know about his stand-up comedy, and got him to post photos of himself at the gym. And suddenly not only is he head prefect, but everyone likes him too. Khalid doesn't mind people knowing about what Scott's done for him. Those two are a mutual admiration society."

"And what's he done for you?"

Euan looks back at the car park. "He did an image overhaul on Frazer for me. People used to take the piss and it got pretty bad. Frazer's too orange, but he's a good teacher. He's embarrassing but he's not mean. Like, he can be a laugh sometimes. Scott planted a few stories, got a few people saying how he was all right really, and everyone backed off. People like Frazer now, and, by extension, me."

I realize that I've underestimated Scott. He's not the school joke; he controls so much of the content the students see, and has a lot of influence. He can plant positive spin stories. Robinson's very own PR factory.

"What did Amber need him for?" I ask, curious. "Or Naz?"

Euan shakes his head. "I can't say – I mean, I really can't, I don't know. I know Scott seems like a massive gossip, but he can be discreet when he wants to be, and so are we."

"Hi, Ruby." We look up and see Georgia and Mara.

They're wearing green tunics over their PE kit. "Guess which school just got through to the netball quarter-finals, thanks to goals by me and Mara?"

"No clue," I tease her, although it's obvious by the sweaty elation on their faces.

"Rob-in-son!" chants Mara. She's studying me a little too intently, I think. I guess she's heard the speculation about me, and was probably in the canteen when Monique went for me.

"Cool," I say. Much as I enjoyed the cheerleading at the athletics event, I've only been at Robinson five minutes and I'm not that invested.

"Great!" says Euan, making up for my lack of enthusiasm by going over the top. It's sweet.

"Thanks," Mara says. "Georgia's the legend. It was two-one. She scored the final goal."

Euan's name is being called from the car park. Mr Baldini is standing by the car and gesturing him to get over there, pronto.

"I'm being summoned," says Euan. "Better go, or he'll drive off without me."

"Come *on*," bellows Mr Baldini.

"He's getting worse," sighs Euan.

"He's all right," says Georgia, "and he's the best geography teacher, right, Mara?"

"Right," says Mara, and Euan gives me the faintest of told-you-so shrugs.

# CHAPTER 12

On Saturday, Mum wakes me up at nine-thirty, reminding me we have a date for mother-daughter bonding in Barchester, and that she's bored waiting. She's dyed her hair a deeper brown colour this morning. She looks happy, I think.

"Hair looks nice," I say.

She smiles. "Hurry up, Ruby."

Forty-five minutes later, I'm showered, dressed, eyebrows looking fine, and in the car with a slice of toast.

We park behind the supermarket and wander down Barchester's high street. It's not a long road, but it's pretty, and there are some great gift shops. Mum buys a blue-and-white striped candle for the living room, and a postcard for us to send to Alice. I pick up eyeshadow palettes and admire a perfume with a glass flower stopper, but put them back down. In another shop, I stroke a gorgeously soft, cream-coloured rug. There's a fruit, veg and flower market at the end of the street, and we wander slowly past the stalls, stopping to taste-test cubes of cheese, and I scoop big juicy olives into a pot to buy. Our old town was on the edge of a city, and it sometimes felt unloved, with closed-down shops and overflowing rubbish bins. It feels as if people pay Barchester more attention, and there's more going on. A couple of shops have posters up for a concert, and the bookshop is advertising spaces for a reading group.

I see a few students I recognize from school, but Mum makes me feel safe, distracting me by asking what I think of an item or laughing at a jokey sign outside a shop.

The day we came here to look at houses, we only drove down the high street because we didn't have time between viewings. We had lunch in the café of a local garden centre, which was dead but had plenty of parking. The town itself has quite a few cafés. Mum wants to try one called Monty's, which I remember Euan telling me is the one he works at. She looks through the window. "Come on," she calls. "I see a free table."

I scan the room as we enter, but I don't see Euan. I'm not sure if I'm relieved or disappointed. A woman shows us to a small table in the corner, and Mum is already cooing about how nice it is. It *is* nice, in an alternative, cool way. She sits down and notes they have five different types of non-dairy milk, including her favourite, soya.

"Are you ready to order, Ruby?" she asks, and I look up to see Euan approaching us. He's wearing a half apron over black jeans. On his top half he's wearing a white polo shirt with *Monty's* written in lime green in an arty font.

"Very professional," I say, and he merely grins back.

Mum frowns at what she thinks is my snarkiness to a stranger.

"I know him!" I say.

"Hi, Ruby," says Euan. He's still smiling, and I'm transfixed for a moment by the clarity of his grey-blue eyes.

"See?" I say. "He's from Robinson. His brother is a teacher there."

Euan smiles at Mum. "Hi, yes, we're friends."

Her face transforms into an expression of delight which brings a sudden lump to my throat. She's never been introduced to a friend of mine before, apart from Luffy, who wasn't up for talking to her with eye contact.

I watch with amazement as the two of them exchange small talk about her stripy candle, then I order the best hot chocolate Monty's can provide. Mum orders herself a soya milk latte and a slice of carrot cake for us to share.

"He seems nice," Mum says quietly, after Euan has brought our order and left a Friends & Family twenty-five per cent discount card on the table for us, which I thought

Mum was going to hug him for – maybe because of the friends thing more than the twenty-five per cent? Who knows. "Have things died down at school, then?"

"I'm not sure," I say. I don't want to burst her bubble. It's worse than ever. Yesterday as I was walking out of school, I was followed by some younger kids who were taking photos of me and talking about how I'd just come out of a young offenders' institution and was wearing an electronic tag somewhere under my uniform.

Mum places her hands on mine. They're warm from cradling her latte mug. "It'll blow over," she says firmly. As always, I am amazed by her optimism.

When we've finished the cake, she pulls a biro out of her handbag and writes the postcard to Alice. She tells her we're feeling at home in Barchester, which is a stretch, and that we're missing her, which is even more of a stretch. She says that her job is going well and adds a smiley face after this. I sign at the bottom, looping the $y$ of my name into a spiral. It's how I used to sign my name when I was about eight, and I know she'll appreciate it.

"I'll buy some stamps, post this, and meet you in the supermarket," she says. "No rush. Here." She winks, then picks up the discount card and gives it to me with a twenty-pound note.

Euan's at the bar when I go up to pay. He asks me how my hot chocolate was, and I give him a full report: that it mostly measured up well against my high expectations, but if I'm being completely honest, I could have done with a few more marshmallows. He shakes a few out of a glass jar on to a saucer for me, and says he has to go into the kitchen to change my twenty-pound note.

While he's gone I perch up on a bar stool. There's a mirror behind the bottles of alcohol on the wall behind the bar, and I can see some of my thin, pale face. People think I have a need to stand out because of my hair colour, or my garish clothes, or the tiny, illegal angry-face tattoo on my shoulder that Luffy's cousin gave me last summer. But the way I present myself doesn't completely match who I am on the inside. I'm not trying to draw attention to myself; I'm trying to warn people that I don't fit in.

"Here you go," says Euan, returning with my change on a little metal dish with the receipt.

"Thanks," I say. It's comfortable on the stool. He picks up a tea towel to dry off some latte glasses. "That conversation we were having yesterday before Georgia and Mara showed up was interesting. About the favours that Scott does for you guys."

He raises his eyebrow in a puzzled way, but I'm pretty sure he knows which conversation I mean. He just doesn't want to go there any more.

"Why is he so keen to help people?"

Euan gives an embarrassed laugh. "You think he's got to have some ulterior motive?" I notice that he glances around briefly to check no one is listening.

"I do, yeah," I say.

Euan sighs. "It's not as calculating as you think. He helped out Khalid because he fancied him and didn't want to lower his own reputation by going out with someone other people thought was a loser. Not," he adds quickly, "that I ever thought Khalid was a loser, but, you know. Sometimes people get these lazy tags." He looks at me and he doesn't need to say out loud that I've been a victim of that, a lazy tag. "And then I guess Scott realized he was good at it – turning around people's images, changing public perception of them. People started to realize he could help them, and it grew from there."

"So, what's in it for him? Do you pay him?"

Euan places the dry latte glass on a tray with three others. "I don't pay him – and I can't imagine the others do. We just help him out with his campaigns. Scott gets a buzz from what he does. He likes trying out new things. Sees people in need as a challenge, you know."

"It sounds like I need his services," I joke.

"You should talk to him," says Euan. I look up and see that he's serious. "He's a clever guy."

I shrug. "I can fight my own battles," I say. Plus, whatever Euan says, I wouldn't want Scott to have any sort of hold over me.

We're interrupted by a young family coming into the café, and I mouth goodbye to Euan as he comes out from behind the bar to show them to a table.

The high street is busier now, and I have to dodge pushchairs, old people's shopping trolleys and a motorized wheelchair. Looking into the bakery, I see the student librarian behind the counter. He clocks me, and waves with manic energy. I hold one hand up, which might be interpreted as a greeting or it might mean *Stop*. I leave it to him to decide.

There's a wide alleyway between two shops that leads to the Tesco car park. As I walk down it, distracted by a little dog in a jumper, I hear a voice calling, "Ruby! Ruby!"

I stop and look around, seeing no one I know. I think it must be another Ruby who's being called, and then I notice Mara trying to get past a family with a pushchair.

"Hi!" she says, reaching me, bright blue eyes shining, pink-cheeked from running. Athletics fiend. "I thought it was you. I'm glad I saw you."

"Hello," I say hesitantly. I can't think of any reason why Mara would be particularly glad to see me. She hardly knows me.

"Can we talk a moment?" she asks.

"Sure," I say. I move to let the family with the pushchair go past.

"Somewhere we're not in the way," Mara says. "Somewhere private."

This is beginning to sound heavy. "I'm meeting my mum in a minute," I say.

"Please. It won't take long." She starts walking and I don't have a lot of choice but to follow.

She leads me to a low wall round the corner, which

edges a triangle of grass, and we sit down. There's a small boy clambering on and jumping off one end of it while his mum holds his hand. His mum tells him it's time to go and he starts wailing.

"There's something I have to tell you and there's no easy way to say it," Mara says. I start to feel anxious, and too hot. She takes a deep breath. "My last name's Cole."

The name reverberates in my ribs. *Hannah Cole.* I brace every muscle in my body. My breath hitches with a terrible anticipation.

Mara clears her throat and says, "I'm Hannah's twin."

# CHAPTER 13

Nothing feels real for a moment. Is this a sick joke? A dare?
I search Mara's face. She's totally serious.

Hannah's twin is sitting next to me. I've spoken to
her, cheered with her, *laughed* with her, all the time not
knowing this one terrible fact.

The colours in the car park become overwhelmingly
bright; there's a dazzling blue car in my line of sight, and
shiny painted yellow lines for the car spaces. The silver of a
trolley being wheeled past glints so violently my eyes hurt.

I can't seem to keep my eyes from returning to her face.
Hannah's twin. Were Mara and Hannah identical? Is this
how Hannah would have looked if she'd lived? Is this the
face of the girl I killed? I suck in more air at the thought.

Those vivid blue eyes, the oval shape of her head, the small nose and two moles on her cheek.

I knew Hannah had had a sister, but I'd imagined her to be older, perhaps because I had an older sister myself.

"I didn't mean to shock you," Mara says. She has her hand at her throat. She's nervous. "Once I knew who you were, I had to say something, and I couldn't do it in front of anybody else. I've been waiting for an opportunity to speak to you alone." She pauses for breath. "It's been so hard."

I nod, my mind clunking madly like our inherited fridge when we open the door for too long.

"You need time to let it sink in. It's not sunk in yet for me either," says Mara.

I search her face again, this time for signs of hatred. Instead I think she looks … awkward. She's looking at me carefully too. "It doesn't feel real, does it?" she says.

"No." I stand, desperate to get away from her. I need to get to the supermarket. I need Mum.

"When you're ready…" says Mara. She pauses. "When you're ready, please can you tell me some more about what happened that day? My grandparents won't talk about it, and my parents weren't there, and I don't want to upset them. Mum and Dad like remembering Hannah, but we never talk about the day she died."

The smell of the play park is suddenly in my nostrils, the metal of the slide and the leafy scent of the trees by the fence. "Yes," I say, because I want to do this for her. I owe her that much, no matter how painful it is for me.

Mara gives a half-smile, then stands. "Thank you. I've wanted answers for a long time. It — it would help a lot. We were identical, you know. Han and me."

Confirmation. Mara's face is Hannah's face, haunting me from the grave.

"Are you going to be OK?" says Mara. She steps closer and I step back.

I nod. I hear myself say I'll have to talk to her another time. I turn and stumble in the direction of Tesco's entrance, and a car blares its horn at me for stepping out in front of it. I hop backwards and see the driver shake his head slowly to tell me what an idiot he thinks I am.

"Wait," says Mara, appearing alongside me. "Please. Let's swap numbers, at least." She has her phone out already.

I want to do whatever it takes to get away from her. I recite my number, which Mara stores, and uses to call mine so I have hers. The ringtone sounds suddenly menacing.

I don't have any other Maras in my phone, and I don't want this one; it's like having Hannah inside my phone, wriggling her way into my life.

"I'll be in touch," says Mara, and I don't reply. I'm looking at the cars curling their way round the one-way system of the car park. I step out into a gap, careful this time where I'm putting my wobbly feet.

Once I'm on the pedestrian path that leads to the Tesco

entrance, I move faster. Faster and faster. The security guard looks accusingly at me. *You are a bad person*, his face says. The colours of the fruit and vegetables, and the pungent smell of the lilies in bouquets in buckets, are too much. Over the tannoy, there's a request for more staff to make their way to the tills. It's too loud. There are too many people.

I can't see Mum. I start to run from aisle to aisle, going back and forth in case I've missed her while she was moving between aisles. I'm running out of breath. There's no more oxygen in my lungs. Finally I glimpse her at the checkout, looking round for me.

When she sees me she says, "What's the matter, Ruby? You look as if you've seen a ghost." I'm aware of the person behind her gawping at me with interest, of Mum's bewildered concern, of the horrible white light attacking my eyeballs from every angle, and I ask for her keys, and say I'll meet her at the car, and I'm sobbing as I run to the exit.

# CHAPTER 14

I'm hunched in the passenger seat crying when Mum reaches the car. She opens the door, crouches down and holds me tight. "Tell me what's happened," she whispers.

I try, but it comes out all garbled. All I can manage are the words *Hannah* and *twin*.

"We can sort this out," she says gently, and I cry even more as she strokes my hair, because she can never sort this out. Mara exists.

After she's loaded the car with the shopping and we're inching in traffic out of the car park, Mum tells me to start at the beginning, and I watch how her face changes as I speak and she takes on some of my pain.

She first became ill with headaches, unexplained

aches and an inability to concentrate when I moved to secondary school. Her high-pressured job in IT wore her out and Dad encouraged her to give up work and pursue something she'd wanted to do for years – make and sell silver jewellery. The problem was after less than a year, Dad left us to pursue his own dreams, and she couldn't afford to keep going with her business, even though Alice and I tried to help as much as we could. She decided she'd have to go back to IT.

Alice's and my biggest fear is that Mum won't cope with her new job, and she'll get ill again. Other people don't always realize she has to take it easy sometimes, because she gives the impression of being as tough as they come.

Mum turns right out of the car park now, accelerating fast into the window of traffic opportunity. "I knew Hannah had a twin," she says. "I should have told you. But what were the chances you'd end up in the same school as her?" Her eyes flick to the wing mirror. "I knew the family lived out this way, but I didn't know where." When she's looking straight ahead again, I see there are tears in her eyes. "It was so long ago…"

Why did we have to wind up here, out of all the places Mum could have found a job? "It's OK," I say. "She wasn't confrontational or anything. It was just a shock."

Mum glances at me. "Do you think she was behind all that business at school? The note?"

"I don't know," I say, and I really don't. "She could be.

She said she just wanted to talk."

Mum grips the steering wheel with both hands firmly again. "We'll deal with this, Ruby. You like this school, and you're making friends here, and I don't think we should uproot you again, OK?" I nod. "If you do want to talk with Mara, I'd rather I was there – at least initially. Or Alice. Even your dad."

"Dad would probably want to write a song about the experience," I say, and it makes Mum smile, though it's a sad smile.

"I'm going to speak to Miss Starling first thing on Monday," she says. "I'm not standing back any longer. This needs to be handled very carefully. Is Mara in lessons with you?"

I shake my head. "She's in the year below."

"That's something, I suppose," says Mum. She gives me a quick, warm smile. "It's going to be OK," she says. I don't know whether she's trying to convince me or herself.

At home, I help unload and put away the shopping, and then I curl up on the uncomfortable, ugly bamboo sofa and watch a home makeover show on Netflix. My mind repeatedly goes back to Mara. I wonder what her house is like, and if there are photos of Hannah everywhere.

When Mum goes out for a run, I turn the TV off and lie in the silence, crying, and hating myself all over again for What Happened.

★

I spend a lot of Sunday crying too, when I'm not writing an essay on how Dickens explores forgiveness in *A Christmas Carol*. Forgiveness is far more complicated than people think.

On Monday morning, I walk, my face pale and fragile like a china teacup, into school. At period three lesson changeover, a boy holds the door for me, then lets it close in my face when I'm centimetres away. I swear loudly at him.

Miss Starling is behind me. "Language," she says automatically.

It's easy for her to say that. If someone had slammed the door in her face she'd be giving them a detention. She sees it's me. "Oh, Ruby – I need to have a word. Come with me."

I follow her down the hall and into her office. She smiles encouragingly as I settle myself in the seat opposite her.

"Your mother told me that Mara approached you," she says. "I understand what a shock that must have been."

*No you don't*, I think. How could she understand?

Miss Starling leans on her elbows and talks about coping mechanisms. She explains she's already spoken to Mara, and Mara has promised to keep her distance. She's also spoken to Mara's parents, and they understand that I have as much right to be at this school as Mara, but they don't want the two of us to have any contact other than that which is strictly necessary to school life.

I get it.

"I'm confident we can manage this situation," says Miss Starling. "I trust you both to keep what has happened with your families out of school." She adds a slight lilt to the sentence to make it a question I agree to. "Everybody involved wants the same thing – for the two of you to get on with school life without any issues. I promise you I will keep this a confidential matter. I have also spoken to Isaac, who I gather foolishly forwarded a malicious text message. He acknowledges he shouldn't have done this, and has been asked to keep away from you too. I hope this reassures you."

I nod. I suppose it does. Slightly. There are no birds on her dress today, but there are polka dots. They appear to bounce in front of my eyes. I stand, keen to get away and slip into my next lesson, for which I'm now fifteen minutes late.

I'm in such a rush I forget to ask for a late note, and my maths teacher says she'll check whether I was with Miss Starling, and if I'm not telling the truth, it'll be a detention.

"Whatever," I say as I sit down, and she glares at me.

When double maths is over, Georgia waits for me by the door and says, "Coming to the canteen?"

I shake my head. "I'm going to do some piano practice."

"Are you OK?" asks Georgia.

"Not really, but thanks." I'm touched she's noticed, but she can reverse out of my personal space right away. "I want to be on my own."

She nods. "See you in English. Hope you've written the essay on *A Christmas Carol*?"

I nod. "Thanks. Yes, I did it."

"Good," she says, just like a teacher.

I walk past Naz and the Glossy Posse on my way to the music room, and one of them says, "I used to have a backpack like that in year seven."

I ignore her, and hear Naz drawl, "If she's trying to be retro, it's not working."

I've started to feel at home in this practice room, but for some reason I can't bring myself to sign up to legitimately use it. After I've played a piece through by heart, a music teacher pops his head in the door and says, "Nice playing. D'you have lessons in school?"

"No," I say, my hands still on the keys, a hint that I'd prefer to keep playing than talk.

"Lessons out of school? Who teaches you?"

"I used to have lessons," I say. "But we don't have a piano at home to practise on any more."

He nods. "I'm Mr Williams. And you're...?"

"Ruby."

"You're welcome to use the room, but students who have music lessons in school have priority. Good to meet you, Ruby. I'll leave you to it." He closes the door quietly behind him.

There's a pile of sheet music on top of the piano. I pull out one of the easier pieces and attempt to sight-read it.

I have to remind myself about the bass clef, working out notes quickly enough to keep the pieces moving along. It keeps my brain busy. After a while my concentration lags. I can't stop thinking of Hannah's face at four turning into Mara's face now. The room is stuffy and small. I stop playing. I need to get out.

It's raining outside, and the communal spaces in the building are packed with people. I walk the length of it instead, stepping over bags, coats and legs. As I look through the door of the performing arts office, I see the back of Scott's head, with its thin blonde hair, and my eyes slide to his computer screen.

I stop. I recognize the article on it. It's the one about What Happened which appeared in our local newspaper a few days afterwards.

It can't have been hard for Scott to find it. He'd heard it was an accident on a slide when I was four, and Amber could have told him roughly where I used to live, having asked me at lunchtime on my first day. A chunk of the article is turning blue as Scott highlights it.

I burst through the door.

Scott jumps when he sees it's me and quickly closes the tab so his screen reverts to the mountainscape wallpaper of his desktop. "Do you always have to make such a dramatic entrance when you come to see me?" he says.

"What the hell are you doing?" I say. "Why did you have that article up?"

103

He sighs as if it's slightly annoying for him to have to explain it. "Fine, I'm interested. I was seeing what was out there about the accident. It all happened a long time ago – so why hasn't the story gone away? It should have done." He has a smug look about him now. "That garden getting trashed didn't help. Did you make any enemies at your last school?"

"It's nothing to do with you," I say. He'd explode with excitement if he knew Hannah's twin was here at Robinson.

"Your story's out there," Scott says. "It's public property now." He scratches the side of his head. "Speaking of which, I understand that Euan has mentioned my sideline. I'd be up for taking you on." He smiles as if he's doing me a huge favour. "You'd need to support my projects in return, of course."

"Why would you help me?" I say.

He raises an eyebrow. "I help people I like."

I roll my eyes. "You don't like me – you like the challenge. I'm a pretty big challenge, aren't I?"

He doesn't contradict me. "You've come with some baggage," he says, eyeing me thoughtfully. "But you're not a lost cause. We could turn this situation around."

"How?" I can't help being intrigued.

"Remind people that the girl's death was ages ago. That it was a tragic accident when you were four years old, for goodness' sake. That you've had to change schools in year eleven, which is a nightmare. Let it be known you're a talented piano player. That you care about causes like Justice for Jim. That's just for starters."

"How do you know I play the piano?"

"I heard you play when I went past earlier. Those rooms should be soundproofed but they're not. I'm an ideas person. I could really help you." He leans back, folding his arms. "And, frankly, you need the help. Interested?"

"Go to hell," I say, as I stride to the door. I slam it so hard on the way out, I feel the vibrations as I walk away.

# CHAPTER 15

As I squeeze on to the bus the following morning, standing in the aisle next to a pole, I'm aware of Euan sitting in his usual seat. I'm determined not to make eye contact with him. I'm suspicious of him suddenly. I wonder whether he's been playing me all along, getting me curious about Scott. Maybe it's like a bizarre pyramid scheme, where each of Scott's disciples has to recruit someone.

The bus lurches forward and I grab the pole to stop myself falling into the person next to me. A few people snigger, including Monique, who is sitting at the back with Jay. I'm skilled at this, working out where everyone is within a couple of seconds of stepping on the bus.

I curl one arm around the pole, keeping my head down, and scroll through last night's conversation with Luffy.

We spoke properly last night for the first time since the move. He finally answered my message *U still alive?* with *Been fishing with my cousin. You all right?*

I've never heard him talk about fishing before, and it doesn't explain why he hasn't messaged for so long, unless he's now living in one of the domed tents that spring up along the river from time to time, which would be very Luffy even though the weather's turning autumnal.

I told him about Mara, and everyone knowing my past, and he'd replied, *That's wild. Ignore the haters.*

Frustrated, I'd called him, willing him to pick up, and he did.

"Hi," he said.

I could hear rap in the background. "That's your brother's music I can hear, right?" I asked, and he laughed. I hoped Mickey wasn't going to be listening in to our conversation.

Luffy told me his brother got off with a fine at court for handling stolen goods and everything was cool in his family. "So. What's up with this twin?" he'd said.

I stood by the window in my room, in front of my sheet curtain looking at the emptiness of my new road. I began to tell Luffy everything that had happened. At several points I had to say, "Are you still there?" because he was so quiet.

When I was done, I said, "What d'you think?" and he exhaled in a way that told me he was smoking.

"I dunno," he said. "I really dunno. You're going to have to see how this pans out, bruh."

I watched a cat walk down the middle of the road, stealthy and purposeful.

"Yeah," I said.

"Take care," said Luffy. "Call me when you need to."

"You don't pick up though," I replied, and he laughed again. It wasn't unkind. It was self-mocking.

We said goodbye, and I went to bed, feeling as if our friendship was evaporating slowly, like the reed diffuser Mum was given last Christmas which started out strong, but after a few months was nothing but a faint smell and dry sticks in an empty bottle.

Now, as I scroll through my texts, a new one slides on to my screen. It's from Mara and it's long. I look up immediately to see if anyone in the bus is reading over my shoulder, but they're too immersed in their own phones, music or conversations.

My stomach lurches as I read it:

*Hope you're OK after my bombshell. I'm sorry. I didn't know how else to tell you. And I know we're not supposed to have contact but I really need to talk to you.*

So much for keeping her distance. I get where she's coming from though. I'd want to know more if I were in her shoes.

The bus comes to a halt outside school and I'm jostled

off with everyone else. As I walk towards the gates, I hear my name being called. I look back and see Euan wave at me.

I stop but I'm not looking at him. Behind him, something intriguing is taking place. Monique is standing by the bus with Amber. As I watch, Monique hands something to Amber. There's something covert about it. There are too many people in between us to see what it is, but it's something small as it disappears into Amber's palm. Drugs?

"What are you staring at?" asks Euan. He looks back to see what he's missing out on.

"Nothing," I say.

"I didn't get a chance to speak with you yesterday," says Euan, "but you seemed down."

"It was nothing." For all I know, he's reporting to Scott. Trying to drum up business.

"Anything you want to talk about?" he pushes.

"No thanks," I say, aware of the non-stop vibration in my pocket. Mara, not taking silence for an answer.

In form, looking at my phone under the table, I read the eight messages she's sent.

*I want to stop obsessing about Han*
*It would help me so much to speak to you*
*Nobody else understands*
*Sorry to bombard u*
*Ur the only one who can help*

*Can we meet somewhere? In Barchester? Or anywhere*

*I won't ask anything you don't want to tell me. Only wanna know the facts*

*Please please please reply*

At lunchtime in the music room, playing the same piece of music over and over, one Alice and I used to play together at different ends of the keyboard, I think about what I should do. I want to forget Mara exists, and that's what Mum wants too. But for that to happen I might need to answer her questions.

I imagine what it would be like to have her in front of me, talking about the day It Happened. I can feel the edge of panic, my heart picking up speed.

*Get a grip*, I tell myself, as I take my fingers off the keys and go to open a window. I gulp in the fresh air and listen to the squawking of a group of boys squirting water at each other.

I open up Mara's messages and tap the knuckle of one thumb against my mouth. I rewrite my response a few times. In the end I go for: *I'll meet you on Saturday in the garden centre café at ten.*

She replies almost immediately: *THANK YOU – I really REALLY appreciate it*

I have a sense of immediate regret, as if I've put something into motion which can't be reversed.

The school gym is packed, maybe because it's raining. All the treadmills and cross-trainers are taken, and there's a smell of stale sweat. Georgia is adjusting the seat on a rowing machine. Amber is on the machine that works the thighs. Isaac lies on the bench press, lifting heavy weights. We haven't had any contact since Miss Starling spoke to him.

Mr Morton, who teaches PE, is spotting for him and counting the reps. "Anyone like to do alternate sets with Isaac?" he calls as Isaac takes a rest.

None of Isaac's mates are here, so no one steps forward.

"Sir, can you look at this seat?" calls Georgia.

Mr Morton asks Khalid to stand in for him for a moment, and I watch the body language between Isaac and Khalid with fascination. Khalid keeps as far apart from him as he can, and he counts too softly to hear.

"Speak up, you moron!" yells Isaac.

"I'm not having this," says Khalid, turning away.

"Unsafe practice!" calls Mr Morton, coming back over.

"That's unfair, sir," says Khalid. "He was rude."

"Right. Listen up, everyone," says Mr Morton, raising his voice above the chatter. "We need a better community spirit in here. We take it in turns to spot for each other. We aren't rude. We say thank you. Georgia? I'll fix that seat while you spot for Isaac for a moment."

I see her face tighten in horror, but she can't refuse a teacher. Instead, she says, "OK," and comes over.

"Thanks so much, Georgia," says Isaac, exuding unctuous politeness.

I admire her. She gets on with it, counting in a clear

voice, adding more weights when he asks her to, checking the different coloured stickers on them to make sure they're the right ones.

I do some stretches on a mat, waiting for a treadmill to be free, and when Isaac finishes on the bench press, Khalid says, "Ruby, will you spot for me?"

"OK, but I've never done it before," I reply.

Amber comes over to help. We smile at Khalid's facial expressions as he lifts the weights, and while we make sure he doesn't drop the bar on to his chest, I silently note his super-expensive Nikes. Amber laughs to see me surprised at the heaviness of the weights as I return them to the rack.

Khalid finishes and thanks us, then his gaze moves past us, and he grins. Scott has come into the gym, in full school uniform.

"Hey, you need to be in correct clothing," calls Mr Morton.

"I'm meeting my boyfriend," says Scott indignantly.

"Meet him outside the gym," says Mr Morton.

Scott reaches for Khalid's hand, and the two of them walk out together.

Naz wanders in, looking incredible in her Gymshark gear. "Lost my PE kit temporarily, sir," she says to Mr Morton, who sighs.

"I'll let you in this time," he says. "Next time, I'll turn you away."

"Thanks, sir," she simpers.

"Looking hot, Naz!" calls Isaac.

"Thanks, babe," she replies, in a clipped voice. She steps on to a mat and stretches, without giving him a second glance.

Later, as I pound the treadmill, I force myself to think about Mara. I could still cancel. Shall I meet her, or not? Isaac steps on the one next to me, randomly shouting "Snitch" at intervals. After 5k, I step down, my decision made.

I'll go. But I'm not going to tell anyone about our meeting until after it's happened. Mum would try to put a stop to it, or insist on coming with me. Alice would tell Mum, and no one at Robinson can keep a secret. And I can't bear the thought that Luffy might not care at all.

# CHAPTER 16

The rest of the week passes slowly. I keep myself to myself as much as possible. In form, from my vantage point at the back, I watch as Amber spends more time talking to Tolla than she does to Georgia. Georgia keeps herself busy with books or fiddling with items from her pencil case. She cuts up abandoned pieces of paper with her scissors, picks apart her eraser with her fingernails and bends paper clips into different shapes.

Since my past was made public, my following on social media has increased. People are intrigued by me. I follow them back. I suddenly feel as if I should know who's connected to whom.

Naz posts a picture of a Halloween Batgirl costume

she's thinking of buying for the school disco, and lots of people pile in to say how awesome it is, including Scott. I see Khalid taking selfies of himself when I'm in the gym, hanging around with the Sporty Lot, laughing and back-slapping.

In history, Khalid and I do our group project presentation on the Globe. It goes well and Khalid and I make a good team. Claudia stands up at the front with us, pulling at a thread on the hem of her school jumper, saying nothing until the end when she adds, "Thank you for listening." Khalid rolls his eyes at me and afterwards he says, "A few of us are hanging out at my house tonight, if you fancy it?"

He says it in the euphoria of the presentation being over, and our mutual annoyance at Claudia. For a moment, I'm caught up in the warmth of acceptance, and I'm smiling a proper smile, and then he says, "It'll be me, Scott, Euan, Amber and a few others," and I'm suspicious. He's either been asked by Scott to soften me up, or I'm being sucked into the Justice for Jim campaign to bulk up numbers.

"Thanks," I say, "but I've got something on this evening."

I wake several times in the night before I'm due to meet Mara, slick with sweat from nightmares. I lie on my back in the darkness, imagining the way she'll look at me as I tell her What Happened. But in my nightmares it's four-year-old Hannah I see, not Mara. I'm perpetually trying to save Hannah from smashing her head on the slide, and I'm always too late. But then, when nobody else is looking, she lifts her bloodied head and laughs at me with evil eyes, missing teeth and a section of her face gone.

The previous evening, Mum asked me what my plans for the weekend were, and I decided to keep to some of the truth. I told her I was going to the garden centre because people at school said there were weekend jobs up for grabs. She asked if I'd done myself a CV and I had to say I'd heard I would only be required to fill in a form, and CVs weren't needed. That's the problem with lies – they start out simple and get complicated.

"Having a CV is a good idea," she said. "Come on, let's do one," and the next hour was given over to examining which CV template on the internet was the best, filling it in and printing it out. I think about how I'd like to have piano lessons again, although I know Mum can't afford them. Each lesson is as expensive as a pair of decent jeans. Me getting a job would really help. Now I have a CV, I decide to actually start looking for one.

In the morning, Mum is up and ready with opinions about what I should be wearing, even though I tell her there won't be an interview. To please her, I wear my black jeans, which look smarter than my blue ones, and a sweatshirt that doesn't have tomato ketchup on it, and I tie my hair up. I spend a long time at the bathroom mirror on my eyes, eyebrows and contouring, until Mum walks in and says in a jokey way, "Are you sure you're not going on a date?"

"In that garden centre?" I reply scathingly, and she says, "Fair comment."

She's humming round the kitchen, scrubbing at the discoloured grouting between the tiles. "I've measured your bedroom window," she says. "Let's order you a blind when you get back."

I watch her, busy and happy, focused on our fresh start, and my chest tightens.

Google Maps says it's going to take me twenty-three minutes to walk there. Listening to music right now would make me associate those particular tracks with Mara, so I leave my earbuds in my pocket and let my thoughts roam. The thought that goes round and round in my head is: *How did Mara know I was at Robinson? Who told her?*

I guess I have questions too.

Outside the garden centre, I stand by the big trolleys, breathing in the woody smell of the sheds for sale. My phone pings and I check to see if it's Mara cancelling or running late. It's Mum, wishing me luck.

I put my phone on silent, and walk in. I need to look in control, and to stop biting the inside of my mouth, which, as Alice has told me plenty of times, makes me look weird.

I'm deliberately ten minutes early. It's the middle of October, but there are Christmas tree lights on display. I see Mara straight away, at a table near the entrance, scrolling through her phone. Her shoulder-length hair hangs down in a smooth curtain; she's straightened it. For this, for me? All other tables are busy and there's a queue of people at the counter.

There are a couple of seconds when I am looking at her and she doesn't know I'm there. I could still turn around and go. Instead, I force myself to keep moving forward, past the stand which announces there's a special coffee-plus-cake promotion this morning.

Mara stands when she sees me. It's awkward. She tries to smile and I do the same. Her eyes are so blue, they're distracting. Hannah's eyes.

"I didn't think you'd come," she says, in a rush. "D'you want a drink? I didn't know whether to wait or get something and in the end I thought I'd shotgun a table and wait, but people keep glaring at me. It's got really busy."

I look at the queue. Being in it will give me more breathing space. "Stay there. I'll get you something," I say.

"A Diet Coke, please. If that's OK," she says, like I might say it wasn't.

"Anything to eat?" I ask. I'm not remotely hungry and I don't suppose she is either.

"No, thanks."

I nod and join the queue, and listen to a man complain the café has run out of his favourite cake. It's nice, the distraction, hearing his voice stop and start, and the placating tones of the older lady serving him. I'm given a couple of two-for-one breakfast vouchers with my change,

118

and when I point out I have an extra one, the lady says, "You keep them both, love!" as if it's my lucky day.

I carry the tray carefully to the table, and Mara thanks me, then takes a sip of Diet Coke from the bottle it came in, and says, "Nice." I didn't want Mara thinking I was a cheapskate, so I've bought myself a hot chocolate, which I don't want.

Mara pulls her thumb and forefinger along a length of blonde-brown hair by her cheek, and says, "Thank you for not bailing." She looks around. "It's the first time I've been here. They're into Christmas already. It's mad."

"I know." I look back at the display out of politeness. "At least there'll be no one here from school," I say, as I take off my coat and let it fall back on the chair and dangle on to the floor. "Hopefully." There's a boy stacking candles on a table near the café entrance, but he's definitely older than us.

"I think my nan comes here sometimes," says Mara. I flinch and she says quickly, "Don't panic. She's gone to Costco with my granddad this morning. I checked. Not that she'd recognize you now, anyway." She bites her lip, as though worried she might have said too much too soon.

A thought shoots like a hard object into my stomach and brain simultaneously. "You're not going to record this conversation, are you?" I ask.

"Of course not," says Mara. She takes her phone from her black cotton tote bag on the floor, shows me a blank screen and places it in the middle of the table. She frowns.

"I wouldn't do that. This is just for me. We've got to trust each other. OK?" She looks at me, those bright blue eyes searching mine. I keep her gaze.

"OK."

Mara takes another sip of her Diet Coke, then wipes her mouth self-consciously with the back of her hand.

"Did you tell Isaac what I ... what happened?" I ask. It's the question I need to get out of the way first.

Her eyes widen. "No. Of course not. Why would I do that? You know what he's like."

"To get at me?" I say quietly.

She shakes her head. "Don't get mad at me, but once I knew that locker with the note on was yours, it crossed my mind that..." She trails off, flushing.

"What?" I say.

"I wondered whether you'd put the note up yourself. Told people about what happened. I thought you knew I was at the school and were trying to bully me..." She sees my horrified face. "I don't think that now."

There's pressure in my temples, a headache brewing. "That's insane," I say sharply, but I check myself. I need to stay calm. "How could you think that?"

"I thought it was the kind of horrible thing you would do. I was taught to hate you by my nan," she says, and looks down for the first time.

*I was taught to hate you.* Those words shock me.

Mara looks back up at me. "It took me a long time to realize it must be her guilt, that she didn't protect Hannah

120

when she was looking after her. Nan told me you were starting at Robinson. Her friend at your old school told her." Mrs Lipperton, determined not to let me escape my past. "I felt sick. And then I met you at athletics club and you seemed … nice. Normal."

"So your parents knew too – before Miss Starling spoke to them on Monday?"

Mara nods cautiously. "My mum and dad had to stop Nan from storming down to Robinson straight away. They calmed her down, reminded her how long ago it was, that it was just an accident."

"So how did Isaac find out?" I ask. Surely Mrs Lipperton doesn't know him?

Mara frowns. "I don't know. It wouldn't have come from my family or Nan's friend. Why would they want to make things difficult for me at school?"

I pick up the long spoon that came with my tall glass of hot chocolate. I stir it round and round, and when I stop the liquid keeps going, spiralling into a point in the middle which disappears. "None of this is very nice for you."

Mara visibly relaxes at that. She lays her hands, palm out, on the table. "It's not very nice for you, either," she says softly. "I don't want people to find out the connection between us any more than you do… It's private."

"So you haven't told your friends?"

"No, not yet. They know my twin died in an accident with my grandparents. They've always assumed it was a car accident. That's kind of what my family implies to people.

121

It's easier. I might tell my friends, but not now – after you've left, maybe. I'd warn you first."

"All right." I can't quite bring myself to thank her, but I know it's a decent thing for her say. "At least we're not in the same school year."

"We should be," says Mara. "I started school later because of the accident. I wasn't ready. I was struggling without Hannah."

I bite down on the inside of my mouth.

Mara leans forward. "I know this is difficult, but I really want to hear about that day. Please?"

I think of the hate Mara's family must have for me, and my stomach aches. "OK," I say. "I can only go through it once, though."

That's not true. I've gone through that day too many times to put a number on it.

"I understand," she says. She picks up her bottle of Diet Coke and takes a larger mouthful than before, and I watch her swallow. She makes it look slightly painful.

"It was in the spring," I begin. I study the few grains of sugar someone spilt on the table earlier in the day. White against the dark wood background. They look like stars in a different galaxy.

"April tenth," says Mara. Of course she knows the exact date. "Sorry," she says. "I'll try not to interrupt. I don't want to stop your flow."

I take a deep breath. "It was a bright day, but quite cold. I was wearing my new coat…"

122

# CHAPTER 17

I was proud of my new coat. It was navy with tiny white flowers, and I'd chosen it myself from a catalogue, circling it with a wobbly black pen. I was four, I had a new coat, and I'd had a breakthrough that day – I'd learned how to move my legs so I could go back and forth on a swing independently. Maybe I hadn't learned on that exact day, but that's how I remember it.

The play park was my favourite. There were two slides, one for little kids and the other much higher and more exciting. I was fearless, always wanting to do what Alice could. I'd been down that big slide loads of times, so many times that Mum and Dad didn't hover at the bottom like other parents, shouting up to be careful, or to take turns. I knew about taking turns. I understood the rules. When a girl pushed past me to go down the big slide,

*I was outraged, but I figured because she was shorter than me that she wasn't four and didn't know how to behave. I told her the rules as she sat down right in front of me, dressed in flowery leggings and a fluffy turquoise jacket with big buttons, and pushed against her feet to launch herself down that big slope.*

*A little while afterwards, as I was standing, waiting until the boy in front of me had gone down the slide, the same girl tried to jostle her way in front of me again. She tugged my ponytail hard.*

*I wasn't having it.*

*This is the part where my memory is sharp. I can even hear the noise again — the wind, my shout that Hannah had to wait her turn. The dismissive noise she made. I shoved her hard. For some reason, I didn't push her sideways where she would have fallen back into metal safety barriers, I pushed her forward, down towards the side.*

*Hannah screamed once and then there was a horrible thud.*

*There was a silence and then a voice said, "Come on, Hannah, up you get," and then more voices and then screaming. And nothing would ever be the same again.*

As I finish, I'm conscious my voice doesn't sound like mine any more. It's croaky, as if the out-loud version of this story is buried away under dry, dusty rubble, and has to be unearthed. I have to stop and cough.

"I'll always regret it," I say. And I will. That shove. That fall. The way she fell like a doll, hitting her head and bouncing a tiny bit, and coming to a complete and final stop.

I look up. Mara has a hand over her mouth and she's crying very quietly.

"What happened afterwards?" she asks. "Please."

I explain how I and all the other kids on the slide were told to walk back down the steps, and were huddled away from Hannah, how the ambulance seemed to be there almost immediately, and how a lady I didn't know told me, "That wee girl is going to be absolutely fine, don't you go fretting," and feeling relieved. I describe how Dad took me by the hand and we walked back to our house in shocked silence.

She died later that day in hospital.

Dad told me at home on the sofa in the living room. He said that the little girl had hit her head really hard, so hard that she couldn't get better. She'd gone to live with the angels. Mum wasn't there and I remember she was cross about that. "We should have told her together," she had hissed at Dad later in the kitchen. I don't think she was happy about the angels part either.

"I would do anything to undo that day," I tell Mara. "I know it's not the same, but I have to live with it, too."

Mara blows her nose on a tissue. "My parents told me Han had gone," she says. "But I didn't know *where* she'd gone. It was confusing. My grandparents cried every time they saw me."

I rub my arms, suddenly cold.

"Mum and Dad had this idea that Han and I needed to spend time with them separately, because we were twins. That's why Hannah was on her own with Nan and Granddad that day. Han really didn't want to go." She pressed her lips together at the memory, then says, "That awful memorial garden. I hate it." She smiles at my shocked face. "It was Nan's idea. She was so upset when it was vandalized."

I say, "My grandma can hardly stand the sight of me. She bought my sister a gold bracelet last Christmas, and I got this horrible cheap metal brooch which I know she regifted. You should see it." I'm embarrassed by my whining, and by giving away too much of myself. I lift the hot chocolate to my mouth for something to do. It is lukewarm and too sweet.

Mara looks towards the flashing Christmas lights. "My nan is the opposite," she says. "She can't get enough of me, and that's quite … intense. My parents only like remembering the good times. They say it doesn't help to get stuck in the past, and I get it, but … I wish I had more memories. Real ones. I can look at photos, but it's not the same, is it?" She drops her shoulders. "Anyway. It's been good to talk to you, Ruby. Thanks."

It's the signal that we're nearing the end of the conversation. It's only now I realize I'm breathing more normally.

Mara bites her top lip. She looks very young all of a sudden. "I was dreading this."

"Me too," I admit.

We both give a weak sort of laugh. Mara reaches for her

puffy pale blue coat and I think of Hannah in her fluffy turquoise jacket with big buttons and the room tilts.

I'm on my feet before her, pulling on my coat, telling her I really need to find the toilets, and she points to them, and says she'll say goodbye now.

"I'll be careful, Ruby, I promise," she says. "I won't tell anyone at school."

"Goodbye," I say, and she says it back, and then I say it again. We're awkward. I want to disappear in a puff of smoke right now.

"See you on…" we say at the same time. Mara covers her face with her hand.

"Monday!" I finish, and the smiles we give each other are genuine.

# CHAPTER 18

Just over forty-five minutes later, I bump into Euan in Barchester high street. Literally; I've been doing the rounds with my CV and I walk smack into him as I leave the shop where Mum bought her stripy candle last weekend. He catches me by one elbow, and says, "Whoa. Oh. Hey, Ruby!"

"I'm sorry," I say, adding another apology to a day already saturated with them.

He lets go of my elbow. "Don't worry about it. I didn't hurt you, did I?"

My nose is tender where I bashed it against his shoulder, but I'm not going to mention that. "No, no."

"I'm on my break from Monty's. Want to walk to

Tesco? A hard-to-resist offer, I know. I said I'd buy my mum some spaghetti."

"Spaghetti?" I echo like a fool. It's a sunny day for October. Light bounces off the shop windows on one side of the street, orange and full of dust particles. I have to squint to look at him.

"Yeah, she's making spaghetti bolognaise tonight. Crazy times." He takes it for granted I'm going to walk along with him, so I do. "What did you come into town for?"

*I was meeting the twin of the girl I killed.*

"I'm seeing if anywhere has a weekend job going."

"Oh? Any luck?"

I shake my head. "I asked at the garden centre and a few of the shops on the high street. They either say I'm too young or I'll need to wait till Christmas."

"There's nothing going at Monty's either," he says.

He said that too fast. I wonder whether he thinks I'd be a liability. We walk several paces without speaking. "By the way," I say, "Scott told me he wanted to 'help' me. You know, sort out my image, given that everyone thinks I'm a violent ex-offender." My expression should give him a steer as to exactly how mad I still am about it.

Euan shakes his head. "Scott can be really insensitive. I'm sorry. But he means well. Usually."

"I think he's arrogant and patronizing, and … yeah…" I stop myself because I don't want to get into an argument with Euan or burst into tears. I feel exhausted after this morning with Mara.

"He's ambitious," says Euan. "He's a good journalist and he gets a kick out of turning people's images round, but he has big ideas about social justice too. I know his manner can be off-putting sometimes. It's gone to his head a bit."

I glance at him. "Do you feel like you owe him?"

Euan considers his response. "A little. But it's all for a good cause. Look at the Justice for Jim campaign. The attack happened just up here." We're at the alleyway that leads to Tesco. "It was here in the porch of this office block," Euan says. "There was one of those yellow police signs up asking for witnesses to come forward for a while, but they've taken it away now. Scott called the police to ask for an update on the case. Obviously they didn't tell him anything that isn't already out there, but they emphasized that people at our school might know the attackers. They were probably aged between sixteen and twenty-four."

I stare at the grey marbled tiles, darker in some places with dirt. They look cold and hard, but I can see why Jim chose this porch. It's wide, with enough room to roll out a mat and sleeping bag.

"Does Scott often phone the police for updates on ongoing crimes?" I say.

"Yes." Euan gives a sort of laugh. "They know him by name now, but that's how he likes it. He's always hoping he'll get a police officer who'll say more than they should." He nods at the porch and says, "This is where we're going to do some busking. We're waiting for permission from the council."

We're walking back to the alleyway now, past the triangle of grass where I sat with Mara. I run to cross the narrow road before we have to wait for a car to go by, and he follows, catching me up effortlessly with his longer legs.

We spend a minute weighing up the merits of short spaghetti versus long, and join a self-service till. There's a bored assistant leaning against a rail, and while Euan pays I ask if you have to be sixteen to work there. She nods, and looks me up and down so blatantly I wish I hadn't asked.

Outside, a couple from our year walk towards us. They smirk at Euan as they go by, and I look to see if he's embarrassed to be seen with me, but he's checking the time on his phone.

"I've got to get back to the café," he says.

"Bye, then," I say, but he doesn't move.

"Ruby, if you want a job, I could get you a few hours at an event next Saturday evening."

"Really?" I say eagerly. "That would be amazing, thanks. What's the event?"

Euan is vague. "A dance thing. You could help us."

"Us?"

Now he does look embarrassed. "My parents run a dance school. There's a show on this Saturday. Frazer and I check tickets, show people to their seats, and run a raffle

131

and sell sweets. Front of House stuff. It's either super-busy or really quiet. Khalid usually helps out, but Scott and him are going out. Nine quid an hour. About four and a half hours."

"I'm in," I say, without thinking about any of it other than the nine pounds an hour.

"No hot dates on Saturday night, then?"

"Absolutely none."

I've never been on a date. Aside from once with Luffy's brother, and that was an accident. I'd spent ages persuading Luffy to come to the cinema with me to see a thriller set in 1970s East Berlin. I'd bought the tickets, and was treating him for a birthday present. We didn't do presents, unless they worked in our own favour, which in Luffy's case meant hippy gigs. But when I went round to his house to pick him up to ensure he didn't miss the beginning, he turned out to be ill with food poisoning. Luffy's brother, Mickey, said since I'd bought the tickets anyway, he'd come.

We didn't have numbered seats, so we sat in the back row, and Mickey didn't even wait until the adverts were over before he put his arm round me. His denim jacket smelled of beer.

"What are you doing?" I whispered.

He removed it. "Don't you want a cuddle?"

I stared at him.

"You're not going out with Luffy, right? He says you're just mates."

That was true. "But you and me – we've never really spoken," I said.

Mickey rejected this with dramatic bewilderment. "Yes, we have! Loads of times."

"I don't mean as in, 'that's a cool jacket', 'the bus is late' or 'where did I put my phone'," I said. "I meant, like a proper conversation."

"That's not me, though, is it? I'm not like Luffy. I don't have big thoughts and that." Mickey glanced at the screen. The trailers had started. His face in profile looked like Luffy's and there was something I loved about it. It was the honesty of it, which didn't make much sense because I knew Mickey sold counterfeit stuff at his college.

Alice was always warning me that Luffy's family were "dodgy", but suddenly there in the back seats of the cinema I desired Mickey. I placed my arm round him and pulled him towards me. He was briefly startled but then he repositioned himself and we kissed. It felt strange and pleasant, and detached. Afterwards, Mickey said he'd walk me home, and I wondered if he'd hold my hand. He didn't. He talked about his PlayStation and then he answered his phone to someone he said he couldn't ignore.

"I've got to go," he said, his body already turning in the opposite direction. "Take care, yeah?"

When he left, I'd felt a wave of loneliness. I never told Luffy what had happened, and Mickey never seemed to be around much after that.

I focus back on Euan. "Just let me know the details; I'll be there."

We swap numbers so he can send me details nearer the time. Having his number gives me a thrill.

"See you there," I say. "Thanks for this."

"Great." He pauses. "Just one thing though, Ruby. My brother. He's doing … like a dance with his partner in the show. He's good. But…" He scrunches up his face.

"Don't tell anyone at school?"

He winces. "Yeah. Obviously, some of our dancers come from Robinson, but they're cool about Frazer. They'd never make fun of him online or anything."

"Don't worry," I say. "I'm really good at keeping things to myself."

# CHAPTER 19

I tell Mum I didn't find a regular job, but I've got a paying event on Saturday. Within minutes, Alice FaceTimes me.

"Congratulations on your first step to financial independence," she says. I don't know why she's being so patronizing – she's existing on student loans.

Raising my eyes to my bedroom ceiling, I notice a patch of flaky paint, like peeling nail varnish. I hope she doesn't notice her boxes are missing. I've put them in the shed for now.

"Perhaps I'll get a decent Christmas present from you this year," she says.

"It's a one-off. Four-and-a-half hours' work," I say, sitting on the floor with my back to the radiator, which is faintly warm. "So don't count on it. But don't worry, Grandma's got your back when it comes to presents."

Alice tilts her head to one side. "Ah, you're still sore about my bracelet. Some years you get lucky."

"I've never got lucky with Grandma," I mutter.

Alice starts laughing. "Remember that football hat and scarf she got you? What team were they for, again? You hadn't even heard of them."

I can't remember now either. "I hate football," I say. I slouch into a more comfortable position.

Alice is in bed. There are fairy lights behind her. She rattles a tube of Pringles to check that there are some left before shoving her hand in and fishing out a small stack, then crunching down, trying to catch pieces as they splinter off. "So how's life, dearest sister?"

"Fine," I say.

"Oooh," says Alice. "You said that a bit too quickly. Trouble at school?"

"No," I retort. "Bet your bed's going to be comfy tonight with all those crumbs in it."

Alice leans closer to the camera. "Stop. Changing. The. Subject."

"Did Mum put you up to this?" I ask. She's irritating me now.

"Nope. If you're going to clam up, fair enough, but don't say I didn't ask about your life."

To my horror, I realize I'm crying, not racking sobs but the silent slide-down-your-cheeks type. "Ruby?" Alice's voice is uncharacteristically gentle. "What's going on?"

I put down the phone so she has a good view of the radiator and not my face, and I tell her about Mara, and our meeting today. When I'm done, I pick up my phone and there's Alice's face, serious and concerned.

"What is she like?" Alice asks.

"She seems all right. Her eyes are how I remember Hannah's were, which spooked me at first. She wanted to know about the day her sister died – I was dreading it, but it wasn't as bad as I thought it would be. Don't tell Mum," I say.

"I won't," says Alice. "But only because she's got enough to worry about. Personally I think you took a big risk meeting Mara on your own, but I'm glad it went OK. I think you're quite brave, actually, and maybe it's been helpful to you as well as her." She pulls a thick garment around her shoulders. It might be a coat or a blanket. She's re-angling her phone. "Wait. Do a three-sixty with your phone." She narrows her eyes. "Where have all my boxes gone?"

I'm jumpy at school over the next few days. I am sure it's only a matter of time before someone makes the connection between Mara and me. Maybe someone saw us at the garden centre. I'm on high alert for Scott to let me know he's linked Mara's last name with the Hannah Cole he's read about. I reckon he's too sharp not to.

The way to get through this, I tell myself, is to keep my

head down, slay my assessments, and spend my lunchtimes in the music practice rooms. Whenever I see Euan he's with other people, often Scott, and we don't exchange more than a few words, but we smile, and it makes me feel less lonely.

After school on Friday, Euan messages that he and his brother will pick me up by car at six the following evening

"You look lovely," says Mum when I ask her to check for loose hairs on my black top, at five fifty-five on Saturday evening. She lint-rolls my shoulders. "Good luck, Rubes, you'll be great."

I twist my hammered silver ring on to my finger; Mum made it when she had her jewellery business. She gave one each to me and Alice after we worked several late nights in a row, packaging up her products.

The doorbell chimes and I quickly pull on my coat, check my keys are in my pocket and hug Mum goodbye. I open the door to Euan, who's in a purple sweatshirt with *Baldini School of Dance* written across it.

"Ready for a wild one?" he says cheerfully.

"Bring it on," I say as I pull the door closed.

Mr Baldini – Frazer – gives me a brief, teacherly smile as I climb into the back seat. His face is more orange than usual and he's wearing a purple sweatshirt too, which only adds to the weirdness of having my form tutor drive me somewhere.

"Here's something for you," says Euan as the car picks up speed. He throws a purple sweatshirt at me. It's slightly more faded than Euan's or his brother's. "It's been through

138

a few helpers, but don't worry. It's been washed."

I bring it up to my nose and it smells of Euan, or at least his fresh washing detergent.

"It doesn't stink, does it?" asks Euan, concerned.

"No, no," I say hurriedly. I peel off my coat and tunnel into the sweatshirt. "I feel like a Baldini now," I say when I emerge. I catch Mr Baldini's expression in the front mirror, and he looks taken aback. It was a silly thing to say.

"I hope you enjoy the evening, Ruby," he says. "We, ah, pride ourselves on polite customer service, by the way."

"Fraaa-zer," says Euan. "Wind your neck in."

"Of course," I say. I bet he's never said that to Khalid when he's helped out.

Euan mutters under his breath, then there's silence in the car until Frazer puts on some Coldplay, which is so predictably tragic I almost start laughing and then I catch Euan's eye and I can't help myself.

# CHAPTER 20

"I apologize for Frazer being Frazer-ish," says Euan as we walk down a path to the theatre entrance with a heavy small cardboard box each, leaving Frazer to follow us with a few bags. "He finds it hard to switch off his teacher brain."

Inside the foyer, strung across the length of one wall, purple and red bunting spells out *Baldini School of Dance*. There's a table with what must be the raffle prizes – a hamper, a bottle of champagne and some beauty gift sets. On another table there's a heap of wands (I do a double take and they're still wands), and on a third, an assortment of Baldini merchandise, most of it purple.

A woman in a tight red dress and black dance shoes comes rushing through a door. Her hair is up in a ballet bun. "'You're here! Fantastic! Ruby, isn't it? I'm Bella Baldini, which is such a mouthful, people tend to call me BB." She takes my hand in hers. "Lovely to meet you. Thanks for helping out. The boys will show you the ropes. Ah, here's Frazer."

So this is Euan's mum. I smile politely and wonder how much Euan and Frazer have told her about me. She disappears off saying something about a problem with the curtain.

We work quickly – apparently there's not much time before the pupils and their parents and grandparents, and whoever else has come to see them, arrive. We shift furniture, fold raffle tickets and arrange merchandise.

Euan's dad, a tall man in a smart suit, comes over and introduces himself as Ronny. He shakes hands with me firmly as if I'm an important business associate, and I see the Baldini resemblance when he flashes me a broad smile. "Great to have you here," he says. He gathers up the wands and takes them backstage. We open the cardboard boxes we brought in from the car. They're full of programmes which we have to place on every single seat of the theatre. Euan and I race up and down the aisles while Frazer moans that our programmes are falling to the floor. Euan says, "Ignore him. He's all stressy because he's dancing later."

The next hour goes in a blur of selling raffle tickets and writing people's names on the back. When I have a chance I fold the tickets up and put them in the box. There are a few students from Robinson with their parents, siblings of

141

the dancers, I guess, but they don't seem to recognize me. Euan sells the merchandise, and Frazer checks tickets and directs people to their seats.

Things only quieten down when a voice over a loudspeaker announces the show will start in five minutes, and music plays inside the auditorium. Euan comes over to help fold the heaps of tickets I've amassed.

"We don't usually sell this many," he says. "You must have some serious sales skills."

"I'm going backstage," hisses Frazer, glaring at us. "Keep it down, OK?"

"Now we need to set up for the interval and wait for the stampede in about an hour," says Euan in a quieter voice.

The dance school doesn't have an alcohol licence, so we unpackage cartons of soft drinks which are piled in one corner and place them on the table that held the wands, along with packets of crisps and chocolate.

"It's a big dance school," I say.

Euan nods. "We went through a bad patch a few years ago, but it's doing well again."

"How come you don't dance?" I ask.

Euan shrugs. "I do. I mean I did. I can dance. It's not my thing any more."

"Let's see you then," I say. I move out away from the front of the table, offering him the floor. "Show me your moves."

"I'm not a performing dolphin," he says, but he moves into the space I've left for him.

"What's your favourite dance?" I ask.

"I love tap dancing," he says, and in his Adidas trainers he does a few hopping movements. His trainers make squeaky noises on the plastic flooring and then he starts calling out the taps, and he looks and sounds so funny I burst out laughing.

All of a sudden, my hand is in his. He's gentle and laughing, and I feel a rush of excitement having him so close up against me. He places one hand on my shoulder and the other round my waist. "Time to dance, Ms Ruby Marshall," he says.

I laugh. "I'm not big on dancing," I say. Alice was the one who craved ballet lessons and writhed around the living room when she was doing Modern, showing us how expressive she could be.

"Prepare to be amazed," says Euan. He runs to open the door to the auditorium, jamming it in place with a chair. Jaunty music pours out. He takes up the same position with me again, and whisks me round the foyer. I know enough about beats and rhythm to feel the dance, even though my feet don't know where to be.

I'm breathless, but when Euan stops I'm disappointed. I step away and brush back my hair. He says, "You're a natural."

"Sure," I say and, horrifyingly, I blush. I hide my face by going to find my phone in my coat pocket and sit behind the refreshment stall. I ignore a message from Dad asking how my new school is. The answer is way too complicated to get into, and also, hello. I've already been at Robinson a month, thanks for asking.

Euan was right about the stampede at the interval. Never has my mental maths been so challenged as the two of us work the refreshment stand. Euan seems used to it, maybe from working at the café. He stays unflappable as little kids push in and people change their minds, or drop coins.

Finally, a bell sounds and people flow back into the auditorium.

"Now we just wait," says Euan. "This is the boring bit."

"Are there any spare seats?" I ask. "We could watch the rest of the show?"

"All right," says Euan without enthusiasm. He's probably worried about me mocking his brother's dance routine. "There are seats up in the circle."

We walk up the stairs to a door that opens to rows of seats sloping down to a shiny brass railing. There are only a few people up here, and they're in the front row, probably other helpers. The view of the stage isn't brilliant, but it's warm up here and the red velvet seats look squishy and comfortable.

We settle ourselves in a couple of seats a few rows from the front. On the stage there are about fifteen dancers doing a dance with the wands. They're very smiley and slick.

Next, introduced by Euan's mum, BB, is a parent-and-little-child dance and it's surprisingly cute and funny. BB appears again and says how proud she is to introduce her award-winning son, Frazer, dancing the Cuban salsa with his dance partner, Lori.

Frazer comes on dressed in tight black dance trousers and an emerald-green shirt open to the waist. His partner is wearing a crop top and a skirt with frills in the same green. They look good together, like a couple from *Strictly*.

I prod Euan and give him a cheesy thumbs up. He pulls an embarrassed expression and buries his face in my shoulder. I giggle and pat his head soothingly.

Euan lifts his head and our eyes meet. Our faces are close, so close I can see a freckle I'd never noticed before by the corner of his nose. I sense he's holding his breath. My stomach twists with anticipation. This is the moment we're going to kiss. I imagine it's going to taste of the Haribos we ate as we packed up. My seat squeaks as I shift my weight, and I'm immediately taken back to the cinema with Luffy's brother. The awkwardness afterwards with Mickey wasn't too bad because I didn't see him often, but with Euan, I have the rest of the school year to get through. Is this a mistake?

The music and the Spanish lyrics cut into my thoughts. Frazer's onstage, moving his limbs in an undulating way I wouldn't have thought possible, and grinding up against his partner. Kissing Euan with my teacher doing this in the background isn't ideal. I shift uncomfortably.

I'm feeling too warm now, wishing I had brought a bottle of water. I sense Euan's confusion and, as Frazer and Lori finish, I clap and risk a sideways glance at him; he's looking straight ahead. The intimate moment has gone.

# CHAPTER 21

The breaking news that Georgia and Amber have had a massive falling out reaches me by Snapchat before I get to school on Monday.

The two of them went to Nando's on Sunday evening, and someone saw them shouting at each other. Allegedly, Georgia left her peri-peri chicken wrap untouched and stormed out. There's blurred footage of her in tears, with a caption saying *Drama Queen* and a crown.

When I enter our form room, Georgia is sitting, pale-faced and reading, at her usual spot. I sit at my desk at the back on my own, doodling in my planner. Amber, who arrives after me, walks in and past Georgia's desk without looking at her. There are murmurs of "Over here, Ambs," and "What happened, babe?"

She mutters to the expectant crowd, "I don't want to talk about it."

Mr Baldini comes in humming. I avoid eye contact because I don't want to think about him in his dancing outfit. He says, "All right, Ruby?" and I mutter, "Fine, sir," and pretend I've dropped something on the floor.

In PE, because it's pelting down with rain, we play badminton in the hall. My partner and I play against Georgia and another girl, and we lose quickly because Georgia slams the shuttlecock over the net so hard we have no chance of returning it.

"Aggressive game, badminton," I observe as I sit on a bench with her, waiting our next matches.

"Hmm," she says. She's retying her laces for the billionth time. When she looks up, the whites of her eyes are pinkish, as if she's trying not to cry.

"Sorry you're having a bad time," I say.

Georgia looks away. I watch the match for a while and when I glance back, she's clutching a hand to her chest. Her breathing is coming in little gasps.

"Sir!" calls the boy the other side of me. "Something's up with Georgia."

Mr Morton comes bounding over.

"I'm OK," she says breathlessly. "It's not an asthma attack. I've had this before. I'm feeling panicky. I just need some air."

Mr Morton hesitates. "You!" He points at me. "Take Georgia to student services."

I help her up. She's sweating. She looks terrible.

Once we're out of the hall, she stops to lean against the wall.

"Can we stay here a moment?" asks Georgia. She's speaking slowly, as if each word hurts. "I don't want to go to student services."

"As long as you don't die and get me into trouble." I sit on the floor, cross-legged, opposite her, and wait for her to speak.

Gradually her breathing slows. "It was a panic attack," she says. "I've had them before."

"Why don't you want to go to student services?"

"Because they'll tell my parents," says Georgia. "And my parents will overreact. It's passed now. Let's stay here until the end of the lesson. It's not long."

The silence hangs between us, like string for me to tug on. "What's going on between you and Amber?" I say at last.

Georgia wipes sweat from her nose with the inside of her sports polo shirt. "Amber told me she'd referred me to the counsellor," she says. "She had no right to do that. She went behind my back. We used to talk to each other about everything…"

"You can talk to me," I say. The words sound small. I've never said them to anyone before. I guess I'm not sure if I really mean them or not.

She laughs, a hollow kind of laugh, as if I wouldn't understand her problems. It makes me want to walk away, but I shouldn't. She slides down the wall to the floor, where she hunches her knees to her chest. We listen to the sounds from the gym, and Mr Morton ordering people to take down the badminton nets, and when we hear everyone traipsing off to the changing rooms, we merge in with them.

"Feeling better, Georgia?" asks Mr Morton when he sees her.

She nods.

"Good stuff."

At the beginning of lunch, I find Georgia by my side. "Can I have lunch with you?" she asks.

"As long as you don't run away and leave me with Isaac Linesman again," I say. She blushes and I regret being so direct.

She buys a main meal and mashes it about on her plate as usual, while I eat my sandwiches. She wants to talk about her A-level subject choices. It seems there's a clash between what she wants to do and her parents' expectations. They want her to take science subjects, and she wants to do English, history and psychology.

The Linesmen are at their regular table, but they leave us alone. The canteen is full and the bad weather means more and more students flood in. They stand with trays, looking for tables. The canteen staff decide it's time to turf out anyone who's finished, including us and the Linesmen, and we end up leaving together.

I'm jostled from behind and I feel a hand grab my bum, hard. I spin around and see Isaac grinning nastily, but the hall is so crowded no one else notices. I turn and kick him in the shin, and he jumps back dramatically on one leg, yelling, "Ow! Why did you do that, you psycho?"

The noise dims, and Georgia freezes beside me. I say, "You know why."

"You going to tell tales again, Granny?" His face is angry.

Not that far away, I see Euan with Khalid and Scott. They're all looking. I can feel myself going red.

"You're getting hot and flustered now," says Isaac. "I think she secretly fancies me, Mon. Georgia's not the only one with a crush."

Monique laughs. "Loyal fangirls!"

"As if," I say.

"I heard another interesting thing about you, Granny," says Isaac, checking he has an audience around him.

"Here we go," I say with an eye-roll, desperate for him not to think I'm intimidated.

"Does the name *Mickey* ring any bells? I heard you and your boyfriend's brother were" – he coughs dramatically and my first thought is who on earth thinks Luffy is my boyfriend, but then I hear the rest of what he has to say – "let's say *close*. That would be like you going out with,

150

say, Euan Baldini, and making out with the Big Orange himself."

The shock takes my breath away, and I can't speak. Someone from my old school must have found out. Seen us in the cinema, maybe. Or Mickey told someone. Did the gossip reach Mrs Lipperton, who saved up every last thing about me? But surely even she wouldn't stoop so low.

"See?" says Isaac, and he looks around him triumphantly. "She's not denying it."

Once again, I would give anything to know who's been feeding him this information.

Everyone in the canteen is watching. I see Euan's frowning face, and I'm so thrown I have to look away.

"Move along. Please don't block the exit," calls a member of staff, appearing from the kitchen area.

I step closer to Isaac, a move he wasn't expecting, and I hiss, "Whoever is telling you this stuff is lying. And you're an idiot for believing it."

He grabs my arm and I spin round in a self-defence move Alice taught me, catching him unawares and twisting his own arm painfully. He screams.

Monique comes to rescue him, and I know I can't manage two against one, so I release him.

"Leave me alone, or you'll regret it," I say.

"I think you're the one who should be scared," he mutters. He steps away though, and Georgia and I walk out of the canteen.

# CHAPTER 22

Miss Starling pulls me out of English. Twenty-nine pairs of eyes look up from *A Christmas Carol* and watch as I follow her out of the classroom.

In her office, she says, "Ruby. I thought we should have a little chat."

"OK," I answer warily. "What's this about?"

"A member of staff was concerned about your behaviour in the canteen." She pauses. "Some sort of altercation between you and Isaac Linesman?"

I set my jaw. "It was nothing."

"What started it?"

I can't stop thinking about Luffy. If rumours were going round about me and Mickey, did he know that we kissed? Did he mind?

"The member of staff reported you as using significant force."

"On Isaac?" I raise an eyebrow. I should tell her that he grabbed me. But I'm scared how he'll retaliate if I get him into more trouble.

Miss Starling nods.

"It was a self-defence move," I say. "And it wasn't *significant*."

"Why did you have to use it?"

"He's bad with personal space."

There's a pause for me to elaborate but I don't. I want all of this to go away. "I see," says Miss Starling. She clicks her biro open and shut and it's like a signal to change topic. "How are things generally? It can't be easy for you, knowing Mara Cole is here."

I have an urge to tell Miss Starling we met out of school and talked, and I think it cleared the air, but a noise outside in the corridor breaks my resolve.

"I'm trying to keep my head down," I say. "I mean, I know it doesn't look like it today … but I'm trying. I want to do well in my exams."

Miss Starling smiles. "I'm pleased to hear that. Mr Williams tells me he heard you playing the piano and you're very talented. It's a shame you're not doing music."

Not taking music was a way of rebelling against Dad. I regret it now. Another regret to add to my list. "I just play to relax," I say.

"Well, you must keep going with it," says Miss Starling, standing up. "Let's touch base again soon." I stand. "And Ruby? No more fights, OK?"

On the way to my locker at the end of the day, I see Euan and Amber standing close together, talking intently. When they notice me, they stop. Neither of them looks at me. They probably think I'm dangerous, like everyone else.

There are a few students near my locker, and something white is smeared on it. It's probably just glue, but I don't dare touch it.

"You all right?" calls a boy at least two years younger than me. He's smiling at his mates now.

"You talking to me?" I reply, as if I can't believe he has the nerve.

He laughs, unsure what to say. One of his mates says, "He fancies you," which the first boy is so deeply offended by, he kicks him.

"Did you see what's on her locker?" someone says, and that reunites them all again in shared disgust.

Life is easier when you show you don't care. I open my locker, take out my PE kit, lock it again and head towards the sports block. I want to work off my pent-up energy from the encounter with Isaac before I slink home.

The girls' changing room is crowded. Georgia catches my eye as she ties her hair up and gives me a hesitant smile. I agree with Amber – Georgia looks like she needs to see the school counsellor. The skin under her eyes is grey and she has a permanently haunted look which has definitely become worse in the month I've known her. As though she's buckling under the stress of perfectionism.

The rest of the school netball team is there too. I change quickly because, although I can't see Mara, she's likely to be around. As I yank my small gym towel from the bottom of my bag, spilling other things in my haste, I overhear someone say Mara wasn't selected for the match. Great. I needn't have rushed. Someone else is complaining that a kid went crazy with his mate's squeezy glue all over her locker. So it wasn't just mine, then. At least that's something.

There are only three students plus Mr Morton in the gym but, just my luck, one of them is Isaac. He's on a running machine. I don't want to give him the satisfaction of seeing me leave because of him, so I choose a cross trainer, the furthest away from him. My anger makes me strong as I push easily through a hard setting.

The two other boys are doing weights, and after a while they stop and discuss whether to go and watch the netball. They shout over to Isaac to see if he wants to join them, and he says, "Netball? Nah."

That's my cue to leave, too – there's no way I'm staying here alone with Isaac. Mr Morton has a habit of wandering between the gym and the PE office. One of them pings something green at Isaac, which lands short of his running machine.

"What's that?" Mr Morton asks. "Pick it up, Archie."

"It's Georgia's hair thing, sir. It's gross." Archie holds up the scrunchie, a ball of hair and dust dangling from it.

Isaac makes an exaggerated gagging noise.

"Lost property box," says Mr Morton. "Think you two were leaving, weren't you?" The two of them go laughing out of the door, and Mr Morton goes round checking the machines. It seems like he's going to be here a while longer, so I linger at the cross trainer, to be sure.

"Oh, Isaac and Ruby," he calls from the rowing machines. "The gym's closing half an hour early today. You need to be out by four-fifteen."

"What?" Isaac slows the running machine, steps off and wipes his face on the bottom of his vest top. "Why's that, sir?"

"I've got to leave early."

"But I want to do my full workout."

"That's just how it is today, I'm afraid," says Mr Morton. "It'll be open tomorrow as usual."

"That's a piss-take, that's what it is," mutters Isaac. He moves to the mat area and looks at himself in the mirror. I restart my workout, then see him lift his top, admiring his stomach muscles as he does squats. He catches my eye in the mirror and winks.

I roll my eyes, wishing I had my phone and earbuds, and go up a level on the cross trainer.

Isaac leans his sweaty back against the wall and looks up at the end of the dangling cable from the CCTV camera.

"Sir, you need to fix that," he shouts to Mr Morton, who calls back, "Yeah, it's on my list. My very long list."

"You could sell my workouts and make some money for the school," he calls while leering at me.

Mr Morton says, "I think I'd get sacked for that, Isaac."

I grip the cross trainer handles hard.

"Granny here flashed her tits at a teacher in her last school. Wish someone had filmed *that*," he says, just loud enough for me to hear but too low for Mr Morton to.

I stumble on the cross trainer and he laughs. I can feel myself losing it. Sweat prickles in the creases of my elbows and the backs of my knees as I step down.

"You are a disgusting, sexist—"

Mr Morton strides over and stands in his black shorts, sinewy, knobbly-kneed legs apart, hands on hips. "That's enough of that," he says. "Come on, get back to whatever you were doing, both of you."

Isaac starts on some sit-ups, and I leap on to a treadmill and run fast. Soon Mr Morton tells us we have ten minutes left. After five minutes I get off the treadmill and wipe my face with my towel as Isaac is attempting to negotiate extra time with Mr Morton from the rowing machine.

"Come on, sir. When I've finished, I can wipe down any equipment I've used and the door will lock behind me."

"I can't allow that, Isaac. Ruby, your lace is undone."

I kneel down to do it, as Isaac says, "I've got to find my phone. I've put it down somewhere."

Mr Morton's voice rises in frustration. "OK. I'm going to pick up my things from the PE office, so make sure you're both gone by the time I come back." He glances up at the clock. "You've got two minutes." The door makes a screechy sound as he pushes it open and disappears.

Isaac says, "See ya, Mr M! Just you and me, then, Granny." He turns, holds up his phone and takes a lightning-quick selfie, catching me in the shot before I stride towards the door and go out without saying a word.

I walk to the gates, wide open now that it's the end of the day. The school looks empty, but I can hear the whistle from the netball game, laughter from a couple of parents in reception and the drone of a vacuum cleaner coming through the window of an upstairs classroom. There is no one around. Only a black crow on a litter bin, staring accusingly at me.

My app says the next bus isn't due for sixteen minutes, so I keep walking. After a mile or so, there's a big crossroads and I'll have a chance for another bus. I've only been driven down this road, and never taken much notice of it until now. The houses with their prickly bushes have a closed-up look – curtains drawn, gates shut.

I wish I hadn't walked. Ten minutes later, a bus drives past me when I'm in between stops, so I have to wait ages at the crossroads. Mum is already home when I get there, and she asks me how my day was.

I say, "Fine," then grab a banana and go upstairs. Ever

since leaving the gym, I've known what I have to do this evening.

First, though, I need a shower. I stand under the hot water so long that Mum bangs on the door and tells me to consider the heating bills. Once I'm in my pyjamas, with my dressing gown wrapped tightly round me, I sit on my bed, swipe to delete Dad's how's-it-going text, and call Luffy.

For once, I'm not sure if I really want him to pick up.

"Yo," he says.

I ramble a little, about having been at the gym, that I had my first paying job on Saturday night, and all the time he says nothing apart from a little "uh-huh" now and then. I ask him where he is, in case Mickey is around, but he says he's on the rec. I imagine him sitting on a park bench, smoking. If I listen carefully, I can hear the sound of traffic in the distance.

I take a deep breath. "Luffy, someone accused me of getting off with my boyfriend's brother."

"Who's your boyfriend?"

"Well, I think they meant you." I hurry on. "You weren't my boyfriend, obviously, but do you remember that time you were too ill to go to the cinema for your birthday and Mickey came?"

"Yeah?"

"Well, I never told you this, but Mickey and I kissed. That's all."

Silence.

"I wanted it to happen. It wasn't anything bad. But we never did it again or talked about it. I wondered … if you knew?"

More silence. Then Luffy breathes out, and says, "No. No, I didn't know that."

"I'm sorry. If you're upset. It's a freaky thing to have told you."

"A freaky thing to have happened," he says slowly.

"Yes," I say. I wish I were there in front of him. Luffy and phones just don't work well together.

"Right," says Luffy. "I need to think that one through."

"OK," I say, and there doesn't seem anything left to add, so I murmur goodbye. There's no reply and I hang up and cry, wondering how much I've hurt him. All those years we were friends, did he hope for more and I never realized?

# CHAPTER 23

Maybe an hour after speaking to Luffy, I decide to check my phone and see if he's messaged. He hasn't. But my social media is ablaze.

*Isaac is dead.*

Euan heard the facts from his brother, and told Scott, who's put them on social media.

At first, I think it must be a prank. But as I read through Scott's posts, my blood runs cold and I can't seem to find enough breath. There was an accident with the bench press. A cleaner found Isaac with the weight bar on his neck, suffocated by the pressure of it against his windpipe. The CCTV was broken so it's impossible to know for sure what happened, but it looked as if he'd been unable to lift the weights.

Which was odd, considering how fit Isaac was.

The cleaner couldn't find a pulse – Isaac was already dead – but the ambulance came with its blue light whirling and siren blaring anyway, witnessed by the girls' netball team. Other teachers in school came to help. Mr Baldini stopped the netball team getting too close when Isaac's body was brought out. A year ten girl fainted when she heard what had happened.

There are hundreds of posts offering condolences. Someone posts a link to a breaking news piece on the local newspaper's website, but the news is only what we already know: a student at Robinson was discovered dead in the school gym.

Isaac must have tricked Mr Morton into thinking he'd left by hiding out of sight, but stayed on to finish his workout. The way the doors worked for the gym and refurbished classrooms was that they locked only from the outside when closed, so he'd have had no trouble getting out.

Scott posts: *RIP to one of Robinson's biggest personalities*

I am stunned, almost numb with disbelief. How can Isaac have been so alive just a couple of hours ago and now be dead?

Underneath Scott's comment, someone called Dylan has written: *THIS IS UNREAL. Me and Archie was at the gym with him earlier. Does anyone know who the last person to see him alive was?*

Was it me? I start to tremble, and I'm still shaking when Mum calls me downstairs to eat. She's standing next to the table, grating cheese into a dish of tomato risotto.

"What's up, Rubes?" she says when she sees me.

"Isaac Lineman was found dead this evening in the school gym. A bench press accident. It's all over the internet."

Mum's hand flies to her mouth. "The boy who caused you all that trouble? How awful," she says. My mind races, "catastrophizing", as Mum would say. *They know about Hannah. Somehow, they'll blame me. It's all going to get so much worse...* "Oh my goodness. What a horrendous thing to happen," says Mum. She shudders. "Surely there should have been an adult in there?"

"There was. Mr Morton, a PE teacher. He told me and Isaac we had to leave, but Isaac must have stayed anyway."

Mum sits down by backing into a chair and thudding down. "Ruby – you were there just before it happened?"

I nod slowly.

"Are you OK?"

Her phone is on the edge of the table, light flashing from the screen. She follows my gaze and leaps for it. "Oh my God, I've missed all those calls. It's been on silent." She takes it off silent, and it rings immediately. She looks at me. "School," she says quietly, then answers. "Hello. Yes, yes... We heard. Ruby saw it online. Tragic... Right." There's a long pause while Mum listens. "Yes. I understand. Of course. Thank you, Ms Laurel. Bye." She lets her hands sink to her lap, still holding the phone. "That was the head. They want us in school tomorrow morning at eight to give your statement to the police."

I look at the risotto, at the heap of cheese on top, slowly melting. "I feel sick."

Mum says, "I'll be with you, don't worry. Did you notice anything different about Isaac? Was he unwell or acting differently?"

"I can't think of anything," I say. I picture him goading me. "He was his usual self."

"It must have been a tragic accident," Mum says. That phrase sounds frighteningly familiar.

I suddenly imagine Isaac's panic at not being able to lift the bar, it moving towards his neck, him gasping for oxygen, the slide into unconsciousness. I don't want to think about it.

Mum pushes the risotto dish towards me. "Eat something. It will help." She turns back to her phone. "Ms Laurel said there was an email." She accesses her emails. "Here it is: *Unfortunately, we need to inform you of the sad and sudden death of Isaac Linesman, a Y11 pupil, following a tragic accident in the school gym. We are working with the police in their ongoing investigation, and we hope to be able to provide more details soon.*" She glances up at me and I nod for her to continue. The next bit is about sending heartfelt condolences to Isaac's family. It finishes with, "*In the meantime, parents and guardians are asked to discuss the contents of this letter with their child, and explain that grief counselling and additional support is being made available for them at school."*

Mum puts her phone face down. "I don't know how it can have happened," she says. "Apparently there's already a lot on social media, which must be very upsetting for his family. I don't think you should look online any more. I know it's hard, but it's not going to do you any good."

Neither of us can eat more than a few forkfuls of risotto. We push our plates away and watch some old episodes of *Modern Family* together to distract ourselves. Afterwards, I give Mum my laptop and my phone because I can't trust myself not to look. But in the middle of the night, I wake up and immediately think of Isaac, so I sneak downstairs to where Mum left my phone. In the cold stillness of the night, with the fridge making a whirring sound and the clock on the window ledge ticking loudly, I learn on Instagram, underneath a photo of Isaac holding up an athletics cup, that now everyone knows what some girl has posted as an "interesting" fact: I was the last person to see Isaac alive.

Morning arrives slowly. My eyelids are itchy and heavy, and my head is aching. Eventually I hear Mum's slippered feet pad into the bathroom. I reach for my phone.

The post about me being the last person to see Isaac alive has been deleted. Someone wonders what time Isaac was found, and Scott pops up to say it was after five o' clock – Scott's been talking to people who were there when the ambulance arrived. People are saying the gym closed half an hour early yesterday, but he has been doing some digging. He's heard Mr Morton had to leave in a hurry for his wife's pregnancy scan. He points out what we all know: that the gym can only be opened from the outside by staff swipe cards if the door is closed. I think about Mr Morton saying he would return to the gym in two minutes. Did he even come back, or rush straight out without passing by and seeing the lights on? I can't imagine how he must feel now: if only he'd made us leave right there and then.

I head downstairs and sit on a chair in the kitchen, huddled in my dressing gown, my knees bent up to my chest, my feet resting on the edge of the seat. I'm so cold. Mum is dressed now. She leaves a voice message for her boss saying she'll be in late due to personal circumstances which she'll explain later. She adds a strange "Byeee" at the end, trying to be upbeat.

We park near school at five to eight. Outside the gates I see a clump of people in black North Face jackets, jeans and grey joggers, and beanie hats in muted shades. There's a woman in a grey trouser suit. They have cameras, takeaway cups and microphones. They rush at a car that is turning into the staff car park. "A few moments of your time," a man shouts.

As soon as they see us walking along the pavement towards them, me in school uniform, they swarm to us. "Did you know Isaac Linesman?" "How are you feeling this morning?" "What year are you in?"

"What's your name, love?" asks one, trying the softer approach. "You in Isaac's year?"

Mum holds my arm tight, close to her, and pushes them away. "Leave us alone. She doesn't want to answer any questions."

"Tell us what you think about Isaac's death," shouts a woman, holding out a microphone. She has a tattoo of a few bars of music which starts on the inside of her wrist. I hear the first notes in my head and they mock me.

Mr Pompley jogs heavily up the path from reception to the gates pulling on a high-vis jacket. "Let these people through!" he bellows. "This is unacceptable."

"Just doing our job," the woman with the musical notes says.

"Thank you," Mum says to Mr Pompley, who nods at us and stands outside the gates, upright and expressionless as a soldier guarding a secure compound.

There are four police cars in the staff car park, blocking in other cars. Yellow Do-Not-Cross tape criss-crosses the sports block entrance. Two officers are standing outside talking.

Inside school, a woman from the front office kindly says, "I'm sorry about the reporters," and takes Mum and me to an empty room in student services. She gives me a quick smile before ducking out again, and I think, *She's nothing like Mrs Lipperton*. We wait to be called in.

Eventually a woman about Miss Starling's age in black trousers and a bright blue, floaty top comes in and introduces herself as a detective constable. Her first name is Carrie, and I'm reassured by her friendly manner. "Please, would you both join me in the meeting room."

We sit opposite her. "Thank you both for coming in. Ruby, how are you holding up? This all must be quite a shock."

"I'm OK," I mumble.

"You're here, Ruby, because we know you were in the gym at the end of the day yesterday. I'll ask some questions, and we'll put together a written statement. It's nothing to get anxious about, just standard procedure when something terrible like this happens."

I talk through my basic movements from yesterday, from getting changed in the busy changing room to my gym workout and my journey home. I'm asked if I spoke to Isaac and I say, "He asked if I liked his abs, and he made a comment about me showing my chest to someone at my old school, which wasn't true."

Carrie nods and writes notes. Mum frowns. "Did you notice anything different about the weights yesterday?" Carrie asks. Her gaze is intent. I feel guilty even though I have no reason to be.

Then I remember: I always have a reason. That one fatal shove in the park.

"Are you remembering something?" prompts Carrie.

I shake my head. "I don't do weights. I wouldn't have known if there was anything different."

"And Isaac was still in the gym when you left?"

"Yes. He was looking for his phone. Or pretending to. He wanted to stay and finish his workout. Mr Morton heard him say that too."

Carrie nods.

After I've signed and dated my statement, she says Robinson has brought in an extra counsellor and I should see them if I think it would help, and no one will expect me back at school until I'm ready.

As we emerge from the meeting room, I glimpse someone from the netball team and her parents in the room where we waited. Outside another room, I see Georgia next to a woman with a perfect, chin-length bob who must be her mum. Georgia's eyes are red and swollen. She gives a tiny wave with a hand clutching a tissue, before dropping the eye contact. Her mum is wearing office wear in beige and white, which looks heaps better quality than the H&M stuff Mum has on, and is speaking very loudly to Miss Starling. "Yes, yes, I know this is a tragedy, but I have to get to an extremely important meeting and I'd appreciate it if we could go in next."

Miss Starling says she'll see what she can do, then catches sight of us.

"Ruby," she says, hurrying over. "Do take today off, if you need to. Would you like to speak to the counsellor?"

Mum looks at me. I just want to go home.

It's strange leaving school when students are arriving. They stare at me. Some are crying and clinging to each other; others look nervously excited by the drama.

Scott, in school uniform plus beanie hat, is interviewing people, filming them on his phone. Amber is stopping students and asking them to give a quote or speak to camera. Teachers are gathering to keep students moving into their form rooms. Mr Baldini yells at Scott to put his phone away or he'll confiscate it. We leave as Scott tries to argue that it's allowed as he's working for the school newspaper.

At the gates there's now a police presence, and the reporters are being held back. Mum and I leave without difficulty, but the traffic is heavy, so she takes a side road. As we wait at a junction to turn, I spot Naz coming out of a block of flats, checking her phone and speeding up as though she's realized she's late. It's a large block of flats in a scruffy area. It can't be where she lives; I've hardly been at Robinson a month and even I've heard all about her massive house. Maybe she was visiting someone before school? I watch her as we drive away.

# CHAPTER 24

The next day I wake early again and stare at the ceiling. I'm not sure whether it's better to be at home or at school.

"Maybe you should go in," Mum says, stuffing some paperwork into her work bag. "Better than brooding at home, isn't it?"

She's right. I can't stop thinking about Isaac, how strange I feel about his death, glad he's no longer around to harass me but sad for him. I think about his family too, the way his death will impact them all, like Hannah Cole's did.

I'll have to go back at some point anyway, so it might as well be now.

In the end Mum says she'll go in late so she can drop

me off at school. The reporters have disappeared. They filed their stories yesterday. Several students had been interviewed for the local TV news, and said variations on, "I can't believe it. Everyone knew Isaac Linesman. He didn't deserve to die." Isaac's uncle, a guy in his twenties with the same smooth mannerisms, gives a statement about Isaac being a being a top student who was always there for other people.

Mr Baldini puts up the day's notices on the SmartBoard and there are howls of protest at the second one:

*The whole sports block is out of bounds until further notice.*

*As a mark of respect for Isaac, the Halloween disco has been postponed to later in the academic year.*

*Anyone with library books still outstanding from before the summer holidays must return them immediately.*

*Anyone found with stolen police caution tape will be dealt with by Ms Laurel.*

Mr Baldini hands out questionnaires from the school canteen for us to fill in as everyone chats amongst themselves. Georgia is one of a handful of people not here. Amber is sitting with Tolla. A boy near them wants to know what questions the police asked me.

I shrug. "I can't remember. I just told them everything I knew." The noise in the classroom fades.

"You were the last person to see Isaac alive, weren't you?" Amber says. Ms *Robinson Record* Reporter of the Year.

The air almost crackles with expectation.

"I guess I must have been," I say. My mouth is dry. These aren't friendly, curious questions. There's insinuation in them.

"You were," says the boy. "Someone overheard Mr Morton say he left you and Isaac in the gym on your own, and that you were both gone when he got back. Man, he must be in trouble."

Mr Baldini clears his throat. "For goodness' sake, people, that's enough. I have one more announcement for you. A few students are going to be busking in Barchester on Saturday morning to raise money for the Justice for Jim campaign. It would be terrific if any of you could come along and support them."

Conversation shifts to how much money can be made from busking if you stand in the right place. Someone asks how a Halloween disco can be *postponed* because it won't be Halloween any more.

A woman in leggings, tunic top and trainers, more casual than the teachers' clothing, comes into the classroom and Mr Baldini introduces her as an external counsellor, called Bridget.

"As you all know," she says, "Isaac Linesman tragically died on Monday evening after school. Some of you may be feeling sad, worried, numb or indeed a whole range of other emotions. He was in your year. Your age. Some of you will have been good friends with him, or had lessons with him. In a minute, we're going to break up into smaller groups, in twos or threes, and we can discuss how you're feeling."

I find myself in a pair with a boy I've never spoken to before called Rohan. "You first," he says. "You were there." He sees my face. "I'm sorry, but it's true, you were."

"I left before anything happened," I say, through gritted teeth. I sigh. "None of it feels real."

"And?" says Rohan, chucking gum into his mouth.

"That's it," I say. "I'm struggling to process it all, if I'm honest. How about you?"

"Devastated," says Rohan, as if he's been throwing that word around a lot. "Isaac was a laugh. I want to know what happened. I mean, I've read about this happening before..." He goes into gruesome detail about bench press accidents. I listen with mounting horror.

"Stop!" I say eventually. "That's horrible."

I'm loud enough for the counsellor to come over.

"How are you two getting on?" she says. "Would you like to share?"

"Rohan's sad," I say. "Devastated."

Rohan nods. "Yeah, and Ruby's finding it hard. She feels guilty about being the last person in the gym."

"I didn't say that," I reply. The room is quiet now, everyone listening to our mini feedback session.

Rohan chews down on his gum a couple of times. "My bad. She doesn't feel guilty at all."

In history, Khalid pokes me in my back with a ruler. I whip round to face him, furious, ready to snatch the ruler and snap it in two, but then I see his expression is anxious.

"How was Isaac?" he whispers. "Before he died?"

"What d'you mean?" I ask.

Khalid is drawing spirals round his notes on sixteenth-century power struggles. "Like, did he seem himself? Something must have been wrong. He lifted weights all the time."

"I wasn't there when he was doing weights. Before I left, he was acting the same as ever," I say. "Trying to wind me up. Being sleazy." I notice the frown on the girl sitting next to Khalid. She's a wannabe Glossy.

"He's *dead*," she hisses. "Have some respect."

Khalid ignores her. "I wish we knew what happened," he mutters.

"I know. Me too." I turn back to my own doodles.

At lunchtime, I practically run to the music practice room. To my horror, it's occupied, but I chuck out the year seven by telling him I have an exam next week so I get priority. I play a C-major scale really fast, my fingers flying four octaves up the keyboard, thumbs tucking under almost of their own accord. My mind is still free to think, which isn't a good thing, so I move on to harder ones. While I'm struggling with B-flat minor, Euan comes in.

"How are you doing?" he asks.

"OK," I say cagily. "How about you?"

"All right. Shocking about Isaac, right? I found out in the performing arts office with Scott and Amber when my brother came to find me. He was shaking."

I look at him suspiciously. "Are you here on behalf of Scott, asking for an interview?" I wish I could be more sure of him.

He half smiles. "I bet Scott would love an interview, but that's not why I'm here. It's about the busking. I'll be on flute, Aaron from my geography class on guitar, and Amber on vocals. We need a keyboard player. Will you do it?"

I shake my head. My piano playing is a private thing for me, something to escape into. I'm not ready to expose myself and worry about how well I'm doing, on top of having random strangers stare at me while I play. "Don't have a keyboard."

"Frazer has one we can borrow."

"I'm rubbish at sight reading."

Euan groans. "Come on. We've got really simple music and you can improvise as much as you like. We'll have a practice tomorrow lunchtime. It'll be so much better with a keyboard."

"There must be loads of keyboard players in school you can ask."

"Yeah, but … they're idiots. And I've heard you play."

I shake my head. "I can't. I'm sorry. Why don't you ask your brother to play if it's his keyboard?"

"We want to raise money, not scare people away." He comes further into the room and leans against the wall. My heart gives a little leap. "Look, in case this needs saying, I know you didn't have anything to do with what happened with Isaac, and—"

"How d'you know?" I say.

"What d'you mean?" He looks so startled that I nearly laugh. "You didn't, did you?"

I shake my head. "No, of course not. I suppose I meant, I'm glad you have faith in me."

He smiles, I think with relief. "Well, then – join us."

I hesitate. It is for a good cause. And it's hard to resist those eyes. "I'll come to the practice tomorrow and see how it goes," I say at last.

"Nice one."

I play a few chords but he doesn't leave.

I find myself playing "Ladders", Dad's piece, and stop abruptly. I stretch my fingers.

"Am I putting you off?" asks Euan. He pushes himself away from the wall. "Sorry, I'll let you get on. I've got to meet Naz now, anyway – she's making some posters for us."

"Bye," I say, wishing I was brave enough to tell him I'd rather he stayed. When he's gone I check my phone. Dad's sent a photo; he's in Bulgaria for a music festival. He's holding up a bottle of beer in the sunshine. He has stubble and some extreme sunglasses, and looks like someone aged forty-seven trying too hard to look twenty-seven. He says he has been booked for a late-night set. I look up the music festival. It's niche and tiny. I bet he's spending more on flights and hotels than what he's being paid. *If* he's being paid.

Scott's leaving the performing arts office at the same time I come out of the music practice room. Behind him, I see Euan and Naz leaning over a computer, presumably discussing the busking poster. What is Scott doing for Naz that she gives up so much time for him, away from her glossy friends? The office, though – it looks inviting. I imagine myself sitting at one of the computers typing out a news story, or planning how the front page will look.

"Wait! Ruby!" calls Scott, bounding over. "I need to touch base. You're a key witness!"

"I can't," I say. Then, trying to think of a way to deflect him, I add, "I'm not allowed to."

Scott blinks. "Oh?" he says. "Why's that, then?"

"Well, the police are still taking statements, aren't they?" I improvise.

"Really? I don't want a full-blown interview or anything," says Scott. "Not yet. I just wanted a steer on Isaac's state of mind when you last saw him? Did he seem himself?"

"Not you as well," I say. "Khalid was on at me in history about this."

Surprise flits across his face. "He was? So how was Isaac?"

"His normal Isaac Linesman self. I don't have any great revelation for you." I start walking. "That's it. I have to go now."

"No worries," calls Scott. "Keep me in the loop."

"Ruby!" calls Mum, when I walk through the front door. "I was just about to call you."

"What are you doing back early?" I ask. I scan her face for the tell-tale signs of illness and exhaustion.

She has her car keys in her hand. "The police called me. They need you to go to the police station. More questions, I'm afraid."

"What?" I say. I'm tired and hungry. "Can't I go tomorrow morning?"

"Apparently not," says Mum. She holds up one of the cereal bars that I need to make her promise never to buy again because they're a skinny knock-off version of my favourites and taste grim. "I've got this for you and a bottle of water. They said we needed to be there as soon as possible."

My heart thuds. All day I've been telling myself that no one believes I had anything to do with Isaac's death. And now I'm not so sure.

# CHAPTER 25

The police station is tucked down a road off Barchester high street. It would look like the world's most boring office block except for the gated car park to one side, which is full of police cars and vans.

After we've gone through the automatic doors, there's a tiny reception area. Mum tells them who we are and we're escorted down a footstep-echoing corridor to a small, bland room with a table and four chairs. There's a window, but it's a normal one, with a view of the car repair garage opposite – no one-way mirror for studying my body language. I notice two cameras, though, in opposite corners of the room.

"Mum, should we have a solicitor with us?" I think of

all the TV dramas I've seen in police interrogation rooms.

Mum frowns. "Oh, Ruby! Of course not. Don't worry, they said they just needed to double-check some things, to be thorough." But I see her tighten her hands, clasped in her lap.

We're left on our own, until a male police officer sweeps in with a folder under his arm and a brisk, efficient manner. He's around fifty, in formal trousers with a shirt and tie, and tells me his name is Mike. Behind him is a younger woman with blonde shoulder-length hair, and a plain black dress, who he introduces as Molly.

We sit at the table, Mum and me facing the other two. Molly smiles reassuringly as she lines up an A4 pad of paper and pen in front of her; Mike looks as if he has about twenty interviews to do today and he needs to get this done, shifting in his chair, hurriedly looking through his folder.

"Right then," he says. "Just a few things to clear up, Ruby. Thanks for coming in at short notice." He gives me a brief smile. "Ready?"

Mum gives my hand a squeeze, and the nerves I've been feeling up to now suddenly sprout new branches.

"Yes," I say. It comes out more quietly than I intend.

Mike explains that the interview will be recorded. Suddenly everything feels more business-like. He turns on the machine and gives the names of everyone present. "We are in the interview room at Barchester police station." He gives the date and the time, and Mum does some muffled throat clearing, as if she wants to have a coughing fit but feels she can't.

Mike opens his folder, leans back in his chair and seems to have all the time in the world now. "Ruby, we heard there was an argument with you and Isaac at lunchtime the day he died. Can you tell me about it?"

My hands are clammy.

"Isaac grabbed my, um, bum at lunch," I say. It sounds wrong in the police interview room. "And then he told me he knew something about me. That I'd gone behind my boyfriend's back and ... got off with his brother." A silence. "I didn't even have a boyfriend," I add.

"But it upset you. Why?"

Molly looks up from her note-taking. Her face is serious.

"I did kiss a friend's brother ages ago, and I didn't know how Isaac had found out and – it freaked me out." This is so embarrassing, with Mum right next to me. "I haven't been at Robinson very long."

"How would you describe this argument, or altercation, with Isaac Linesman?"

"It was minor."

"And yet we have several statements saying you used *significant force*." His manner is bland, but my heart flops like bread dough. Not again.

Mum shifts in her seat. I'm grateful she's here, but I wish she didn't have to hear all this.

"Isaac was a bully," I say. "Lots of people will tell you

182

that. Like I said, before our argument, he'd grabbed my bottom."

"Did you report him for this, or for any previous or subsequent bullying behaviour?"

I shake my head. "No."

Mike looks down at his folder. He says, "I'd like to move on to Isaac himself. What can you tell me about his behaviour the day he died?"

I sit up straighter. "There wasn't anything different about him. Why?"

Mike ignores the question. "And you had another altercation with him in the gym, didn't you?"

I frown. Mr Morton must have told the police that. In my statement I'd said it was a comment. "It was … banter."

"Right." Mike stares at me. "Can you describe this banter."

"He asked if I thought he was attractive. He said he knew that I'd flashed my – um, breasts to someone at my old school. Which I didn't."

Mum draws in her breath but says nothing.

"I see," says Mike. His face is expressionless. "How often do you do weights at your school gym?"

"Never." I wait for his response.

"Have you ever put the weights back on the rack?"

"No. Oh wait – one time," I say. "I was a spotter for another student." My heart picks up a faster rhythm.

Mike nods. There is silence, and my anxiety mounts.

"And do you understand how the different-coloured stickers correspond to different weights?"

"Yes," I say, slowly. What are they getting at? "Please can you tell me what you think happened to Isaac?"

"Not yet, I'm afraid, Ruby," says Mike. "We're still waiting on the full post-mortem report." He glances at Molly.

I think about Khalid and Scott and how desperate they've been to know how Isaac was behaving before he died. Maybe they think that he took something, a drug? Maybe they know what he took.

"Just a few more questions to go and then we're done," Molly says easily, taking over from Mike. "You say you left the gym at almost four-fifteen after your PE teacher, Mr Morton, but before Isaac. But you didn't get home till about an hour later. How come?"

"I got my bag from the changing room locker—"

"The changing room was empty?" Molly has a gentle way of speaking, but her gaze is intense.

"Yes, and then I walked instead of getting the bus. I told Carrie, the last police officer. I wanted to get the bus, but the app said it would be sixteen minutes, so I walked."

"I see," says Molly. "So you walked home because the bus didn't arrive?"

"Actually, it did about ten minutes later. But by then I'd already started walking ... I was in between bus stops."

Mum interjects with, "She's told you that she didn't want to wait sixteen minutes for the bus."

Molly nods. "We appreciate that, Mrs Marshall. But, Ruby, you say the bus actually only took about ten minutes to arrive?"

"My app was wrong," I say.

"Why don't you check out the app," says Mum. "Instead of interrogating my daughter." She speaks stiffly.

Mike sits up and interjects. "Of course we can do that." He looks at Molly and she nods, as if to say she's finished. "One last question," he says. "Were you aware of a cable being loose in the gym CCTV?"

If I say yes, will this implicate me in some way? Show that I knew whatever happened when it was just me and Isaac in the room wasn't being recorded? Mr Morton will probably have mentioned the discussion between Isaac and me about it.

I nod.

Mike blinks at me. "For the recording, Ruby is nodding her head."

My mouth is dry. "Yes," I say. "I was aware of the cable being loose. Everybody was."

"Did you discuss it that day in the gym?"

The police must have compared Mr Morton's statement with mine. Does it look bad that I didn't mention it earlier? "Isaac was joking about it and Mr Morton said he'd get round to it sometime."

Mike gives me a professional smile. "That's all for now. Thank you, Ruby, for your patience."

*For now?*

Molly picks up her notes. Mike looks up at the clock on the wall, says the time out loud and ends the interview. I suddenly want to cry, and I turn to Mum, searching for her reassuring look. She gives me a nod. *Well done, Rubes. You did the best you could,* it says.

We walk the short distance back to the car in silence, in some kind of shock.

In the car, Mum says, "Are you OK?" and I answer, "Yeah."

Mum clicks her seat belt into its case. "I thought we *were* going to need a solicitor for a moment back there," she says, forcing a smile. "I suppose it's their job to go over things again and again, but that's all it is, Ruby. You're not in any trouble. I'm beginning to get a better picture of Isaac." She squeezes my hand. "I'm sorry you've been caught up in this."

I nod. I want to say I'm sorry she's caught up in this too, because of me.

We drive home listening to Mum's ancient Spotify playlist. It keeps playing songs that she used to play when Dad left, and eventually I give up trying to skip to something decent.

"I heard you were called in for more questions," says Scott.

It's the following morning, and he's ambling past my locker. It's not a coincidence though; he's been waiting to speak to me.

I stop stuffing my coat into my locker and study Scott's face as I say, "Yes, they're waiting for the post-mortem report." I pause. "They think Isaac might have taken something."

This isn't what they said at all, but it might be true and I want to see what he says.

"Wow." His eyes widen. If he's acting, he's good. "Wonder what it was."

"Why did you ask me yesterday how Isaac was behaving before he died?"

Scott runs a hand through his hair. "That's a pretty standard question, isn't it? I wanted details." He looks at me for a moment, half-squinting. "Look, I get it: you think the stuff I do is a joke. But I don't think it's a joke. Journalism's important, even if it's at school level. And I'm good at it. Look at how the Justice for Jim campaign has taken off. Another couple of schools have joined. I'm really proud of that."

"I expect it will be global soon," I say, banging my locker door shut.

Scott doesn't react to the sarcasm. "You should check out the website. I've also heard from a *protected source* ..." Scott lingers awhile on that phrase. "... that the police think there may be a fourth member of the gang that attacked Jim. One CCTV shot they've managed to get shows a possible human shadow."

"Keeping a lookout?" I ask, interested in spite of myself.

"Or filming the attack," says Scott. "Jim doesn't

remember how many people he saw. All he remembers is that the attackers were 'young'. That's it." He cocks his head to one side. "Hey, I hear you're going to be busking at the weekend – nice move. Amber and I are going to meet Jim at the hostel next week to hand over the money we've raised so far."

"That's great," I say.

I'm not being sarcastic for once, but his face flickers uncertainly. I mess this up all the time. People are never quite sure of me.

Scott's defensive now as he says, "We're making a real difference to that man's life."

"I know," I say. But he's off, walking away down the corridor.

# CHAPTER 26

I sit quietly at my desk before registration, listening to the gossip that swirls.

"Anyone know if Naz is having a Sweet Sixteen party? Let's hope it's so big even I get invited," says Rohan.

"I heard she's having a fancy dinner with the Glossies," says Tolla.

Georgia is still off school, but word is that Monique is back.

Someone says he witnessed Isaac and Monique having such a massive slanging match on the bus into Barchester a while ago that the driver stopped and made them get off.

Tolla says they had a *volatile relationship*.

I see Monique for myself outside the classroom for

English. She walks right up to me, and I see that her hair is loose and puffy, and she's taken out her trademark hoop earrings. She's wearing trainers instead of school-approved shoes, but I don't suppose anyone's going to challenge her over those today.

"Granny, I want a word with you," she says. She tilts her head for me to step aside, and I comply, mostly because I don't want everyone else to hear.

We walk round the corner, and she somehow manages to pen me into the gap between the stairs leading to the maths corridor and the wall. I should have seen it coming.

She slams my shoulder against the wall. "What happened to Isaac?" she asks.

She's wild-eyed, make-up-free. The holes where her earrings should be are red.

"I don't know," I say.

She slams my shoulder again. "I think you do," she says.

"I really don't. I wasn't there when he died," I say. I look over her shoulder but there's no one else around. I avoid eye contact, and let her pin my arms to my side. It's hard to take, but I wait for her to say what she wants to say.

"You're involved somehow. I just don't know how yet." She knees me in the stomach and I gasp for breath, dropping to the floor. I don't want the humiliation of throwing up.

"Be careful, Ruby," she warns. "I'm watching you." She walks away.

I stay there on the grimy floor, clutching my stomach. The pain lessens over the next few minutes and eventually I drag myself to English. I have no sensible reason for being late, which means I'm given a lunchtime detention. Monique doesn't show up at all.

The lunchtime detention means I can't rehearse with the busking group. I only remember this as the bell goes to signal the end of lunchtime, and I send a quick Snapchat to Euan explaining why I wasn't there. As I'm on my way to science, I see him heading in the opposite direction.

"Euan!" I say, catching him up. "I'm so sorry I missed practice, I—"

"Don't worry about it," he says, rather stiffly. "Actually, Mr Williams saw we were without a keyboard player and came into the practice room with a year nine girl who's apparently desperate to busk. I explained you were already on board but he said the more the merrier. He's a bit overexcited by the event. He's been spreading the word for us and we're expecting a big turnout. So – she's doing it now." He hesitates. "You could still come along and play, though?"

"OK, I will," I say. "If I'm feeling brave enough."

He widens his eyes in disbelief. "Ruby! Course you're brave enough. You'll be amazing."

Euan sees Amber ahead and calls to her to wait, saying a quick goodbye to me. I watch as they walk away, heads close together.

I make it to the lab in time, and find my seat in the prescribed seating plan next to Naz.

"How are *you*?" she asks in a loaded way.

"Good," I say in a carefully neutral voice. I don't want to give her the impression I'm too intimidated by her to ask questions, so I add, "You?"

"I'm all right," she says. "Scott says you're playing keyboard in the Justice for Jim event?" She seems mildly impressed.

"Yeah. Maybe." The more I think about playing in front of a crowd, the more nervous I feel. "Are you going to be there?"

"No," says her fellow Glossy, Penny, who's turned round from the table in front. "She's not. It's her birthday."

"I might go for a bit," says Naz. "I'll see. I want to support Scott's campaign."

"But you'll be getting ready for your dinner," says Penny, all smiles. "Hair, nails, pampering."

"Where are you going for dinner?" I ask. I bet it's the swanky little hotel you can glimpse on the road from Barchester to the racecourse.

Naz takes a deep breath, and Penny jumps in. "The flat she's living in while their new house is being remodelled. You're getting caterers in, aren't you, Naz?"

She nods. "It's more private at home. Just my closest friends."

Penny gives a smug smile.

"Is Scott one of your closest friends?" I ask. I might never have another opportunity.

Naz looks uncomfortable. "He's not coming to my birthday dinner, but he's a good friend," she says. "I like to help him out when I can."

"I don't know why you bother," says Penny. "He's odd, and he thinks he's better than everyone else when" – she does a textbook fake laugh – "he *so* isn't."

"He gets me," says Naz.

Penny frowns. "I don't like him."

Naz shrugs and flips open her science book. The subject is closed.

Alice phones me on repeat as soon as the school day's over. I ignore her. She needs to butt out of my life. I know she's wanting to get my side of the story of what happened at the police station, but I don't want her to treat my life like some TV drama. She's not here, so she doesn't get to be part of it.

*Call me urgently,* she texts.

*I mean it,* she texts a few minutes later.

If it were that important she'd tell me what was up. It's a trap. She's luring me in. She'll have already heard Mum's version of everything. I don't want to go over it with her; I just want to forget about it.

Instead, I lie on my bed and look up Scott's website for Justice for Jim. There's a big photo of Jim, the same one that was in the school newspaper. There are photos

193

of fundraising activities from three schools, including the cake sale. There's a link to the article Scott wrote for the school newspaper, and there are smaller follow-ups. The latest one, dated yesterday, is titled BREAKING NEWS and announces what he told me this morning, about police believing a fourth person may have been involved.

There's an *About Me* page detailing Scott's credentials. I skim-read it, cringing because it's written in the third person, but I know Scott's written it, describing himself as "one of the most well-respected student journalists in Britain today."

I ignore Alice's FaceTime again, and to keep myself busy I google the most profitable busking tunes. *Don't Look Back in Anger* by Oasis is allegedly one of the biggest crowd pleasers. I hear the music in my head, and feel the heaving of my stomach at the thought of performing in public.

I send a link to a good article to Euan, and I add, *Also I've been thinking about the busking and I've decided I can't do it. I'm very sorry x*

He replies immediately: *What can I do to change your mind?*

Me: *Nothing. Go and make lots of money!* I push my phone under my pillow and feel a rush of relief. And underneath, familiar, bitter disappointment.

# CHAPTER 27

At a whole school assembly, we walk in to find an enormous photo of Isaac projected on to the wall. Ms Laurel, who has a different-coloured cardigan for each day of the week, is wearing a black one. She first tells us about the busking event in aid of Justice for Jim.

I look anxiously around to find Mara, to be sure she's far away, but can't spot her anywhere.

"It's encouraging that in such difficult times there is always good to be found, and I want to thank the students who organized this," she finishes.

I'm sitting behind Scott and Khalid. Khalid is fidgeting, shifting around in his seat and examining his fingernails. He looks jumpy.

There is a silence. We all know what is coming.

"This has been a very sad week for the school," says Ms Laurel. "I know you are all grappling with the news of Isaac's tragic death, and I want to reassure you that counsellors trained in grief and trauma counselling remain on the premises. Please do make an appointment to speak with them if you need it. And my office is always open." She hesitates. "The police inform me that they will be able to tell us more about the accident very soon, and I will pass this information on to you via your parents and guardians as soon as I can. We don't want any rumours getting out of control, and we'd ask you not to speculate about anything out of respect to Isaac and his family."

After a pause, she moves on to the upcoming careers fair and how year tens and elevens need to return their forms indicating which talks they wish to attend.

I see Scott take Khalid's hand and Khalid stops fidgeting.

When assembly is over and we're all filing out, I see Mara on the other side of the hall, looking sombre. I hear Scott say quietly to Khalid, "The police are releasing a statement at lunchtime. We'll know then." He calls to Amber. "Hey, newspaper meeting at lunchtime, OK?" She nods.

I keep my head down all morning. At lunch, I see Euan. "I'm still gutted you're not going to come busking," he says.

There is a cluster of students ahead of us in the corridor, all whispering excitedly.

"What's all that about?" I say, nodding at them.

"Scott got hold of a copy of the police statement," Euan tells me. "Isaac had taken steroids, and his chest was badly bruised from the weights crushing him, but the cause of death was from the weight bar suffocating him."

I watch as Khalid stands apart from the group, and I can't quite pin down the expression on his face. Could it be relief? I think about his beat-up phone, which he has alongside his brand-new one. Does he have something to do with the steroids?

I don't mean to turn up to the busking, but I'm in Barchester on Saturday morning shopping for Alice's birthday present. I need to buy orange-flavoured Lindors to go with the lip gloss, bought online, which she specifically requested.

It's an autumnal day gone rogue. The sun is bright enough for people to be wearing T-shirts and sunglasses. When I come out of Tesco and go through the alleyway, I see a big crowd, and hear "Don't Look Back in Anger". The vocalist is great. Can that really be Amber? I move cautiously to the edge of the crowd to take a closer look.

It *is* Amber. She sounds relaxed and confident, effortlessly in tune. She's wearing black jeans and a black T-shirt, red DMs and several inches of silver bangles. I take in Aaron on guitar and the year nine girl on keyboard, who has jaunty bunches sticking out of her head like a children's entertainer. But I'm drawn to Euan, the melancholy of his flute. A few people are singing or mouthing the lyrics. The girl playing the keyboard has a cough and at one point she has to stop playing.

There are a lot of people I recognize from school. Scott, Khalid and Naz are going round with collection buckets, and most people are chucking in some coins. I fish my purse out of my bag; I'll give some money and leave.

"Ruby!" I swing round to the familiar but out-of-context voice. It's Miss Starling, with a little girl in a red pinafore and rainbow-striped tights by her side, the girl from the photo on her desk. "Good to see you here supporting the campaign. This is my niece, who's staying with me for the weekend."

A new song starts. My mind is distracted. It's Ed Sheeran, but I can't remember the name of it. I smile at Miss Starling's niece, who smiles shyly back.

The music stops. The girl on keyboard is standing up. A woman, probably her mum, hands her a bottle of water.

"That girl needs to go home," says Miss Starling. "Ruby, why don't you step in? I've heard such great things about your playing." Before I have a chance to stop her, she calls, "Ruby'll take a turn on the keyboard." I thought teachers weren't supposed to touch students, but her hand is very firmly on my back as she pushes me forward.

The coughing girl gives us a grateful thumbs up, and Euan beckons me forward. "You're here! Fantastic!" Amber and Aaron give me brief waves. I find myself taking a seat at the keyboard. I look out towards the audience. Fear squeezes my throat.

"We'll start that one again," says Euan. "Ready, Ruby?"

I look down at the music. Euan counts us in, and my fingers freeze. Sweat breaks out on my forehead. I want to move them into position but they're stiff and slow. It's easier to make no noise than the wrong noise.

I look at Euan, who's standing the other end of the porchway, and his eyes are on me. He's already playing. He widens his eyes and nods towards the keyboard.

*Play*, he's telling me. *Just play the effing notes. You'll be fine.*

I take a deep breath, and try to think of Jim in this porchway, soaked in urine, bruised and battered after the attack. Of course I can do this. I spread my hands outwards and follow the notes on the music, and then I lean, sinking into a chord. I remember an interview I saw once with a musician saying he was just a vessel through which music flowed. My fingers dance on their own, connected to the black dots on the page on top of the wobbly music stand. For a moment, it feels like an other-worldly experience, and then it's over and people are clapping.

"Well, you got there in the end, Ruby," mutters Amber. "Relax. It's a friendly audience."

"You all right, Ruby?" says Euan.

I nod.

"On to the next one?" he suggests.

199

As I play the next song I try to capture the same feeling of music flowing through me, but it doesn't happen. Instead I have to concentrate hard on translating the notes, and I fumble a few times. I keep up with the others, though; I even get up enough confidence to memorize a few bars so I can look up and see Amber holding the mic with both hands, singing with an emotional intensity that has the audience rapt. Aaron is concentrating on his playing, but Euan is looking directly at me. He holds my gaze and I don't look away. I have the sensation that it's just the two of us with everything else muted, transported somewhere else, somewhere calm.

And then the moment breaks because Amber puts her hand on my shoulder, and I'm back in the porchway, and I realize with a lurch that this arrangement has given me a solo, and here it is, and it's like reading out loud, being scared of the notes like I sometimes am of words, waiting for them to trip me up.

I think of Dad, and how smug he'd be seeing me playing the piano. Smug, or proud? I don't want to think about him. I hate how often he comes into my thoughts when he doesn't deserve to be there, taking up space. I have to concentrate, but I can't. And then I make the mistake of glancing into the crowd and there's a face which overloads my already clogged brain. *Mara.*

I can't be here. I mouth "sorry" to Euan, get up and push my way past Miss Starling and the others and run.

# CHAPTER 28

I sprint down the crowded high street to the bus stop at the end. There's nobody waiting, which means I've just missed one. I'll have to wait, and other people will turn up, and I don't know who those people will be. I'll walk to the next bus stop, which is always less busy, and if there are people I know on the bus when it comes, I'll … cross that bridge when I get to it.

I walk for a few minutes, allowing my heart-rate to return to normal, consumed with embarrassment about what I've just done. I should have pulled myself together and carried on.

"Ruby!"

I wheel round. Mara is jogging towards me, not out

of breath at all. It's all that netball and athletics.

"I'm sorry, I know it's my fault you stopped." She walks slowly now, approaching me like she would a frightened dog. "I didn't know you were going to be there." She holds her hands out in some sort of peace-offering gesture. "You were amazing, by the way."

I turn and carry on walking and she catches up. "Have you been playing since you were small?"

"Please leave me alone," I say. "We had an agreement."

"I only wanted to say sorry," she says. "I'm doing my best."

"Go away," I say, my voice flat, like it gets before I cry.

"It's hard for me too, you know." She says it in a resigned way and I look at her. She's wearing jeans and a sweatshirt printed with Minnie Mouse. She dresses in that way that's either cool or tragic, depending on who you are. In her case, I don't know, and I don't want to.

Up ahead, the next bus stop looms. I falter. Archie, who was in the gym the day Isaac died, is there, a skateboard under his arm.

"He's in your year, that boy, isn't he?" says Mara, shielding her eyes from the sun. "You want to sit by the river for a couple of minutes, till the next bus comes? There's a bench down here, and we can just … sit. We don't even have to talk." She points towards a path across the road.

I check the app on my phone. I have thirteen minutes before the next bus. "All right."

The bench is surrounded by cigarette ends, but sunshine is bouncing off the water. Swans on the river glide close to the edge nearest us, wondering if we have bread.

"Hope they don't get out," says Mara as we sit down. "I'm scared of swans. They can be super-vicious."

OK, I guess we are going to talk. I put my head in my hands and sigh. "I feel an absolute idiot running away like that."

"They might think you were about to be sick?" suggests Mara. "Anyway, you stepped in for that other girl. People will think you were brave for having a go."

"No, they'll be talking about what a weirdo I am," I say. "But I'm used to it."

"Why?"

I pull back my hair as if I'm going to put it in a ponytail but then let it flop, as I try to find words. "I don't fit in like other people. Not like my sister. She's really..." I trail off. "Sorry. I didn't mean to talk about..."

"Sisters? Don't worry." She hugs her little black backpack. "Don't take this the wrong way, but I'd love an older sister. I mean, me and Han, we didn't always get on."

Being with Mara is so hard, but as soon as I think that I feel as if I'm a horrible person. I get to my feet, leaving my bag on the bench, and wander towards the water's edge. There's all sorts of green stuff waving around in there, making everything murky.

"It's bad about Isaac Linesman, isn't it?" asks Mara. "I knew him from athletics. He was really good at high jump."

I look round. "He took something," I say. "Steroids. You heard that?"

Mara nods. "Doesn't surprise me, if I'm honest."

My stomach clenches. "It seems I was the last person to see him alive. I got asked loads of questions, but I didn't know anything."

"What sort of questions?"

*If I'd ever touched the weights at the gym. The argument I'd had. The loose CCTV cable.* I say, "Just our conversation in the gym. Stuff I said to him."

"Stuff you *said*?" Mara says.

Suddenly I'm back in the play park all those years ago and I'm yelling at Hannah to take her turn. I didn't just yell that. I screamed she was stupid and mean.

I walk unsteadily towards my bag, and double-check I haven't lost the Lindors. If I hadn't come into Barchester for them, none of this other crap would have happened. And if I hadn't gone to the gym that evening, people wouldn't be whispering that I had something to do with Isaac's death. My life is a series of "ifs" gone wrong.

Alice and I once spent an entire summer obsessed with making Shrinky keyrings. We'd colour in pictures on special paper, and put them in the oven, watching them shrink through the glass door. Sometimes they wavered and wobbled as they shrunk.

I have the strongest desire to shrivel to a fraction of myself.

"It must have been strange," says Mara. "Talking to the police. Were you scared?"

I nod. I don't want to relive any of this. "The bus will be here in a moment, so I'll..." I indicate the path to the bus stop.

"Sure," says Mara.

"Thanks for not telling your friends," I say. "You kept your word. I wasn't sure if you would."

"That's OK," she says. "They did notice something was up for a while, when you first came here and I thought you were getting at me. I told them I was worried about Granddad – he's been sick. And then..." She flushes. "Well, after we talked and I realized you were actually OK, I'm back to my normal self."

I think about this. "I'm glad you think I'm OK."

She grins shyly. "If you were in the athletics club or something where different years mixed, I think we might be friends, don't you?"

I smile. "I hate competitive sport."

She shakes her head as if she doesn't truly believe that. "Mr Morton makes it fun though."

Mr Morton has been off school since Isaac's accident. Everyone says it's stress. "I don't want to miss the bus," I say. "But thanks for coming after me. It – well, it meant a lot."

"No worries," she calls as I cross the road, then, "Hey! Come and cheerlead any time." She starts up a chant: *"Rob-in-son – Rob-in-son!"*

Despite my horrible morning, I'm grinning as I reach the bus stop.

# CHAPTER 29

My mood dips again once I'm home. I lie on my bed and let my head pound with embarrassment and failure as I look through social media posts about the busking. There's footage of me doing a runner, hurrying clumsily through the crowd, and the views are stacking up as I'm watching it. There's no footage of me actually playing. Even Scott would have a hard time trying to rehabilitate my image after this.

I should be doing homework or wrapping the chocolates and lip gloss for Alice. As I think this, she attempts to FaceTime me again. She's not going to leave me alone. I decide to make a bad day worse, and pick up.

She's in her bedroom, sitting on the floor against a wall. I can see some postcards and photos on it. I squint at the photos, but I can't see who they're of.

As expected, there's an angry *why-have-you-been-ignoring-me* rant which eventually burns itself out.

"Is there a reason you've been stalking me?" I say, when I think she's finished.

"Yeah," Alice says. "I'm worried about Mum."

"What are you on about?" I say. I feel uneasy. I've been so wrapped up in everything that's been going on that I haven't paid much attention to Mum.

"She's on a probation period of three months," says Alice. She's speaking more slowly now, as if I'm a complete idiot. "If she takes too much time off, not only will she jeopardize her work, she'll be stressed, and we both know that stress makes her ill."

My head pounds more painfully. "None of that's my fault," I say.

"She needs this job, Ruby," says Alice, lowering her voice, and glancing behind her, probably to check her bedroom door is shut. "You moved to Barchester for it. She can't afford to lose it. *We* can't afford for her to lose it. It's not just you who needs a fresh start."

"What exactly are you expecting me to do?" I ask.

"Don't give her any more to worry about," Alice says. "Don't screw this up for her."

"Thanks and goodbye," I say, cutting her off. I throw my phone across the bed, roll over and bury my face in my duvet. A few minutes later, I lean down to the floor and haul up my bag. I take out the Lindors, open the packet and eat three in quick succession.

It's tempting not to go to school on Monday, but I tell myself I have to tough it out. As I cram on to the bus, I deliberately stand where Euan won't be able to see me and delete a text from Dad asking me to give him a call.

After waiting in the toilet until the very last minute, I go to my form room just before the bell. As I push the door, Mr Baldini sweeps in behind me and says, "Everything OK, Ruby? That was a hasty exit from the busking," and I'm flooded with fresh shame. He must have been there too, supporting Euan.

"Stage fright," I say.

"Happens to the best of us," he says, not unkindly, and in the same breath calls, "Settle down, you lot."

After he's done the register, Amber comes over to my desk.

"What happened to you on Saturday?" she says. There's a low level of conversation. Most people are tuning in to this one though.

"I'm sorry," I mutter.

"You made us look ridiculous," she says.

"I got stage fright," I say. If I repeat it enough times, it'll be true. "Your singing was incredible," I add.

She rolls her eyes, thinking I'm just saying it to placate her. "You should have stayed," she says. "You were good."

She goes and sits down, and Rohan says he heard Naz's dinner for her girlfriends was suitably over the top. He's seen screenshots of her private Instagram. Naz's uncle is a celebrity chef.

I notice then that Georgia's come in late. That's unlike her. Isaac's death must have hit her really hard, even though he was so awful to her all the time. I wonder if I should feel more upset than I do. When Mr Baldini reads out a notice telling us Isaac's funeral will be on Friday and anyone in our year can attend, I see her wipe her eyes.

As we both walk in the same direction to maths, we end up next to each other. "You OK?" I ask. "You looked upset in form."

Georgia stops momentarily to re-angle her bag on her shoulder.

"You know, Isaac wasn't always horrible. I knew him from primary school. You won't believe me, but he was all right then. He changed."

I remember Amber teasing her about having a crush on Isaac. I wonder if her crush on him had never quite gone away.

"Monique changed him," says Georgia. "She got her claws into him in year seven and never let go. That's when the Linesmen thing started. He got mean after that."

I glance at her. It seems a bit too easy to me, to blame Monique; Isaac seemed like he was capable of being obnoxious all on his own.

If I thought the rumours about me might have died

down, I was wrong. Throughout the whole maths lesson people whisper about me. When the teacher turns his back to write on the whiteboard, a group to my right throw rolled-up pieces of paper, which bounce off my head and shoulder. One hits my cheek. It's wet with something. Saliva? Gross. I stick my finger up at them and carry on writing, to the sounds of muffled giggles.

In English, Monique spends the lesson staring at me. Her hair is greasy and she still hasn't got her hoops back in. Her staring is so obvious the teacher asks her to turn to the front, which she does for a few seconds, before switching her gaze back to me. Even when she's asked to read a paragraph from a printed-out extract, she looks up at the end of it and I feel her gaze on my lowered head.

We're given twenty minutes to answer questions on the extract, and halfway through I risk a glance at Monique and she's still looking at me. Her exercise book is empty. When I stare back at her, she gives me a long slow wink, almost as if she's flirting with me.

"I'm watching you," she whispers in my ear as we all rush to the door at the end of the lesson.

The teacher says, "Monique, I'd like a word, please."

I hear the beginning of the conversation as I leave. "Monique, I know you're coping with a lot at the moment, but I need you to focus on your work. This is an important time for you..."

It was never going to be, *Will you stop intimidating Ruby Marshall.*

# CHAPTER 30

I know I can't avoid Euan for ever, but I'm going to try. Instead of the music room, I go to the library at lunch instead, where Library Kid tells me if I start any arguments I'll have to leave.

I write notes for a history essay. After that I move on to the crossword in a newspaper which is three weeks old. Somebody has already filled in one answer. I find myself looking up at the door constantly, and after a while I realize I want Euan to find me. It's Scott, though, who comes looking.

"Ru-by!" he sings.

"What do you want?" I ask.

"A word with you," he says. "I need to tell you

something important." He looks at the girl further down the table who's pretending to be immersed in her phone. "In private."

I follow Scott out of the library, and as soon as we get into the corridor outside, his manner totally changes. His smile drops and he looks around, tense.

"So?" I ask. "What's so urgent?"

"Not here," he says. "The performing arts office is empty." If he's trying to spook me in some way, he's going the right way about it. My hands start getting clammy, and I have to wipe them against my skirt.

In the office he indicates I should sit down on one of the ordinary school chairs, and he sits on the big padded swivel one, scooting it on its wheels closer to me. "I discovered what the police are currently thinking about Isaac's death."

"OK," I say cautiously.

"They think he was crushed by a heavy weight, far heavier than the ones that were found at the scene."

I stare at him.

"He couldn't have added the heavier weights himself. Someone else must have done it. They put the extra weights on, then they left him there to, well ... and then they took the weights off and put them back on the rack. I reckon they switched the stickers over or peeled them off, so Isaac didn't realize the wrong weights were going on."

I swallow. "So that means..."

"Yeah. It looks like it was someone he knew, otherwise he wouldn't have trusted them to spot him. He'd have let them into the gym as well because unless they had a staff swipe card, they couldn't have got in."

This was why I was asked about the weights at the police station. "So it's … *murder*?"

Scott nods. He's watching me carefully.

"Is this a wind-up?" The room's too hot. Scott's eager expression is making me very uncomfortable.

"Nope. There's a police statement up. It doesn't go into specifics, but they're treating it as a suspicious death."

"Show me."

He pulls up a website for local residents. I scan through it. He's right. The police have posted a statement asking for any information from the wider community now that Isaac's death is being treated as suspected murder.

Scott is still watching me. "I've spoken to a contact of mine on the local newspaper and he told me the theory about the weights."

"And you're telling me because…?"

Scott throws up his hands. "I'm being helpful, Ruby. I'm giving you a heads up."

"Why would you do that?" I say coldly. "Tell me what your real motive is here. Come on."

"Why are you so suspicious?" says Scott in such a calm voice I want to throttle him. "I thought you might want to hear this now rather than in, I don't know, let's say an

English class with Monique in it. Be prepared."

The door opens. It's Mr Pompley. "Ah, Ruby. There you are." He gestures for me to go with him. "You're needed in the front office."

From the front office, I'm taken by Miss Starling to an empty classroom, where a tall woman is talking to Ms Laurel, who looks anxious. The woman has short hair and a very straight back, and is wearing trousers and a polo neck.

This unsmiling woman introduces herself as Detective Chief Inspector Kath Ward, the senior investigating officer in Isaac's case. She indicates that we both sit. Miss Starling leaves, but Ms Laurel stays, sitting apart from us, very still – except her foot, which twitches back and forth.

"Hello, Ruby," says Kath. She looks at me as if she knows my height, my weight and my star sign but what she really wants is to get inside my head. "Thank you for your statements. I want to tell you this news before it becomes common knowledge: the cause of Isaac's death isn't as straightforward as it first appeared. We believe another person was involved, adding extra weights with malicious intent."

She waits for my reaction. The thing is, I already know, so my body language is probably muted as a result. "That's shocking," I mumble, folding my arms and curving my shoulders forward.

"We're interviewing everyone who was in the gym

that day again," says Kath. Her level of eye contact is unnerving. "You may hold a clue to what happened in the gym to Isaac without realizing. It's my job to go over every little detail."

I nod. Fear settles like stones at the bottom of my stomach. I have no alibi and a motive – everyone knew how much Isaac wound me up. I also have a reputation for being aggressive.

"We've already contacted your mum, and arranged for you to come to the police station tomorrow morning." She flashes a brief, not very reassuring smile. "I'm sure you're feeling the strain of all this, but we're doing everything we can to find out what exactly happened. Any questions?"

"No," I say, my voice cracking.

I'm walked to my French class by Ms Laurel, which pretty much equates to having a police escort the way everyone is looking at me. I sit in class and let the teacher's words float around me, each one disconnected from the last, making no sense at all. A teaching assistant tries to coax me to copy down information from the board but I sit in a daze. I want to go home and think through what I've just learned.

*Murder.* Kath Ward didn't say the word, but that's what Isaac's death is now. It can't have been premeditated because no one could have known the gym would be closed early and Isaac would have hidden in there. Was the person constantly watching and waiting for an opportunity? Either way, they returned the extra weights to the rack. Lots of people disliked Isaac, but how many of them would have wanted him dead, and were prepared to murder him in such a brutal, ruthless way?

When the final bell goes, and everyone streams out, I feel my phone vibrate in my bag against my ribs, and I pull it out. It's a message from Mum. She says the police have been in touch, and she hopes I'm all right. She's working late tonight to make up for taking tomorrow morning off for the police station. There's pasta and a jar of pesto sauce in the fridge. She says to ring her if I want to talk and that she loves me.

At my locker, I send a thumbs-up emoji to her as if everything's cool, and I try to call Luffy. His phone rings out. He's turned off voicemail.

I don't want to get on the stuffy, crowded bus with everyone's eyes on me. And I don't want to go home. I decide I'll walk into Barchester.

It's a long walk. I can see why nobody ever does it.

Eventually, I reach the bus stop near the bench where Mara and I sat on Saturday. I take off my coat and stand by the bridge, watching the swans glide past on the murky water.

As I carry on up the high street, I see someone familiar leaving Monty's: Euan. It's too late to turn round. He's seen me and gestures for me to hold up.

I wait while he jogs across the road to reach me.

"Just collecting my tips from the other day," he says. He

holds up a little plastic bag of coins and a ten-pound note. "I was looking for you at lunchtime. Wanted to check you were all right."

There's a big fat awkwardness between us and it looks like it's down to me to confront it. "I'm so sorry about the busking," I say. "I didn't mean to ruin it for you guys. I ... panicked."

"You looked terrible when you ran off." He flushes. "Sorry. I didn't mean that. Just, you seemed really stressed." He pauses. "I should have messaged but I thought I might say the wrong thing. I wished you'd stayed longer – you're great on keyboard."

I should have messaged him first, apologized before now. "I hope you raised lots of money," I say. It's stilted. Too polite.

"Two hundred and eighty pounds. Can't believe it!"

"Well done."

Euan throws his tips bag a little way into the air with one hand and catches it with the other. "I, er, heard the latest about Isaac from Scott. That's a shocker."

"Mmm." *Shocker.* Understatement of the year, I think.

"You look pale. Want to go into Monty's and have a drink?" says Euan.

"No, thanks, I'm getting some steps done. Gotta do something now the school gym's closed."

"Wanna walk with me this way?" asks Euan, pointing to a side street. "I have to go to my parents' dance school and turn off the heating, and scan a certificate because –"

He flicks his hand up. "It's too boring to explain. Come on."

I fall into line next to him, and we match each other's pace within one stride. Euan points out the odd house here and there where a student or teacher at school lives, or where a significant Barchester event happened, such as the house where someone drove into the living room ("Nobody was in, thank God," says Euan) or the pretty Thai restaurant which had a whole series about it on Channel 4.

"I learned to ride a bike on this hill," says Euan, pointing at a little incline that leads to a small park.

"That's not a hill! It's barely a slope," I say.

"Felt like a hill," says Euan. His face is so expressive, eyes lighting up at a memory, mouth lifting in a wide grin. And it stops me thinking about Isaac and his last moments in the gym.

After about ten minutes I see a huge sign further down the road above a small hall, which might once have been a chapel: *Baldini's School of Dance* is written in huge purple letters.

"There it is," says Euan, needlessly.

The brickwork is a lighter colour than the houses near it, and the windows look new. "Mum and Dad spent years renovating it," says Euan. "That's why it was so hard when…" He stops.

"When what?"

Euan scrunches his face up as if he doesn't want

218

to think about it. "Isaac Linesman accused my dad of touching his older sister inappropriately a couple of years ago. She was getting married and wanted to learn a dance for the wedding. She went for an extra lesson on her own one time because she had a complicated part in the middle, and Isaac told me at school that my dad had groped her. When you do ballroom dancing, you have to touch your partner, but my dad's never done anything inappropriate in his life. Isaac and I got in a fight about it at school. Isaac repeated it enough times that it became this terrible rumour in Barchester and kids started withdrawing from classes. My dad had to get in touch with Isaac's sister, who agreed nothing had happened but said Isaac would never have bad-mouthed Dad. It's taken a long time to undo the damage."

"Why did Isaac do that?"

"He found it funny, I think." His voice is bitter. "It nearly broke Dad."

"Your poor family," I murmur. It must be hard for Euan and Mr Baldini to see Isaac every day at school. Credit to Mr Baldini, I'd never have guessed from how he treats Isaac. He's always fair.

And now Isaac is dead. Murdered. I feel a chill creeping down my neck.

Euan unlocks the extra-wide front door, which is black and glossy. "It's all in the past. Isaac can never hurt my family again." Catching my horrified look, he says quickly, "I'm just saying I'm not crying buckets

219

over Isaac being gone. You know what a jerk he was." He pushes the door open and steps inside the studio. He spreads his arms wide and looks around. "Mum and Dad are super-proud of this place." He sounds proud himself.

Then he says, "You coming in?"

# CHAPTER 31

"Where is everyone?" I ask, as we step into the silent lobby area with its gleaming wooden floor, purple sofa, and white walls covered with noticeboards and posters.

"There's a competition this evening in Wallerton so there are no classes tonight. Costs a fortune to keep this place warm, so I need to turn off the heating. Mum left it on." He goes to a cupboard and flicks a switch. "There. Where would they be without me?"

I push open a set of double swing doors and admire a large dance floor. There are chairs round the edge of the hall. At one end, steps lead up to a small stage where there's a microphone on a stand. Near the stage is a shiny black grand piano.

I walk over to the grand piano and reach out to touch it. I've never seen one in real life before. My fingerprints leave a mark. I slip my arm out of my coat and use my blazer to rub them away.

"Play it, if you like," says Euan. He sees me hesitate. "I've got to go into the office to find some paperwork. I'll be back in a moment." He walks off before I can say anything. "There's music in the piano stool," calls Euan as he goes out of the swing doors.

I dump my coat and bag on the floor, and lift the piano seat. It's crammed with sheet music. I pull a handful out and place the sheets on top of the piano, but the urge to play a piece I know by heart wins. I sit on the piano stool, lift the lid of the piano and play a C-major chord to warm up. I play rippling notes up and down the keyboard. The keys are more responsive than the piano we used to have at home, or the one in the music practice room. The sound is bigger and richer.

The piece I most want to play is one that Dad taught me years ago. It's not one of his own compositions; it's by Bach. It comes back to me in a rush like a memory appearing. However much I hate that it makes me think of Dad, it also reminds me of a much simpler time, when Alice and I were both at home and I thought Dad would always be there for me, and Luffy too, and I'd never heard of the Linesmen.

After I've played it through once, I play it through again in a different key. The more melancholy minor key suits my mood better. I play with my eyes closed, imagining the notes soaring from the keys and hovering in the room, and when I open them again on the final chord, Euan is next to me.

"That's beautiful," he says. "What is it called?"

"I forget," I say, because I don't actually know.

Euan is sifting through the pile of sheet music that I've left out. "This is one of my favourites," he says, showing me something which looks like a classical piece. I play the first line – it has an epic grandeur about it.

"Like it?" asks Euan. "It was used for that Netflix series." He names something I've never heard of.

I nod and carry on, my left hand stumbling but picking it up again as I reach the haunting refrain.

"Keep going," says Euan. He walks away, his school shoes squeaking slightly on the floor, and he's back within a couple of minutes with a flute.

The first notes he plays make my skin goosebump. I keep my eyes on the music, letting my fingers move almost independently from my brain, finding the notes with very little conscious effort, and that glorious feeling I had when we were busking on Saturday returns.

The end of the piece comes too soon. As soon as we play the final note, I start at the beginning again, and it's as if I'm in a bubble where nothing can hurt me and the piano and flute together is the most incredible sound I've ever heard. I don't want it to ever stop, but we finish the piece for the second time and Euan says, "That was awesome."

"Yes," I say, and then because there seems to be a gap to fill, I add, "I can see why you like it." I get off the stool. I feel lighter; the horrors of the school gym are in a different part of my brain right now, tucked away. "This floor is very shiny," I say. "Is it slippery, too?"

"Give it a try," says Euan. He's smiling as he disassembles his flute.

I'm not normally the sort of person who would do something like this, but I toe my shoes off and rearrange my black trainer socks. Being in an empty hall like this is giving me a weird sense of freedom. I walk to the swing doors and count down, "Three, two, one, go!" Then I run as fast as I can to the middle of the floor before bending my knees a fraction and sliding towards the stage for a couple of metres.

"Woo – did you see that?" I know he did, of course. I get a kick out of the fact he's watching me, that he's smiling at me as if I'm actually entertaining. As if I'm light and fun, not some troubled problem girl.

Euan takes off his shoes, jogs to the start point by the door, and I count him down. He runs, squealing because his glide is much faster than mine was, because he's put more force into it. He skids towards the stage at an alarming speed and has to grab hold of the edge to stop himself slamming into it.

He stands shocked for a moment, before giggling like an idiot, and I join in. "That was terrifying," he gasps.

"Have you never done it before?" I ask.

"Nope. My parents are really strict about health and safety, and people breaking arms or toes." He nods to the stage. "They go bonkers when kids jump off the stage instead of taking the stairs." He takes a step back and then does a running leap up on to the stage, almost falling over as he lands. "Yeah, I shouldn't have done that in socks," he says, bending over with his hands on his knees to catch his breath.

I take out my phone and glance at the time. As nice as this has been, I should probably get back. I walk towards the piano where I left my shoes.

"You have to go?" calls Euan.

"Yeah," I say, sitting on the floor to tie my laces.

He's done his own up by the time I've finished. He gathers up the pages of music, and I scramble to my feet to open the lid of the piano stool so he can stuff them back in.

"Thanks," he says. Standing this close, I can see the different greys and blues of his irises. There's a gold colour in there too. I see the little freckle by his nose that I first saw that time in the auditorium when I thought we might kiss. We're centimetres apart. My heart is ba-booming and my skin is alive to the possibility of being touched.

He looks stricken with nerves. "Ruby?" he says.

I answer by stepping forward and nodding. He leans down slowly, so agonizingly slowly, to put his lips on mine. There's a lift in my body when he finally, finally touches me, on my lips, and he pulls me close to him. We kiss, slowly at first and then more urgently. I feel an exciting rhythm between us, the pushing of our bodies and tongues.

"Guys?"

We look up and Mr Baldini is standing in the doorway, holding one of the swing doors open with his body.

He does a double take when he sees me. His face falls.

A full-on body blush engulfs me.

"You can't use this place as a hang-out, Euan."

Euan clears his throat with embarrassment, and follows it with a theatrical sigh. "Mum and Dad asked me to turn off the heating and pick up some paperwork." The tips of his ears are red.

"Right," Mr Baldini says. "And Mum needs that certificate scanning over by five o'clock or some of the dancers will be disqualified." He moves further into the hall.

"She didn't specify a time," says Euan.

"She didn't think she *needed* to, because you knew it was for today's competition."

I leave them to bicker and quietly pick up my coat and bag, and move to the swing doors. "I need to go," I say. "Bye."

"Hang on, Ruby," says Euan.

"Mum's expecting me," I lie.

"See you tomorrow, Ruby," says Mr Baldini, switching

226

from his arguing-with-his-brother voice to that of form tutor.

I remember I won't be in tutor time tomorrow because I'll be at the police station, and feel sick. I rush past Mr Baldini and out of the front door. I run to the high street, putting an extra spurt on when I see a bus about to pull away from the stop. I'm lucky – a couple in front of me have also run to catch it and it stays there long enough for me to leap on as the doors are shutting.

# CHAPTER 32

The bus is rammed with people on their way home from work, so I go up to the top deck of the bus behind the couple who also ran to catch the bus, and take a seat near the back.

As I sit down, my phone vibrates in my pocket.

Euan: *I could kill Frazer*
Euan: *Sorry. Bad choice of words*
Euan: *Were you running away from a) me b) Frazer c) my inadequate kissing?*

I can't help smiling at that.

Me: *b) of course*

Euan: 😌 *See you tomorrow x*

I bite the inside of my lip as I think of tomorrow.

Me: *I'll be in late but see you tomorrow x*

I lean my head against the cold window, snuggling my neck against the faux-fur of my hood, thinking about that kiss. It's like my body has been chemically altered by it. I'm lighter, more connected, more alive. I replay the moment his lips moved towards mine, and my stomach does a tumble-turn as I remember the actual kiss.

But then it's swiftly followed by a sinking feeling as I remember Mr Baldini interrupting us. The look on his face. It wasn't just surprise, or annoyance. It was horror. Horror that it was me with his brother.

I'm trouble.

Someone thumps themselves on to the seat next to me. It's a woman with three shopping bags and a coat that flops over my lap. She shoves two of the bags towards my feet, and hugs the other one to her so her elbow is touching me. I edge away, and that's when I see them: Amber and Monique, sitting together on the second seat from the front, on the other side of the bus.

Amber is by the window, Monique by the aisle. I slide back down in my seat, but I'm fairly confident they didn't see me walk by. Monique would be making it clear if she had. Subtlety isn't her thing.

I watch them. They're not laughing or joking or acting especially like friends, but Amber doesn't look uncomfortable either. They're sitting alongside each other, talking.

The bus goes down the high street, turns right at the church and enters North Barchester. Monique stands up for the next stop and steps out into the aisle. Amber bum-shuffles across the seat, and then she too stands up. I've no idea where either of them lives, but I know they don't travel on the same bus to school because I travel in with Monique.

I pull up my coat hood so they're less likely to spot me as they turn to go down the stairs, but they're still deep in conversation. I think about the time I saw Amber meet Monique off the bus at school and hand her something, and how Amber was able to pull Monique off me that time in the canteen without Monique retaliating.

When they've gone downstairs, I hunch close against the window to watch them get off. The light in the bus is brighter than outside and I have to wait a second until my eyes adjust. The two of them walk across the road towards a parked car. I strain to see who's driving it, but I can't because of the angle and the gloomy light.

Amber opens the front passenger door and gets in. Monique climbs into the back, and the car moves off.

I message Euan.

Me: *Just seen Amber and Monique sitting together on the bus. Talking, like they don't hate each other. Didn't know they were friends.*

Euan: *They aren't*

Me: *They got off the bus and into the same car*

Euan: *For real?*

Me: *ikr*

*Weird*, I think. Something connects Monique and Amber; I just can't imagine what.

When Mum comes through the door much later, she looks exhausted. She comes into the kitchen, where I'm staring at a sheet of maths on the table, and sags into a chair, still with her coat on and her bag slung over her arm. "Long day," she says.

I've already made the pesto pasta and eaten my portion. I reheat hers in the microwave and place it in front of her with a bowl of sliced tomatoes, a fork, and a glass of wine. She eats it with her coat still on, but I don't point it out. As she takes her first sip of wine, I worry that I shouldn't have given it to her. She's been drinking more recently. She doesn't binge or anything, but how much is too much when you've had a long-term fatigue condition like she has? When your daughter is still causing you anxiety?

After she's eaten, she finally peels off her coat and I make her a cup of tea, and tell her I'm going to my room.

"Listen, Ruby," she says. "I've arranged for a solicitor to come with us tomorrow, when we go to the police station. She's a friend of a colleague."

I freeze. "Why?" I ask.

She shrugs. "Just for peace of mind. We might as well play it safe. We'll leave here at nine tomorrow morning," she says. "We can have a mini lie-in." Her positive spin doesn't fool either of us.

A solicitor. Suddenly, everything feels much more serious.

Upstairs, my phone pings with a notification.

Euan: *Update on your surprise sighting. Amber messaged me about our geography project. Told I thought I'd just seen her on a bus with Monique to see what she said. She said it can't have been her as she went home straight after school ?????*

# CHAPTER 33

Mum and I are in the police station again, with Detective Ward and the solicitor, who is called Tamsin. She's around Mum's age with untidy brown-grey hair tied back in a low ponytail, wearing a black jacket with a few white dog hairs attached. Isaac's cause of death has been officially confirmed: a crushed throat, which triggered a heart attack.

The questions have more edge today, I think. Or maybe I'm just paranoid.

*Have you ever picked up the weights in the school gym?*

*Did you pick them up that day?*

*When did you first notice the CCTV cable had been pulled out?*

*Tell me what machines you went on that day?*

*How would you describe your relationship with Isaac?*

*When you left the gym, did you speak to anyone? Did you see anyone?*

A couple of times Tamsin objects to a question because she says it's confusing, and she takes notes. Lots of them. I wonder how much Mum is paying her to be here. When I asked, she said it wasn't important.

On the way in, Tamsin told me not to worry, that I am helping the police uncover new evidence that will lead them to the culprit and a conviction. I don't feel as if I'm helping, though. I'm frustrating them. How can I know nothing? What am I hiding? They don't ask these questions, but they hang in the air like an unpleasant room spray.

Afterwards, Mum and I have a coffee and a hot chocolate in Monty's even though I should be at school and she should be at work. I send Euan a Snap of my hot chocolate: *Guess where I am?* Perhaps I shouldn't have sent it; it might seem as if I'm not taking the murder seriously if word gets out that I've been at the police station this morning. What if he shows it to Scott?

The thought of Scott lodges in my mind like something caught between my teeth, irritating and slightly uncomfortable.

A screenshot shared by Tolla catches my eye. It's Monique ranting on Snapchat that everyone knows I'd taken against Isaac as soon as I arrived, and I must have stayed on in the gym and tricked him into lifting heavy weights and watched him die.

Mum asks me if my drink is too hot because I haven't started drinking it yet. Being with her out of school like this reminds me of the times she used to take me to orthodontist appointments and we'd stop by a café before she took me back to school. No matter how crappy she was feeling with her fatigue, we always did it. I can't remember what we talked about then. Today, we discuss doing another trip to the dump at the weekend to take the remainder of the broken garden furniture and chipped patio pots.

Mum reaches for my arm and squeezes it. "We'll get there with the house," she says. "Imagine sitting in the garden next summer with everything sorted. You, me, Alice, having a drink on a sunlit bench in the evening."

"We don't have a bench," I say. "Is the garden even facing the right way to get sun in the evening?"

Mum smiles. "Listen to you! Yes, the garden's facing the right way, and I'm going to find us a garden bench on Freecycle."

I think for a moment. "Lemonade. Sweet chilli popchips in the turquoise bowl."

"Of course."

We haven't even found the turquoise bowl yet in all the boxes. Alice and I gave it to Mum on her last birthday after Mum had seen it in a brochure which fell out of a magazine at the doctor's surgery. Alice had been with her and she told me how Mum had swooned over it so much it had taken her mind off waiting for her latest blood tests. Alice is like that, noticing things and acting on them. The thoughtful one.

Rather than dropping me at school and driving on, Mum insists on coming into Robinson to speak to Miss Starling.

"But you're so late for work already," I say as we walk into reception.

"I took the morning off," says Mum. "Unpaid leave."

I'm costing her in so many ways. "OK," I say, and hug her goodbye.

"Rubes?" says Mum, as I pull back. "Things will improve, you'll see. You're a bright girl. Concentrate on your schoolwork and revision. Promise?"

I nod, sign in and hide in the toilets until my next lesson because I just can't face walking into a classroom right now.

My stomach is jittery as I go to the music practice room at lunchtime; I really want to see Euan, but I feel nervous too. What if things are awkward between us now that we've kissed?

He's there before me, playing scales on his flute while he looks out of the window. I watch him through the glass in the door, looking at the way he moves as he plays, the shape of his body, thick and solid, especially his shoulders. When I open the door, he stops and turns in one movement, and his face lights up.

His face lights up for *me*. My stomach becomes jittery in another, better way. "Hi," I say, dropping my bag next to the piano.

"Hey. You OK? Why were you at Monty's this morning?"

"Another lot of questions…" I don't want to say the words *police station*. I don't want Isaac to get in between us. What I want is to lean into him and reach up to his mouth.

Euan moves closer and he reaches for my face with one hand, his fingers moving exquisitely down my cheek. I tilt my head and stretch a little to kiss him. At first it feels so good, even better than yesterday, but then he stops without warning, and I pull back. I move the wrong way, and very nearly knock the flute from his hand.

He gasps and we both apologize at the same time, and I'm embarrassed that despite him first seeming to be up for it, he changed his mind.

"I'll let you get on with your practice," I say, looking round to see where I dropped my bag. I swing it over my shoulder, and he leans against the wall, next to where I'm standing.

"I've got my grade seven exam soon and I'm still struggling with my scales. I'm going to fail if I can't sort them out."

"Want me to test you?" I dump my bag down exactly where it was before, and sit on the piano stool, holding out my hand for his book of scales. He hands me it and our hands touch. It radiates through my whole body, spiralling and exciting, but I get a grip. I open the book slowly, calling out the first scale I see: "D-flat major melodic. Go."

There are so many scales and arpeggios that the bell for afternoon lessons rings before I've called out even a third of them. Euan packs his flute away quickly, pushing down the final clasp with a loud *click*. "Thanks for this. I'll make it up to you when the exam's over."

"It's fine. I don't mind… I *want* to." *I'll make it up to you.* I want to ask what he means.

"See you tomorrow?" he asks. He touches my face again, and I nod. And smile. I watch him go, and it's only when someone tries to get into the room a few moments later that I realize I am still just standing there, a foolish grin on my face.

# CHAPTER 34

My English teacher announces that the *Robinson Record* needs more students on the paper – presumably things have stepped up a bit, what with an actual murder in the school – and that anyone interested should speak to Scott at the end of the day.

Her words go round my head. I've always thought about joining the newspaper, but I'm realizing it would be strategic for me to be involved in shaping what everyone reads: everywhere I go there are whispers about how I don't have any witnesses to vouch for me after I left the gym. Other people who were in the gym that day, who were also called in for more questioning with Kath Ward, can prove where they were. Archie and Dylan have made a big thing about how they were watching the girls play netball.

I go to the performing arts office after final period, still not sure if I'm really up for it. Scott was keen for me to join before, but now would he see it as a conflict of interest?

He sees me through the window straight away, and he bounces out. "Oh my God, Ruby! You have made my day. You're my third person. Come in!" He opens the door, and I see the boy who was playing guitar at the busking event, Aaron.

Next to him is Mara.

I stop.

Mara's face jolts in sync with mine, but Scott is in full Tigger mode and doesn't notice. "So you and Aaron have busked together," he says with a slight wince, probably remembering my embarrassing exit. "And this is Mara. She's the year below us, but she's helped out before. She's good. Whip sharp."

Aaron nods at me, and Mara says "Hi" as if she's never spoken to me before. Her eyes hold steady. *I'm not going to say anything*, they say.

Why hasn't Scott made the connection yet with her last name and Hannah Cole? I wipe my sweaty palms on my school skirt. I remember there was no mention of Hannah's twin in any of the news articles. Scott's mind has been focused on Jim's attack and Isaac. And Cole? It's not such an unusual last name.

Scott sits in the swivel chair and indicates for us to pull our chairs forward. "Thrilled to have you three on board. It's gone mad since the Justice for Jim campaign and ... well, since Isaac died. I need help with research, proofreading and page layout. If you want to write an article, that's great, but it won't necessarily be published and it'll be edited by me or Amber. Opinion pieces particularly welcome."

I was silly to think I might have a hand in shaping the news content. "I'm not sure I'm the right person for this," I say, still standing. My mind spins, searching for an excuse. "For a start, my spelling's really bad."

Scott waves his hand dismissively. "We've got spellcheck. It's more about consistency, house style and whether things make sense. We need help with layouts too – the programme we use is easy. Also, the newspaper is crying out for a piece from a new year eleven student's perspective."

"I don't want to write anything from a personal perspective," I say.

Scott laughs. "I'll keep working on you."

Mara smiles and pushes a chair towards me. Under her breath she hums the Avon chant while Scott answers a question from Aaron, and I feel myself relax enough to sit.

After Scott has talked us through a few things, I say I'll do a few shifts after school and see how it goes. I leave with Mara and Aaron, both of them joking that having Scott as a boss is good prep for the demanding bosses we'll have when we start working. There's a camaraderie between us already, even though I'm quiet.

"See you tomorrow!" says Mara, going the opposite way out of the gates.

Aaron and I get the same bus home, sitting next to each other, but each with our earphones in. It feels light and companionable.

When Mum arrives back a short time after I do, she has something for me wrapped in pale grey tissue paper. It's the soft, cream-coloured rug that I loved in the shop in Barchester. "For your bedroom," she says. "Very impractical colour, but it is beautiful."

I hold it to my face, loving the softness. "Oh, Mum! Thank you!"

She smiles. "You deserve it, Rubes. You're doing a good job of coping with everything."

I put the rug on the table, throw my arms round her and we squeeze each other tight.

The following lunchtime, in the music room, I tell Euan I'm helping Scott, and he laughs as he slots the pieces of his flute together. "Seriously?"

"I know," I say, settling down on to the piano stool. "I surprised myself. Ready for some scales?"

He lowers his face to mine and we kiss for a short, blissful moment, before he straightens up and says, "Let's do this."

★

242

Over the next couple of weeks I fall into a pattern of making eye contact with Euan when I get on the bus in the morning, and walking into school together at the other end; helping him with his scales at lunchtime; and staying after school in the performing arts office, working on the paper. I get a feel for the layout templates straight away, and I find it satisfying cutting the text to fit. There's a skill in slashing words in the right places, knowing which ones won't be missed.

Scott is always in the office, his mood easy to read when you walk in. He's usually either overexcited, or on edge. He reads messages and squeals, and speaks to press officers and contacts on the phone. Amber is there about fifty per cent of the time, and tends to keep to herself. She sits and types and discusses articles with Scott, but doesn't interact much with the rest of us. When I see her during the school day, she's with a relatively hard-working but carefree group from our year which includes Tolla. Georgia has withdrawn into her studies. She barely seems to notice me any more, but she still looks too pale to me.

Aaron, Mara and I share the remaining couple of computers or sit at the round table. Slowly, Mara and I become used to each other. She writes a piece about fostering cats, which she asks me to read before she submits it to Scott. We have a laugh finding some cute and crazy cat photos to illustrate it. She finds me an online discount code for a really lovely print of the colour wheel for my bedroom, and I help her revise for a French test.

The gym reopens, but I know I'll never set foot in there again. Scott asks Mara to take some photos of the dangling CCTV cord before it is reattached, and write a caption asking readers if they can remember when it was disconnected. He argues with Ms Laurel about what he is and isn't allowed to cover in the newspaper, on fire with his defence of freedom of speech.

At home, I write what it felt like to be confronted by Mara near Tesco, and to talk to her in the garden centre café. I only do it to get my feelings on to paper, but I find myself rewriting it a couple of times in my notebook. Maybe one day I'll let Alice read it.

I avoid Monique wherever I can, although I have to be in the same room as her for English. When she leaves a chewed piece of pizza on my desk, I take it to the bin, wrapped in an old tissue from my bag, and push her water bottle over on my way back so it lands on the floor with a huge *clunk*. She shouts with such venom at me, she's sent outside to calm down for five minutes.

Isaac's funeral passes without incident; Monique attends, and Jay and Dani of course, along with a number of staff including Ms Laurel. Scott and Amber go for the *Robinson Record*. Scott orders new sunglasses for it.

One lunchtime, in between scales, I ask Euan why he thought Amber had lied, that time. He looks up at me confused.

"When did Amber lie?"

"About being on the bus. I saw her with Monique,

remember? And she told you it couldn't have been her…"

"Oh, yeah." He goes back to his scales. "Maybe you made a mistake."

"I didn't make a mistake," I say. "It was Amber and Monique, sitting together. Then they got off the bus and into a car. I'd swear it in court. She lied."

I must sound over the top because he blinks. "I heard Amber's parents are going through a messy divorce. You should cut her some slack. Things are tough for her."

"Oh." I know how a messy divorce feels. How it has potential to spin you the wrong way.

During another practice session, I say, "Georgia told me Isaac used to be all right until he came here and met Monique."

Euan pulls a face which tells me he disagrees. "Really? I was at the same primary school as Isaac too. Marchwood Primary." He moves his fingers on the flute, practising the beginning of a scale, clamping down the keys, making a series of metal thuds. He says slowly, "There was this one time…"

I sit very still because I sense an interruption of any kind will make him clam up.

"…Khalid and Amber were also there. They were different to most people in our year. They were liked, but Amber was into indie bands which no one had ever heard of, and kind of gender-neutral. Khalid was quiet and nerdy. Isaac used to tease them, say they were gay, like it was the biggest insult. One Friday at the end of the

245

day, Isaac locked both of them in the stationery cupboard. They were returning art supplies. He turned the key when no one was looking." He looks at me. "They had a light in there but Khalid said they thought no one would find them until Monday. It was in year six – their parents didn't realize they were missing at first. The caretaker found them about three hours later, and they were both traumatized."

"That's horrific."

"Isaac got a bollocking by the head, suspended for a couple of days, wasn't allowed to go to a school disco or something like that, but he didn't care." He stands up, flute in position by his mouth. "I'm going to try that last arpeggio again," and the notes pierce the air – short, brittle and defiant.

# CHAPTER 35

Things gradually go back to normal. Sort of. The Halloween disco has turned into the Apocalypse disco, rescheduled for the end of November. Everyone is feverishly discussing costumes.

Scott is keen to promote the disco heavily. I don't understand where his enthusiasm for a school dance is coming from until he tells me it's been agreed that fifty per cent of profits are going to the school newspaper.

I watch him monitor social media on his big computer screen, and send complaints to Instagram.

One day, when I arrive at the performing arts office after school, it's more crowded than I've ever seen it. Scott, Amber, Aaron and Mara are all there, along with a year ten who is waiting for Scott to interview him about winning a rap contest, and Naz, who's working on some Christmas graphics to use in the December issues.

Scott looks up from his keyboard and spins his chair round to face me. "Ruby, I need someone to research criminal profiling for a fact-box to go alongside an article I've written. The history of it and some juicy facts. All the computers here are taken so you'll have to use a laptop in the library."

I frown. "Will Ms Laurel let you publish that in the *Robinson Record*?"

"Who says it's for the *Record*?"

"You want me to do some research for a different publication?" I say.

"That's a bit cheeky," says Mara. Aaron doesn't look round, but Amber nods to show she thinks it's a bit off too.

"It'll be good experience," insists Scott.

I roll my eyes.

The library is full too. Some Glossies are by the door, taking photos of each other and squealing, waiting for Naz. I glance out of the window. It's raining, that's why everyone is inside. Most of these people will empty out when it stops.

There are still a few laptops free, and a spare study space between Georgia and Khalid. Khalid waves at me. He's doing maths, waiting for Scott. Georgia barely looks up. She's frowning over a textbook, and fidgeting with her green hair scrunchie.

Monique sits in the corner on the comfy chairs, finishing a bag of crisps by shaking the crumbs into her mouth. She's with Dani and Jay, and the three of them have their feet up on the low round table in front of them. Monique catches sight of me and says, "Granny better keep out of my way or I'm going to kick off," and the others tell her to ignore me, that I'm not worth it, and I'll get what I deserve soon. She says, "Hmm," and drops the empty packet of crisps next to her water bottle on a bookshelf behind her.

Library Kid is at the far end of the library processing donated books, which involves intermittent thumping with a school stamp. Mr Baldini sits at the main desk inputting data into the computer that only teachers are allowed to use.

After I've almost finished the research for Scott, Naz comes in, followed by a loud group of year seven boys in PE kit saying their match has been cancelled and they have to wait for their parents to pick them up. They have a football which they kick around until Mr Baldini confiscates it, and they roam the library looking for something else to kick.

The Linesmen get to their feet and announce loudly they're off to Nando's now that the rain's stopped. I realize the Glossies have already gone. The year seven footballers take over the comfy chairs and play an online football game on their separate phones. Soon they are arguing over who has the best score.

Georgia looks up and tuts, then a few seconds later she sighs loudly, twisting her scrunchie round her hair. At least she's not going to distract me by playing with it any more. But I still can't concentrate. I take a break and go to the toilet.

I'm washing my hands when I hear Monique's voice in the corridor outside. I'm frozen for a moment, unsure whether to hide in a cubicle or leave the toilet and risk bumping into her. I decide to make a break for it.

When I emerge, I'm on high alert, but there's no one waiting to jump me. I go back into the library and see Scott and Euan chatting by the newspapers. I recognize Scott is in excitable mode – he is waving his arms around and talking fast – and Euan is nodding politely. I catch Euan's eye and he immediately smiles and comes over as I make my way back to my workspace.

"Scott's got Robinson Reveals back up," he says. "He's very pleased with himself." He pushes a loose piece of hair away from my face, and in that moment, in the middle of the library, it feels like an achingly romantic thing to have done.

I notice Georgia has packed up and left, and Khalid has seen Scott and is piling his things into his bag.

Behind us, there's some kind of commotion going on.

Monique, Jay and Dani are back, hovering over the year sevens.

"Where is it?" snaps Monique.

Mr Baldini gets to his feet. "Leave them alone,

Monique," he says wearily.

"I'm just looking for my water bottle, *sir*," she says. She turns back to the boys. "I'm not going to ask you again. Where is it? It was on this bookshelf."

They shrink away from her, shrugging. Luckily for them, she sees the bottle, which is under one of the chairs, and pounces on it.

"Bet it's not water in there," says Euan under his breath as the three of them leave.

Alcohol in the library. And they think *I'm* bad news.

Mr Baldini calls out that there's five minutes until we have to leave, and I quickly finish up and send my research document to Scott.

"I'll see you at the car, Euan," calls Mr Baldini as he goes out of the door with a box of books and two bags. He doesn't look at me. I cringe whenever I think of that moment in the dance studio.

When he's gone, Scott holds his hand up to everyone who's still in the library. "Public service announcement, people. Search for Robinson Reveals 2.0. We're back in business!"

There are a few whoops and scattered cheers as people disperse.

And it's on Robinson Reveals 2.0 that most of us learn, the following morning when we wake up, that Monique is dead.

# CHAPTER 36

All we know is what we can glean from social media and the news. The ambulance was called in the early evening and overnight Monique was in a critical state. By morning her vital organs had stopped functioning. Scott puts that last piece of info up.

Amber posts below: *Are we looking at a serial killer on the loose at Robinson?*

Mum has already left for work. I stay hunched up in bed for a while. I'm shocked more than sad, and I feel guilty because of the lack of sadness. Nausea rises as I get dressed slowly. What is going on? Am I in danger, too, or is it just everyone who interacts with me?

When I step on to the bus there is a dip in the frenzied

conversation levels, and it's as if I've been slapped. I can't even meet Euan's eye, though I sense him trying to get my attention.

I hear one of the whispers: "Ruby was in the library with Monique yesterday," and I look at the floor for the rest of the journey.

I was in the gym before Isaac died. I was in the library before Monique died. And I had fallen out with them both.

Euan's waiting for me when I step down off the bus. "Are you OK?" he says gently, and I can't stop my eyes filling up.

"Yep," I lie. "You?"

"Just about." His face looks drawn and serious. "Can't believe the news…"

We stare at each other momentarily, caught in the awfulness of the day, and I can't think of the right words to say as we're funnelled through the gates by four uniformed officers, shielding us from the reporters who stand on the pavement outside.

In tutor time, we sit glued to our phones. "Put them away," says Mr Baldini, but it's half-hearted and we ignore him. He's quiet, pale under his tan. Georgia and several others are crying quietly.

"Which of us is next?" someone asks loudly, and I shiver. Amber is the only person in our form not here. I'm surprised more people haven't stayed away, but I suppose it's easier to be at school than out of the loop at home.

"Enough," says Mr Baldini. "Everyone needs to be sensible. This is not an easy situation for any of us, and being hysterical isn't going to help. Instead of period one we're going to the hall for assembly, and we'll hear the latest then." He forces a reassuring smile.

The minutes tick by until nine o'clock and the bell goes for the first lesson.

We troop into the hall in silence. The teachers whisper to each other. Miss Starling is wearing a black trouser suit instead of one of her dresses. My stomach jolts when I see the woman on the stage next to the head. She's in non-police clothing, as she was before, and she seems to be searching for me as we file in. Our eyes meet and she gives me a nod. I feel sick.

"Did you see that?" says Tolla in the row behind me. "That woman totally clocked Ruby."

*Detective Chief Inspector Kath Ward.*

I try to ignore the fluttering in my ribcage. I was in the library with Monique, but so were many others. There are plenty of witnesses who can say I didn't do anything wrong. She went on to Nando's with Dani and Jay. Anything could have happened after she left.

Scott sits in the row in front of me, and I see he has his phone discreetly on his lap, finger poised to press record. Ms Laurel stands expectantly for complete hush, and it happens immediately. Everyone wants to hear this.

"Year eleven, I know that many of you will have heard the truly terrible news." Her voice shakes and she

254

pauses to regain her composure. "At six forty-six this morning, Monique Lavalier died in hospital. She was a student with a lot to give, full of life, and a close friend to many of you, and I know that you will be in shock. Please do know that you have our support today and going forward as we try and deal with a second death in our close-knit community here at Robinson." She glances at the detective, who steps forward. "I'm now going to pass over to Detective Chief Inspector Kath Ward."

For a moment, whispers fly round the room. What was the cause of death? Did Monique take her own life? Silence descends again as Kath Ward clears her throat.

"While we establish the cause of Monique's tragic death, we would appreciate your cooperation. We have traced Monique's movements yesterday afternoon, following the end of the school day. We know she was in the school library after lessons for a short period of time, then left with two other individuals and got as far as the canteen before realizing she didn't have her water bottle. The three individuals returned to the library, located the water bottle, then went back past the canteen along the maths" – she turns to someone at the foot of the stage for confirmation – "yes, the maths corridor, and exited the building by the resources room. Monique then took the bus with the same individuals to Barchester, where they went to Nando's." She looks out at us. Her expression is completely neutral. "I will need to speak to anyone who saw Monique in any of these locations, starting with your year group. If this is you, please stay behind after this assembly."

She pauses and the room becomes alive with everyone discussing what Kath Ward said and dissecting what it means. I hear the words *serial killer*, and people stare at me.

In front of me Scott mutters, "They think she was poisoned."

*How does he know?* His words ripple outwards into ever more feverish murmurs, as Ms Laurel asks people to join her in a prayer.

*A second murder. I was in the gym before Isaac died and the library before Monique died. I'm the common factor.*

My clothes suddenly are scratchy, my vision blurs, my guts liquefy and I need the toilet immediately. I'm not certain my legs are stable enough to get me there.

I stand. Everyone moves aside immediately as if I'm contagious. I rush to the toilet on wobbly legs.

Miss Starling is waiting for me outside. She leads me to the meeting room in student services, past a couple of members of support staff. One of them mouths "Do you need backup?" to Miss Starling, and her response is too quick for me to catch. I sit on a chair and take deep breaths. Last time I was in here, I was talking to the other detective, Carrie, giving my first statement, naïve in my belief that everything would be resolved quickly.

"Talk to me, Ruby," says Miss Starling, pulling up a

chair beside me. Does she think I'm about to confess to her?

"I'm scared," I croak. Saying these words out loud adds to my fear, makes it larger.

Miss Starling nods. "It's OK. You're safe here. I'm going to stay with you."

Words tumble out, shaky like my hands. "This situation… Monique… It doesn't seem like a coincidence that I was near both of them just before they died… It's like I'm being set up. I can't explain it."

Miss Starling hands me a tissue. "I'm going to call your mum," she says gently. I shake my head vigorously at that.

"Please don't," I say. "She can't afford to keep taking time off work."

"The police need another statement from you," she says. "She'll need to be here."

"You can be my adult," I say. "I'm nearly sixteen. I can make up my own mind."

"I'll have to give her a ring to check."

"No," I say sharply. "Don't."

Miss Starling frowns. She says in a voice she might use for a toddler in meltdown, or a rabid dog. "Let's stay calm, Ruby—"

There's a knock on the door. It's Kath Ward.

Miss Starling overrides my wishes and calls Mum, who says under no circumstances am I to speak to the police without her and Tamsin being present. I wonder how long it will be until it leaks out at school that I have a solicitor.

Within a couple of hours, I'm sitting opposite Kath Ward again. Tamsin asks about CCTV footage in the school, and Kath sighs and says, "I'm told the school couldn't afford to upgrade their system and let the current one fall into disrepair. The cameras only work in certain areas. Of course we're going through everything we've got."

Tamsin raises an eyebrow as if she's deeply unimpressed.

"I can't believe that," says Mum.

Tamsin nods in agreement, and says, "OK, that's all I have to ask at the moment."

Kath begins: she asks lots of questions about Monique's water bottle and I tell her about Monique coming back to the library for it.

"Was she poisoned?" I ask, my hands immediately clammy. I must have walked past the bottle on the way to the toilet. I would have had the opportunity to slip something into it.

"I'm afraid I can't say at present," she says, and then asks if my fingerprints would be on Monique's water bottle.

I say no. Then I remember. "Maybe. I pushed it over once a few weeks ago when she annoyed me. But it was a while ago. She'd have washed, wouldn't she?"

Kath says, "OK, so if we find any trace of your fingerprints, they'll be round the side only?"

"I think so," I say.

She narrows her eyes. "You think so?"

Her accusing stare makes something slip in my brain, and I snap, "If I'd put poison in Monique's water bottle, I'd have used gloves or wiped it," I say. "I wouldn't have left fingerprints."

Kath writes something on her pad of paper and I could cry. Tamsin puts a hand on my arm. I shouldn't have lost my temper. I should have stuck to simple answers, like she told me. I am a self-saboteur.

"May I remind you that Ruby hasn't been accused of doing anything wrong," says Tamsin.

I can almost see three letters floating like helium balloons above my head: *y e t.*

Robinson Reveals 2.0 is full of theories, but everyone has piled on to the favourite – that I went back to the gym to continue an argument with Isaac, found he was there on his own and pretended to help him with the weights, loading up the bar with heavier ones than he'd requested so he was dangerously trapped underneath. Monique somehow had evidence and was going to take it to the police, but I stopped her by killing her in plain sight by poisoning her bottle in the library, taking it off a bookshelf while people were distracted and then rolling it under a chair after I'd done it. Monique thought I was responsible for Isaac's death. She'd said so on Snapchat. Someone helpfully provides the screenshot Tolla shared a few weeks ago.

I climb into bed and pull the duvet up to my shoulders. I was allowed home after speaking to Kath Ward. School was closing at lunchtime anyway. The reporters were multiplying and parents kept arriving to take their children home, scared of the killer stalking the school corridors.

Unlike everyone else, I have no idea who the killer might be, just a deep fear that I'm involved in a way I don't understand.

I keep being drawn back on to my phone. It's like peeling back a dressing to look at a terrible wound.

*It's the only theory that makes sense,* someone writes.

*I agree,* writes Naz, *but why would Monique have gone to Nando's before turning in the evidence?*

*Because that's exactly the sort of thing Monique would do,* another Glossy replies.

No one has defended me. I search through the followers of Robinson Reveals. Pretty much the whole school is on here. I thump my phone face down on the duvet and stare at the patch of flaky paint on the ceiling. It's grown bigger. I wonder at what point the flakes will start raining down on me. How common are miscarriages of justice? I google it and the results aren't reassuring. I pull the duvet closer round me. I don't think I'm paranoid to feel targeted. But why me?

My phone vibrates. It's Euan. I decline the call. I really want to speak to him, but I'm scared to. What if he thinks the same as everyone else?

Alice calls next. I decline her even faster.

I want to speak to Luffy so I can hear his calm voice, but he doesn't want to speak to me, not since I told him about Mickey.

Downstairs I hear Mum on the phone to her office, asking them to forward her some documents because she's working from home. Loneliness creeps over me like an extra layer of skin.

A message comes through from Mara: *Are you doing OK? You probably don't want to hear from me, but my parents are out tonight if you want to talk? Because I've got an idea...*

# CHAPTER 37

I think about Mara's message while Mum and I eat jacket potatoes with cheese and beans and I come to the conclusion there's no harm in finding out what her idea is.

We arrange a video call. I sit on my lovely rug, against the radiator, and wait. All she'll see is me and a few rust patches on the radiator.

My heart beats a little faster as the app makes little bubble noises, and as I connect my stomach lurches. Mara's in her bedroom too, on her bed, which has loads of cushions, fluffy and sequinned. Fairy lights, switched on, loop above her head, and half her face is in darkness. I notice all this in the time it takes her to say, "Hi, Ruby. How are you doing?"

"I've been better." I add. "You?" There's every chance she's secretly gloating over my situation.

"I'm all right, thanks." Mara adjusts the angle of her phone, so I can see her face better. She doesn't look like she's gloating. She looks concerned.

"I know this must be really difficult for you."

There's a pause.

"It is, yeah. What's your idea?" I ask. It sounds more abrupt than I mean it to.

"I feel so bad about this crap you're getting at Robinson," she says.

"You feel bad?" I say.

"Yeah." She gives me a faint smile. "What happened to Han was an accident, and if I can put it in the past, everyone else should be able to. We don't owe each other anything, but I feel sort of … responsible for you. I know that sounds crazy." A tabby cat jumps on to her bed and climbs on to her lap. "This is Stanley, by the way. So, my idea." She leans forward, face intent. "We should look into things ourselves. I could help."

"Investigate? I mean, the police…" I'm completely baffled by the suggestion.

"What have they turned up so far about Isaac?" she asks, raising an eyebrow. "Nothing that helps find the killer, as far as I can see. And they're letting everyone think it was you, and that's not fair."

I swallow. "You don't think I had anything to do with it?" I say, in a small voice.

263

"No!" She sounds startled. "No, I don't think you're capable of murdering Isaac and Monique."

"And you want to help me?" I ask as her cat rolls on to his back and stretches, displaying white fur.

"Look, I'd be a great detective!" she says, full of enthusiasm. "I'm methodical. Scott's not the only one who's good at digging around for things on the internet. Plus we have actual insider knowledge — the police don't know the school like we do. You helped me by talking to me about Hannah. I could help you with this."

I'm silent a moment, emotional with gratitude, but unsure. "Where would we begin?" I ask.

Mara rubs her forehead. "There must be something we know that the police don't," she says. "We saw Isaac and Monique every day."

I think back to the interview with Kath Ward this morning, the way she was pushing me to remember everything about yesterday in the library. "I was there, on the spot, both times. I feel as if I must have seen something, some clue," I say slowly. "I wish I could work out what I know. There must be things that are more significant than I realize."

"Exactly," says Mara.

"It would be better to do something rather than nothing," I say.

"As long as Nan doesn't find out," says Mara. "No offence, but she's probably already reported you to the

264

police on Crimestoppers for the murders just for being at the same school." She sees my face. "I'm sorry, Ruby." She picks up a packet of Maltesers by her bed. "I'd give you some of these to cheer you up if I could. Watch this." She shakes a few Maltesers into her hand — maybe four? — and juggles them quickly, opening her mouth after a bit and ending up with them in her mouth. "Life skills," she says, through a mouthful of chocolate.

"Impressive." I hear Mum's footsteps coming up the stairs. I don't want to have to lie to her about who I'm on a call to, so I say, "Gotta go, but I'll do some digging too. Somehow."

"Write down everything you can remember about the days Isaac and Monique died. Time to fight back against the haters," says Mara, holding up Stanley's paw so it looks as if he's waving goodbye. "Catch you later."

After the call ends, I stay still against the radiator for a few moments. I haven't committed myself to anything yet, but for the first time in a while, I don't feel quite so powerless any more. Mara's optimism might just be catching. I reach under my bed to find my notebook and start jotting things down, relieved at actually doing something and not feeling so alone.

In the morning, Mum wakes me to tell me Ms Laurel has sent an email to say school is open as usual. I read through it on her phone.

*A security firm has been brought in and will maintain a*

*discreet presence while the investigation of Isaac's and Monique's deaths continues.*

*No students are permitted to remain on site once the school day has ended.*

*All before- and after-school clubs have been suspended.*

*Some lessons have been rearranged.*

*Parents and guardians are encouraged to drop off and pick up their children.*

*Students are reminded to be careful when posting on social media.*

*It is very much hoped parents and guardians will support the school in maintaining a sense of calm and purpose during this deeply sad and regrettable period.*

All the empowerment I felt last night talking to Mara is gone as I realize how serious this is. When I tell Mum I can't face school, she sighs and says she understands and at least it's Friday and I have the weekend ahead. She goes to work in such a rush that she leaves her phone behind and calls me from her desk in a panic to talk me through how to forward her calls.

I spend the day lying in bed, reading the news reports and monitoring what people are saying about me on Robinson Reveals. Some students are saying they won't go back to school if I'm there. A girl in Mara's year says she heard I'm not in school today, so perhaps I've finally cracked and confessed.

I keep hoping Euan will try to get in touch again, but he doesn't, and I can't make up my mind whether I should forget about how close he is to Scott and message him. I think about contacting Luffy, but I reckon he's still angry with me.

Meanwhile Alice bombards me with messages, and in the end I reply.

Me: *I bet Mum's told you I'm not in school today. That doesn't mean you can harass me.*

Alice: *Only checking up on you.*

Me: *I don't need you to.*

A pause, and then,

Alice: *You need to go back to school, Ruby. You'll lose it if you stay at home too long, living in your own head. Do you want to end up like Dad?*

Me: *I've taken one day off. ONE DAY. Leave me alone.*

Silence.

I stay in bed until I hear Mum's key in the lock at six-thirty. As I walk into the kitchen she leaps on her phone and starts scrolling through it.

"You could have put the dinner on," she says absently.

"You could have asked me to," I snap.

She looks at me, and I see too late how tired she is, with

dark rings under her eyes. "I didn't have my phone," she says, her jaw tight with tension. "Honestly, Ruby, you can be so thoughtless."

"And you can be so pathetic," I say, feeling more hurt and furious by the second. "And you know what? I hate it here. I hate this ugly house, I hate that stupid school. You should never have taken that job."

She walks out of the room without saying anything. Silently I make two omelettes and a salad, leave one for Mum outside her door, and take my plate into my room.

# CHAPTER 38

The weekend passes slowly. I do homework, sleep, watch Netflix, dye my hair a neutral brown – maybe I'll blend in more at school – and keep out of Mum's way. We're speaking, but barely. She goes to work on Monday before I wake up. I decide to go back to school; I need to sometime. I decide to take a later bus, though.

At the bus stop, I jam earphones in and stand like a shadow behind the old people waiting at the stop. When the bus arrives, it's so empty there are seats to choose from.

The two women in front of me are talking about "the Robinson deaths".

"The killer's going to strike again at the rate the police

are solving this," says one. "I wouldn't have my kids in that place if you paid me."

"Shocking," says the other.

At Robinson, I walk off the bus to flashing lights as if I've stumbled on to a red carpet for an event. "Did you know Monique Lavalier?" a reporter shouts from behind a metal barrier that's new. I feel the eyes of everyone left on the bus on me.

"Did you know Isaac?" "Do you feel safe at school?" "Were you in the library three days ago?" "Do you know Ruby Marshall?"

*Do you know Ruby Marshall?*

My hair might be a different colour, but it won't be long before they recognize me. Robinson students have been posting pictures of me online.

A police officer motions for me to go through the gate, which has been left open, and I run along the path to reception to sign the late book. I go straight to history. There are only a handful of people in the class but their mistrust of me burns brightly. The teacher nods curtly as I apologize for being late. He's going through a PowerPoint about 1930s Germany.

At the end of the lesson, Khalid comes by my desk. He doesn't look his usual immaculate self – his hair is rumpled, there are dark shadows under his eyes. "Ruby, can I talk to you for a second?" he asks.

"Sorry," I say, heading past him. "I need to see Miss Starling."

I don't see Miss Starling. Instead, I hide out in a toilet cubicle.

I catch sight of Mara in the corridor at lesson changeover and she acknowledges me with her eyes. I feel ridiculous about our conversation on Thursday night. Who do we think we are?

At lunchtime I go to the practice room. I play through the show tunes the last person left on the stand. Mr Williams comes in and says, "Interesting choice of music," and I stop. I realize too late I was playing upbeat songs at a time when everyone else is subdued and worried. It's disrespectful and suspiciously out of step with the mood.

Where's Euan? I play a chromatic scale from the bottom of the keyboard all the way to the top and then I remember: he had his flute exam on Friday and I didn't even wish him good luck, or contact him over the weekend to ask how it had gone.

Eventually, he turns up, out of breath.

"How was your exam?" I blurt out. "I'm so sorry I didn't wish you luck."

"It was bad," says Euan, and I can tell it's not false modesty. "Scales were good — thanks to you — but I screwed up my second piece. Hopefully I did enough to pass, but I'm not sure. I've been down about it all weekend." He reaches for me and we hug, and I feel guilty for being so wrapped up in myself.

"Nice hair, by the way," he murmurs after a little while, stroking it before he kisses me.

271

There's a loud rapping sound on the glass window of the door. We look round to see Mr Williams. "This room is for music practice only," he says loudly. Great, first I'm playing happy tunes, and now I'm snogging a boy; what must he think?

"Shall we go out this weekend?" asks Euan when Mr Williams is gone. "Pizza in Barchester?"

The bell goes, and I plant a kiss on his nose and say, "Yes!"

At the end of the day, with no after-school clubs or activities, the corridors are heaving with everyone making for the exits. That, and the fact my head is so full of thoughts twisting every which way is the reason I don't register what's on my locker until I'm right up close to it. Big black capital letters, written with marker straight on to the locker.

*I KNOW YOU DID IT*

I rub frantically at the words with my jumper sleeve, willing them to smear into a black mess, but it's not that sort of marker. People are staring.

Quickly, tears pricking my eyes, I open my locker, grab my things then slam it shut, yanking the key from the lock. I can still hear the reverberations of the slam as I run out of the building, reaching inside my bag for my phone.

I try Alice. She doesn't pick up, but she sends a message saying, *I'm in a lecture. What's up?*

I reply, *Don't worry.*

I'm walking fast towards the school gates but there are reporters up there, and parents whose children no doubt want to point me out to them. There'll be members of staff helping and probably a police officer, but I can't face it. I want to be with someone who doesn't have any doubts about me, and although I don't have much faith in her investigation idea, I could do with Mara's positivity. I turn round and go back towards the empty netball courts, writing a text message to her: *Can you meet me on that bench by the river in Barchester?* I run round the other side of the netball courts to the wooden fencing. Behind it are private houses. I drag a litter bin to the fence, climb on to it, check that the house doesn't look occupied, and drop down into the garden. I run the length of the untidy garden, and shakily unbolt the gate so I can walk out into the street.

I've never been this way before, but I have enough of a sense of direction to know which way to go to avoid the reporters. It's impossible to rebolt the gate, and I wince as I pinch my finger trying. I suck on it as I walk away briskly. If I break into a run I'll draw attention to myself.

Usually the roads would be full of kids walking or on their bikes, but it's creepily empty. I guess all the parents are driving their kids now. What's the murderer doing at this moment? Laughing at me?

I reach the bench by the river sooner than I expect. The air is damp and earthy here, the bank dotted with white

273

flashings of duck droppings. The adrenaline starts to wear off, and I'm exhausted with a headache. My phone buzzes against my thigh in my coat pocket.

Mara: *There in three mins.*

She arrives noisily, her footsteps thudding on the concrete path, a bag on her shoulder hitting an A4 folder in her arms as she half-jogs. I stand up as she approaches and her face is a question: *What's up?*

"I've had a bad day," I say as we sit down together and she takes a can of Diet Coke from her bulging blazer pocket. She pulls the tab and offers it to me first. I shake my head. "Everyone thinks I'm the killer, and I don't know how to change that."

"Right," says Mara. Her eyes are gleaming. "Enough time-wasting. If the police aren't going to solve this, then we'll have to." She glugs some Diet Coke, then sets the can down on the arm of the bench, and brings out a small notebook and a pen with a red fluffy pom-pom attached to it from her bag. "Let's talk suspects."

# CHAPTER 39

"Who even is a suspect, apart from me?" I ask Mara.

"First off, the person isn't necessarily from Robinson," she says. "It could be a randomer. Both murders happened after school when the gates were open, remember. There were loads of after-school things going on. Somebody could have got hold of a visitor lanyard and nobody would have looked twice at them if they went into a side door that was open. But they would have had to have persuaded Isaac to let them in the gym. Also, the poisoning might have happened in Nando's. So again, it could have been someone we don't know. But it's most likely someone at school. *And* the murders must be connected. What are the chances of two separate, unrelated murders in the same school? And if they're from Robinson..."

I push the palm of hand into my right eye socket to try to ease my headache. "I guess we should start with Isaac's murder. Dylan and Archie were in the gym with me, but they left to watch the netball match. I suppose they might have returned after I left. Maybe Isaac messaged them?"

Mara scribbles Dylan's and Archie's names in her notebook. "The police must have Isaac's phone, so they would know if he messaged anyone. I wish we knew if they found anything. Who else?"

I say, "There was the entire netball team … but they were playing netball. Georgia's on that team. You must know the rest of them?"

Mara nods. "We could also find out if any of the PE staff had any reason to hate Isaac or Monique," she says. "What do we really know about Mr Morton?"

I almost laugh. "I know Isaac was annoying, but I don't think Mr Morton would have killed him for it." Mr Baldini had more reason, given the trouble Isaac had caused his parents – but surely that's not enough reason to want to kill a student? I'm not going to mention that information to Mara though, not yet. Euan doesn't want it spread around.

Mara looks annoyed. "You never know." She sounds really young for a moment. She taps her pen against her mouth. "Scott and Amber were working on the *Robinson Record* that afternoon."

"Euan was with them," I say, and I feel weird watching Mara write his name down next to Scott's and Amber's. "I don't know if Khalid was still in school but he often waits for Scott to finish, doesn't he? Isaac locked Khalid and Amber in a cupboard in primary school. Maybe one of them – or both of them – have been waiting all this time for revenge."

Khalid and Amber get stars by their names.

"If Khalid did it, then I bet Scott would do anything to help him," I say.

Scott also gets a star.

"I checked the school calendar on the website for the day Isaac died," says Mara, flicking to a different page in her notebook, and reading out her list. "There was maths clinic, chess club and debating team trials, plus a talk for students going on the trip to Paris, and their parents. And then there are cleaners and the maintenance team…" She looks momentarily overwhelmed.

"Let's move on to the library the day Monique died," I say. "We can see if there's any overlap. Who was there?"

"Aha!" says Mara triumphantly. She turns to the back of her notebook and pulls out two photocopied lists. "I have the list! Are you impressed?"

"What on earth…"

"Scott got these from Ray," says Mara. She sees my puzzled look. "You know Ray, the student librarian?" Ah, Library Kid. "I copied them when Scott left them on the desk on Friday in the performing arts office.

You weren't in. I've been desperate to show you. The originals are with the police, but Ray had the good sense to make copies. Apparently he helps Scott out with research from time to time, and he knew Scott would want them."

"Wow," I say, impressed in spite of myself. "You really would make a good detective." I examine the long list of names and linger on Naz's.

"Put a star by Naz," I say. "That whole group... I wonder if they all had a reason to hate Isaac?" My skin prickles. Naz, Euan, Amber, Khalid and Scott. Is a mutual hatred of Isaac the thing that bound Scott's unlikely group together so tightly?

"Isaac had that effect on people," says Mara. She turns the page of her notebook. She's drawn a map of the library and marked where the Linesmen were sitting. "This isn't finished yet. I want to put where everyone else was positioned. People kept moving around though."

"You could draw different maps that correspond to different times." I frown, thinking. "Both crimes had to be opportunistic. There was no way the killer could have planned for Isaac to be lifting weights on his own, or to know they'd get a chance to put the poison in Monique's bottle, if that's what happened. They must have been watching Isaac and then Monique, and acted when they had the opportunity."

"Like a stalker?" asks Mara.

"I suppose so. If the CCTV was working properly in Robinson we wouldn't be having this conversation."

"Everyone at school knows the cameras are rubbish," says Mara. "And someone has taken advantage of that fact. This is a bit of a strange question, but do you think the police know what they're doing?"

"Yes," I say quickly, because it's scary to think otherwise. I look at her intent little face. "But I wonder if they're missing things. Like," I lower my voice, even though there's no one else around, "I'm pretty sure Khalid has a burner phone. I wonder if it was him supplying Isaac with steroids, even though he hated him. I know that wasn't what caused his death, but Khalid might be holding something back because he doesn't want to admit that fact."

Mara flips back to the previous page and draws another star next to Khalid's name.

"Double star Georgia's name too," I say firmly. "She hated Isaac, but she also blamed Monique for changing him."

Mara swings the pom-pom on her pen. "We need to focus on investigating Scott's crowd first, I reckon."

I nod. "Did you know he helps them fix their reputations around school, and then they have to help him with his projects?"

Mara catches the swinging pom-pom with her other hand. "Seriously?"

"Seriously. We should start with Amber," I say decisively. "She and Monique supposedly hated each other, but I saw them together on a bus, and then getting into the same car, and she denied it. I even saw Monique hand her something a while back which, I dunno, might have been drugs."

Mara circles Amber's name. "Amber doesn't say much when we're working on the paper. She seems very private. I'll do some delving." She looks up. "Anything else, or is that it for today?"

I half-smile. "I think that's it. Thank you."

Mara snaps her notebook shut. "Thank me when we've identified the killer. If my friends ask why we're meeting up, I'll tell them we're working on a *Robinson Record* feature or something. By the way, did you hear? Scott's going to publish the foster cat article. Stanley. Is. Thrilled!"

She beams and I find myself laughing at how quickly she's flipped from hard-nosed to bouncy. But all the same, I'm glad I've got Mara in my corner.


"Sorry I'm late," I shout as soon as I get in. The door wasn't double-locked, so I know Mum's home. "I was chatting with someone on the way home because I needed a rant and I lost track of time."

Mum's in the kitchen at her laptop with a mug of tea. Things between us have been more normal since the weekend. "I was just starting to get worried because I knew there were no after-school activities. What were you ranting about?"

280

"Another message on my locker. *I know you did it.*" A fresh wave of inexplicable shame goes through me as I picture it again.

Her jaw tightens. She holds out her hand. "Give it here, I'll take it to Ms Laurel."

"It was written straight on to my locker. In marker pen."

"Oh, Ruby."

"Yup." I lean against the cutlery drawer.

Mum pushes down the lid of her laptop. "The school sent an email just now. Monique died from poisoning, and it's unlikely to be self-inflicted."

I put my face in my hands, and Mum stands up to give me a hug. She doesn't speak; there's nothing to say. As we release each other, she adds, "Perhaps we should think about you changing schools again. It's such a terrible time to do it though. Once was bad enough…"

The first thing I think of is Euan, and how if I leave Robinson I won't get to hang out with him in the music practice room. "Let's talk about it another time," I say. I flick the switch down on the kettle to make myself some tea.

"All right." She goes back to her chair. "I've got some news though, Rubes. Guess who'll be here the day after tomorrow?"

*Please let it not be Grandma.*

"Who?" I say cautiously.

"Alice!"

This is mixed news. It's a strangely comforting thought that she's coming, but I'm going to have to share my bedroom, and if I'm really honest I'm jealous that Mum looks so happy. Alice is the good daughter, the one who doesn't get mixed up with the police.

"How come?" I ask.

"She's got no lectures this week. A couple of essays which she can do here. So she's coming for a few days. We'll pick her up from the station tomorrow evening."

I get my regular bus the next morning. I'm nervous about what the day will bring, but underneath it all I cling on to the fact that Euan and I are going to go out on Saturday. I manage to wriggle through the other people standing so I'm closer to him. He beams at me, and it calms me.

The reporters at the gate have grown in number. There's a big police presence, and I'm seized with panic. I want to melt to the floor, but when the bus stops, Euan says, "Don't get off the bus without me," and barges through a couple of people to reach me.

The noise from the reporters grows as the bus doors snap open. I tell myself I can tough this out.

I'm grateful for Euan, though, as we step down from the bus together, for his solid calm and how he squeezes my hand. Having the hood up on my coat just draws attention to me. A camera flash temporarily makes everything red, and I hear a policeman loudly telling the reporters to keep their cameras behind the barriers, and I feel Euan's hand pulling me until I'm almost running, and Mr Pompley's voice shouting, "Come along, come along. Get inside."

When we're inside and I've pushed my hood down and everything isn't so red any more, I see my locker, and the words *I KNOW YOU DID IT* are still there.

# CHAPTER 40

After the register, Mr Baldini calls me up to speak to him.

"I saw your locker," he says, and I wait for something more from him. Sympathy, I realize, when he says, "Very disappointing."

"Yes, disappointing," I repeat.

"Did you report it?"

I shake my head.

"You should have done, Ruby. The cleaners have specialist products that can remove it. I've spoken to them about it. And – well, this isn't on. I'm very sorry indeed that you've had to go through this."

I blink. He sounds as if he's on my side.

"OK, well, it's being dealt with now," he says. "Please let me know if anything else like that happens again, though. And – remember. You can always talk to me."

Everyone's seen the locker. By break the specialist cleaning products still haven't materialized. Georgia, making her first appearance since Monique's murder, comes over and says she's sorry about the graffiti. There are tears in her eyes, as if she was the one who did it.

"I'll get over it," I say. I should ask her if she's OK, but I don't. Instead I walk to class.

In history, Khalid leans across to my desk. "Have you heard anything from the police?" he asks.

The anxious way he says it annoys me so much, I snap, "No, have you?"

He leans back, startled. "Why would I? I mean, yeah, I gave two statements. That's all they wanted."

"Just, you know, you seemed pretty anxious about how Isaac was before he died," I say, keeping my voice low. "You kept asking me. Were you worried he'd taken something? Something that someone at this school might have given him?"

"It's perfectly reasonable to be anxious about someone who died," Khalid says. There is sweat on his forehead.

"Except you hated him, didn't you?" I say. "He locked you and Amber in a cupboard that time."

His eyes glint angrily at me. I shouldn't have said that. He'll know that Euan told me.

285

I turn away and raise my hand to answer a question, to the history teacher's surprise, and get it right, to her even greater surprise. Khalid doesn't look at me for the rest of the lesson.

As soon as it's lunchtime, I go to the music practice room. Euan doesn't show up. I don't know what to think about that. Has Khalid already talked to him about what I said? I eat a bag of crisps slowly – too slowly, because Mr Williams sees me through the door and kicks me out for eating.

"Sandwiches I can just about turn a blind eye to, Ruby," he says, "but crisps. *Crisps!*"

There's nowhere to sit without groups of other students staring at me, and the library's still shut, so I walk the corridors as if I have a purpose.

I come across Euan sitting alone on a window seat in the DT corridor. He looks at me without really seeing me, and it shocks me.

"What's up?" I say.

"Oh, hi, Ruby." He acknowledges me with a slight tilt of his chin. "Nothing. Just wanted some space, you know."

It sounds like a brush-off, but I perch next to him anyway. "What's going on?" If this is about Khalid, I need to at least apologize.

He looks at his hands. They're big with knobbly knuckles. He's squeezing them, as if he's warming them up before playing the flute. I want to place mine on top of his.

"I'll leave you alone if you want, but I'd rather stay." My

chest tightens, as if I have a cough but I'm trying hard not to actually cough. Is this about us, whatever "us" is?

He looks up from his hands. "I saw your locker. That's rough for you." He leans back against the window.

"What's going on?" I ask him again.

"It's hard to explain," he says.

"Try me."

"You can't tell anyone." His direct eye contact is like being touched by something too hot for my skin.

Well, at least this isn't about me telling Khalid I knew about him and Amber being locked in the cupboard. I swallow, and say, "OK."

He takes a deep breath, then says, "I was working at Monty's on Saturday. Gabby, the manager, was going through the CCTV from a couple of months ago – after Jim Mason was attacked. The police wanted it, to see if it had caught anything interesting over the last few weeks, even though it's up the other end of the street. Gabby called me over because there was a guy joy-riding a mobility scooter, which she thought was hilarious." He stops. "But then I saw something strange."

"Yes?"

Euan hesitates a moment.

"I saw Scott with Isaac and Monique." His voice is so low I can hardly hear.

"What were they doing?"

"It looked as if the three of them were arguing. Isaac lunged out at Scott, and Scott shot his arm out to

287

block him." Euan demonstrates and I move back.

I wait. Euan rubs his face. "Anyway, I thought it was probably nothing, but maybe I should give Scott a heads-up because the whole section of footage went to the police. He's a mate, right? I told him about it in maths this morning, and he laughed, and said it was nothing. He'd bumped into Isaac and Monique and they were having a go at him for being gay." He screws up his face. "Which sounds plausible. Trouble is, I don't believe him."

"Why?" I asked.

"I saw the footage. It wasn't like that at all: Scott was the one in charge. He was telling the two of them something they didn't want to hear. Isaac was mad about it." He rubs his face again. "So Scott didn't want to tell me what it was really about. I'm worried."

I look at the scuffed wall opposite us, where hundreds of bags, hands, and phones have dragged along it. "Everything's so screwed up," I say quietly. I take his hand finally and hold it in mine.

Euan moves closer and time stretches like chewing gum. Our hands loosen as we turn into an embrace. Slowly, his lips meet mine. The anticipation of what's to come shoots down my body.

A noise makes us both look round. Mr Pompley is striding down the corridor towards us. "You two – you can't hang out here. Move along. And ask yourselves, is this appropriate behaviour for school?"

★

At home, lying on the lumpy bamboo sofa, I scroll through social media. I've told myself to avoid it, but I can't. As I read how many people hate me and can't understand why I haven't been arrested yet, the tightening in my chest worsens. It's not just about what I've done or how evil I am.

*Thinks she's "quirky"*
*Ugly as*
*Wouldn't go near her*
*Her clothes are rank. She smells like a guinea pig.*

I sniff my blazer. Does it smell of guinea pig? If this is what people think of me, why would Euan ask me out?

A message pops up, from Mara.

Mara: *I have news. You're gonna be shook. Ready?*

Me: *YES!!!*

Mara: *Monique's mum is living with Amber's dad*

Me: *OMG. So Amber and Monique were sort-of step-sisters?!?*

My phone rings, and Mara launches straight into an explanation of how she worked it out through online stalking of Monique's and Amber's families. "Monique's mum is all over Facebook and Instagram with photos of her and Amber's dad. Took me a while to realize who he was because he doesn't have any social media. They've been together about six months. It looks like Monique lived with them too. Amber lives with her mum but sometimes stays over at her dad's."

"That explains a lot…" I run my hand along the shiny arm of the sofa and it hits a knot in the bamboo. This explains why they were travelling together. I wonder how Monique made sure Isaac didn't find out, or if he knew, how she made him keep quiet. To be associated with Amber wouldn't have looked good for either Monique or Isaac, I suppose. They thought she was odd, a geek. It worked both ways: people would have found it amusing that Amber had to spend time with Monique out of school. The two of them must have come to some sort of understanding. I remember Amber pulling Monique off me in the canteen. I wonder if Scott knew? Actually, I reckon Scott was probably the only person who did know, and was keeping it a secret. Maybe that's how he knew Monique had been poisoned before anyone else did: Amber must have known via her dad, and told Scott.

"I'm not sure whether that makes Amber more or less likely to have been involved in Isaac or Monique's deaths though," says Mara. I imagine her twirling her pom-pom pen.

"It's information," I say. "We just don't know how or if it fits in, yet."

"Who should we look into next?" says Mara. "Euan?"

"Naz," I say firmly. "Why does she come running

290

every time Scott clicks his fingers?"

"She could hang out with anyone she liked," agrees Mara.

"All I know about her is she's living in a flat while her house is being renovated. Oh, and she had a dinner for her sixteenth birthday – her uncle's a celebrity chef," I say.

"She has a sister in the year below me," Mara says. "I'll look at her social media. That might give us a lead."

"OK," I say. "Let's keep digging and meet after school tomorrow in Barchester to discuss."

"Operation Naz," Mara says solemnly, then breaks into a fit of giggles.

This is all so weird. But at least I find myself laughing, and I've missed that.

# CHAPTER 41

Euan isn't sitting in his normal seat on the bus the next morning; he's standing in the aisle so he can take my hand as soon as I get on. I see other people from the bus give us the side-eye. It's raining outside and the windows are all steamed up. Someone has written with their finger *WHO'S NEXT?* in wonky capitals on the back window.

"What's your favourite pizza?" Euan asks, as the doors open and we have to face the press.

The reporters have large umbrellas but the camera people don't seem to notice the rain.

"Mushroom," I say. We're looking down, walking as fast as we can. We couldn't even run if we wanted to because the others in front of us are in a bottleneck by the gates. "I'm a vegetarian."

"Me too," he says. "How come I didn't know that?"

A reporter calls, "Morning, mate," from the barricade. "Are you dating Ruby Marshall? Give us your name."

*Are you dating Ruby Marshall?* The reporters talk as if they know me. So much for changing my hair colour.

"Tell me your favourite foods," Euan says gently, ignoring the reporters.

I keep going. I tell him I like sushi and halloumi burgers, and how I reckon I've got the gene that makes coriander taste like soap. I talk mindlessly, about tofu, Fox's chocolate rings, which have less chocolate on them than they used to, and sweet chilli popchips, as we walk past my locker, which has been cleaned, and on to my form, where Euan squeezes my hand and tells me to stay strong.

In form, I watch Amber with Tolla at the back of the room. The shock of Monique's death must have been harder for her than anyone realized.

Mara messages me at lunchtime, as I'm walking to the practice room.

Mara: *Where d'you want to meet? Monty's?*

Me: *Not Monty's. Euan might be working there after school. Tesco café?*

Mara: *OK. Guess what? Your co-investigator has news!! Catch you later alligator!*

There are people singing in the practice room. Four of them, and one of them isn't in tune. When I interrupt to tell them I've booked the room, Mo, probably the tallest boy in the year, tells me I can't have because Mr Williams told them it was free and if anyone tried to chuck them out, to let him know.

"As if," I say.

"Please go," says Mo. "Like, immediately."

Euan wanders up to the door. "There's a problem?"

I pull him away. "No point arguing with this lot. Come on."

We kick away a half-eaten apple and sit side-by-side outside the art room. Euan puts his arm round me.

"Reporters were bad this morning, weren't they?" I say.

"Don't let them get to you," he replies.

I wriggle more upright. "Naz and Isaac. Did they get along?" I ask.

"Where did that come from?" he asks, turning to face me.

I shrug. "I'm going through people's possible motives."

"Leave it to the police, Ruby."

"They're taking too long," I say. "Tell me how Scott helps Naz, then. What stories does he plant about her?"

He frowns. "He rates her design work."

I pull my phone out and I'm looking at her Instagram feed. It used to be about parties and holidays. Now there are more arty shots and the occasional selfie. There's a photo of the table for her sixteenth birthday. It looks very fancy with crystal glasses, pink linen napkins, silver-rimmed plates and a big vase of pink and white roses.

Euan says, "Her house is massive. It's next to the golf course. A house with a turret. Like from some fairy tale."

"Ah yes," I say. I've found a photo of it further back in her photos. "Not a bad pool either."

"She had a massive pool party in year seven. I was gutted not to be invited," he says.

"You're mates now, through Scott," I say. "You'll be invited to the next one after the renovations. You're in with the in-crowd. Maybe you'll be allowed to bring a plus one?" I immediately regret being so jokey. "Not that anyone would want a suspected murderer there, obviously."

He pulls his head back with a don't-be-so-ridiculous face. "Ruby, of course I'd take you as my plus-one. I wouldn't care what anyone thought. You had nothing to do with Isaac's and Monique's murders."

There's a melting feeling in my stomach. "You really think that? You promise?"

He nods. "I promise." He takes my hand and squeezes it.

Next lesson, English, when I'm supposed to be

doing silent reading, I search for more pictures of Naz's house. Except I don't think it's her house any more because it's listed on Zoopla as having been sold three months ago.

When I meet Mara at the café in Tesco, we coo over a photo of Stanley before I tell her my bombshell news about Naz's house being sold. I've been desperate to tell her ever since I sat down with my smoothie and cookie.

Mara high-fives me. "Wow. Good work, Ruby. My news is kind of similar." She takes a quick sip of her Diet Coke. "Naz's uncle, the one who cooked her birthday meal, is a wedding photographer. He's definitely not a celebrity chef, despite what her friends are saying online."

"Something's happened to Naz's family's money," I say. Mara nods.

"And Scott's helping her manage the situation," I say slowly. "He's told her to post different sorts of things on Instagram now. More arty stuff. Deflecting from what's really going on..." I tip my bottle of strawberry and banana smoothie into the tall glass that came with it.

"He's maintaining her image as queen bee of Robinson. Stopped gossip about her on Robinson Reveals, too," says Mara.

Of course. "Maybe Isaac found out about the house being sold?" I suggest. How far would Naz go to protect her reputation?

"Maybe," says Mara. She has her notebook open and she's writing quickly and neatly. Naz has her own page.

"Are you sure you can't get more information from Euan?" She gives me a meaningful look, as if to say she's seen us together.

"Euan's very loyal," I say.

"Too loyal?" says Mara.

"I don't think so," I say. "He's worried though. He saw something on CCTV at Monty's…"

I stop because I made Euan a promise. But Mara looks past me. I turn round and see Euan. It's as if my throat and stomach muscles give way at the same time, and everything drops. My face burns.

"Hi," he mumbles. He's lugging a basket full of non-dairy milks. "I just … er, thought I'd say hello. Just picking these up for Monty's. The wholesaler let us down."

He clearly heard me talking about him. The closeness we shared just a few hours ago has evaporated.

"Sorry if I'm interrupting something," he says, finally making eye contact with me briefly before looking at Mara.

I wish I trusted Euan enough to tell him the connection between me and Mara.

"We were talking about the murders, looking at motives and opportunities," says Mara. "Want to join us? You can tell us about the CCTV footage from Monty's."

*Stop, stop.*

The whole of me squirms.

His facial expression shifts. "That's private, I'm afraid." He says something about having to get the milk back to Monty's, but I'm not listening to his words. I'm reeling from how furious he looks and sounds.

"I should be going too," I say once he's gone, bending down for my bag. I'm glad I have a moment to compose myself. "My sister's coming back from uni today."

"That's nice," says Mara, and I immediately regret bringing up the subject of sisters. It's on the tip of my tongue to say, "Sort of, if Alice remembers she's my sister and not my second mother." But I can't say that to Mara.

I glance at my phone. "I'm late, in fact."

Very late. Alice's train was due in five minutes ago. Mum's sent three texts asking where I am.

"What was so private about the CCTV footage?" asks Mara.

"He didn't tell me," I lie as I wriggle into my coat. "Like he said, it's private."

Mara doesn't push me for any more. "I know the two of you are close, but it'd be wise to keep an eye on him," she says. "Just ... be careful."

"Cheers for the warm welcome home," says Alice. She's cross-legged on one of the bamboo armchairs. Her hair looks longer in real life, and she's swapped her nose ring for a purple stud, but she looks as effortlessly pretty as ever. "I wasn't expecting party poppers at the station, but I thought you might at least be there."

"Ruby?" calls Mum from the kitchen. She comes into the living room. "What happened to you?"

"I was doing something for the newspaper," I say,

298

remembering too late she knows after-school activities are cancelled. I carry on quickly. "And then I got talking to someone and I forgot about meeting Alice's train."

"You forgot about me?" Alice chucks a floral cushion at me. A cloud of dust is released as it hits my chest. As I cough, she laughs. "Cool rug in the bedroom, Rubes – and Mum showed me the navy blind you've ordered. Very nice. I've got you a little housewarming gift. Sorry, didn't have time to wrap it."

She throws something in a clear plastic bag at me.

It's a folded-up piece of cotton. A pillowcase – with Alice's face printed on it, in close-up, pulling a goofy expression. "Er…"

Alice is in fits of laughter. "You can snuggle up to me when I'm not here! Or dribble over me. Don't worry. I'm only on one side. You can turn me over."

"It's horrendous!" But I'm laughing. I've missed her. A little bit.

"Mum's got one too!" says Alice. "She loves it, don't you, Mum?"

"I do," says Mum. "It'll make me smile every time I look at it. Now, who wants a takeaway to celebrate us all being together?"

It's late by the time we go to bed, due to Alice telling us about her course, the people on it, the people in her shared house, her nights out and the customers in the shoe shop where she does sixteen hours a week. It's interesting to hear more about her uni life, but whenever I remember

299

Euan overhearing the conversation in the café, my stomach clenches. Now, with Alice lying on a mattress in a cleared space at the side of my bed, the room is no longer mine, but I'm pleased to have her distracting company.

"So the real reason I'm back," she says into the dark, "is to help you."

"Really?" I say. "Who are you – a member of the parachute regiment? Dropping in to rescue me?"

I hear Alice roll on to her side, cursing softly as she's caught up in the thin duvet and two layers of blankets on top of her. "FYI, I think you should stop posting on the music sites…"

I'm glad she can't see the shock on my face. "What are you talking about?"

"I was stalking Dad the other day, and there were comments from a couple of accounts that sounded like you – you've never been able to spell 'absolutely'." She makes a *hmm* noise which indicates she's very pleased with herself. "I'm not saying Dad doesn't deserve those comments – his music is shite – but honestly, Rubes, you've got to let the anger go. It's not doing you any good. Maybe you should text him back once in a while?" She blows her nose and mutters about the dust.

"How do you know whether it's doing me any good?"

"Ha, I knew it was you," she says triumphantly, as if she'd laid a sophisticated trap.

I don't care that she knows. To be honest, I don't even care if Dad knows it's me writing that stuff. "I know you think you can help," I say as I roll on to my side, away from her. "But you do realize I'm being framed for double murder, don't you?" I say it like a joke, but the words are more horrifying when said out loud.

"That's ridiculous. You've got to stop letting other people get to you. You've done nothing wrong. Keep holding your head up, Rubes." Alice has always been an advocate of tough love.

"I'm serious, Alice. I had rows with Isaac and Monique, and I walked home with no witnesses when Isaac died, and I was at the scene where Monique was probably poisoned, and apparently had the opportunity to slip the poison into her water bottle."

Alice lets out a little gasp. "Don't panic. It'll be OK," she says but her voice is softer and less confident.

"I hope so," I reply, and we lie in silence after that, consumed by our own thoughts. When I see my phone screen flash, I reach for it and see Euan's messaged me. I have a bad feeling as I open it, and I'm right.

*Hi Ruby. Sorry. Got to cancel pizza on Saturday. Mum and Dad need me to go to a dance competition with them. Speak soon.*

He should have been more honest.

*Cancelling pizza on Sat because I hate you for talking about things you said you wouldn't.*

I turn my phone over without making a sound. I'm two-faced and can't be trusted. If I had been alone right now, I might have allowed myself to cry into her stupid pillowcase, but I can't. My sister has bat-like hearing.

# CHAPTER 42

I wake the following morning with a massive stomach lurch. Two things hit me at the same time. 1) Mum (and I) forgot to set my alarm and 2) Euan cancelled our date on Saturday. Alice is fast asleep, splayed across some of the floor as well as the mattress.

Mum's already left. I'm so late anyway, I decide I may as well take a leisurely shower. For breakfast I eat leftover vegetable biryani and consider staying at home for the day, but Alice will give me a hard time once she wakes up, so I brush my teeth, grab my bag and leave the house quietly so she doesn't hear me and know I overslept.

I get a seat on the bus. The woman next to me says, "You're at Robinson?" and I nod because I've forgotten to do up my coat to hide my uniform.

"My friend told me a reporter and a photographer got on the bus with all the school kids this morning. That's shocking, isn't it?"

"Seriously?"

"Yeah, getting quotes and that."

I let her tell me about her grandson who started in September and has been having nightmares since the murders. I wish I'd stayed home now, even with Alice there. Facing the reporters without Euan is a terrifying prospect. But I don't want to think about him because it's too upsetting.

"Here you are, love," says the woman as Robinson looms in sight. "Have a good day."

I stand unsteadily, peering to see how many reporters there are. A lot. Even more than yesterday.

"You'd think they'd go home after school's started," the woman says, half talking to me and half to the man behind her.

"The police just put out a statement saying they reckon the poison was put in that water bottle on school premises," says the man, waving his phone to indicate how he knows. "Rat poison, apparently."

The bus squeaks to a halt, the door slides open, and I see the familiar faces and North Face jackets, and a few new ones. A ripple of *Is that Ruby Marshall?* goes through the pack. It's too late for a police officer or teacher still to be on duty.

"Ruby?" someone says, and stupidly I look at them. The doors shut behind me with a mechanical *clack*, and I'm surrounded. I'm aware of the bus lumbering away down the road.

I push through the crowd to the gates, which are locked. I jab at the intercom.

Cameras click and whirr and hundreds of questions fly at me. I hear fragments... *you were there... is it true you moved schools because... bullying... other students have said... you knew the deceased...*

"Will you please stop pressing the button," comes a voice through the intercom. "How may I help?"

"Please open the gate for me," I say.

"Name?"

I close my eyes and say it as quietly as I can.

"I didn't hear that."

"Ruby Marshall," I say. "Please open the gate," and there's fresh energy in the crowd, a surge of excitement that I've confirmed my name for them. Cameras, shouts that other people are getting into their shots, calling for me all the time to look at them.

The gate makes a buzzing noise and I push it and run.

The lady on the front desk says, "I'd have let you in sooner if you'd spoken up the first time. Sign the late book." Another person comes out of the office. "Ruby, Miss Starling left a message for you. She wants to see you in her office."

I scrawl my name in it so messily I take up two lines

and walk slowly through the empty corridors to the stairs up to Miss Starling's office.

Glancing through the window, I see she's already got someone in there with her. A parent who is jerking her hands around as if she's used to being listened to. I give the parent a second look – I'm fairly certain it's Georgia's mum. I recognize that perfect chin-length bob. Miss Starling sees me, and holds up her hand in a gesture which means *Don't go away,* so I settle on to the blue fabric-covered chair outside her office.

I don't want to look at my phone, to read about the latest developments in the Robinson double murder case. I'm too wired to do anything other than listen to the sounds of school: the maths teacher's voice through the open door explaining a graph, the shuffling of books and pencil cases, the clicking of heels the other end of the corridor, belonging to a woman I've never seen before but with a yellow lanyard showing she's a permanent member of staff, the ticking of the radiator near me, and the banging of a window not properly shut.

Miss Starling's door eventually opens and Georgia's mum appears. She places her hand on the door handle, a chunky silver bracelet dropping down her wrist, her back to me. She's wearing dark-navy jeans and a loose pink denim jacket. This must be her dressed-down look. "So you'll have work ready for Georgia by the end of the day?" she says. "I don't want to wait until tomorrow. As I said before, it's essential her grades don't drop." Is she wearing a more casual outfit because she's working from home to keep an eye on Georgia?

"Yes, I'll do that. Thanks for coming in. I'll take you along to reception. I hope the reporters don't make life difficult for you again. They've been very insistent this morning."

Georgia's mum shakes her head slowly. "You'll have them around a while yet until the police make an arrest."

Miss Starling acknowledges me with a nod of her head and says, "I'll be back in a minute, Ruby."

Georgia's mum snaps her head and shoulder round at the mention of my name, and stares unashamedly at me.

I glare back.

Miss Starling says brightly, "This way please," and the two of them walk towards the stairs, talking about the congestion on the way into Barchester due to roadworks.

About seven minutes later, I'm sitting where Georgia's mum was and Miss Starling is telling me that, at the staff meeting this morning, it was decided I should do my work in the focus room.

The thought of being discussed in a staff meeting is horrible. The focus room sounds like a punishment.

"We're aware that things have been, and may continue to be, difficult for you," says Miss Starling. She has both forearms on her desk because I'm way less intimidating than Georgia's mum. "And," she says in a casual tone which tells me *this* is the point of it all, "it might be better for everyone."

306

No one wants me in class with them. That's the real problem. I gaze at a couple of thank-you cards Blu-tacked to her wall. If I was in here on my own, I'd read them, find out who thinks she's so great that they'd send her a card. "I'd rather work from home," I say.

Miss Starling moves her arms off the desk. "OK," she says. "That's certainly something to think about, and I can raise it with Ms Laurel. Until it's been signed off, though, you need to stay in school." She's all smooth and calm and head-of-yearish.

"Can I ask a question?" I go right ahead without pausing. "Why don't you have proper CCTV in this school? They have it all over Barchester. A working camera in the gym and library would have saved a lot of investigation." I choke back a rogue sob. "It would have helped me."

Miss Starling looks embarrassed. Quietly she says, "We got quotes to upgrade our system, but it was expensive so we put it on hold. I'm so sorry we failed you." She picks up a pen and takes a deep breath. "So. Shall we say you'll work in the focus room this morning? I have a sheet here of what work your teachers would like you to cover."

I keep my head down in the focus room, not writing anything but letting my thoughts spin round and round. At lunchtime, I make my way to the performing arts office. I want to speak to Scott, to see if he will tell me everything he knows in exchange for a quote about how it feels to be the last person to see Isaac alive, and one of the last people to see Monique alive. As I walk past the practice room on the way there, I see Euan outside.

"The singing group is in there again," he says. He looks as awkward as I feel. The cancelled date hangs between us. If he didn't want to talk to me, he wouldn't be here, though. I cling on to this thought, but then I see a girl sitting against the wall with her friends filming me. I give her the middle finger then regret it because she's delighted to have caught it on camera.

"Euan, I'm so sorry about yesterday," I say, turning my back on her and speaking in a low voice in case she's still filming. "I shouldn't have told Mara… I messed up. But I didn't really tell her anything."

"What are you and Mara up to?" He holds out his hands, as if he's frustrated. "This isn't a game, Ruby. This is serious. You need to leave it to the police."

I bristle. "Why would you say that, Euan? I know it's not a game, but my life is being destroyed and I'm not going to sit back and do nothing. I don't know why you're being so patronizing – it's not as if you haven't interfered in the process."

"What d'you mean?"

"You warned Scott about the CCTV footage, didn't you?"

"Yes, but—"

I don't listen to his justification. Something has occurred to me, and if I'm right, I won't need to give Scott a quote. "I've got to go," I say. I jog to the performing arts office to see if Scott's there. He is, and so are Amber and Aaron. All three turn to look at me as I walk in.

"Ruby!" Scott says. "Can you read a proof page for me?"

"Can I speak to you in private?" I ask him.

Amber and Aaron exchange a glance.

"Yep, no probs," says Scott. "Give us a minute, guys?"

When they've gone, he grins happily at me. "What can I do for you?"

I glance at the glass window in the door, to check there's no one looking in. "I'm sure you know withholding information to the police is a crime."

He makes an exaggerated face of not understanding me. "Of course. But I don't see what that's got to do with me."

"You discovered something about Isaac and Monique before Isaac's death. That's what you were talking about together, that day in the street."

Scott frowns. "Whoa. I was with Isaac and Monique? Back up, where's all this come from?"

"The CCTV footage from Monty's."

He laughs. "Oh, that! Has Euan been blabbing?" I think I see his eyes narrow, but then his expression clears. "Isaac was being his usual douchy self. And I'd had enough. That's all."

"I don't think it is. You were telling him and Monique something they didn't want to hear. I've been wondering what it was. And now I think I know."

If Scott had the upper hand in that meeting which was picked up on CCTV, it was because he had knowledge of something. Something the other two didn't want him to know about. Something they'd done. Scott was like a terrier when he got his teeth into a project, I knew that much. And his obsession at that time was the attack on Jim Mason.

"Can you pull up the CCTV image the police released of the attack on Jim?" I say, walking to his screen.

"There are several, Ruby," says Scott. His face is less relaxed.

"The clearest one. Please, just do it."

Scott moves his mouse and within a couple of seconds, a black-and-white photo is on his big screen. "This is the best. None of them show more than a shoulder and arm of the third person," he says.

I tilt the screen a fraction, to ensure anyone looking in doesn't see. I need to work through this without any outside interference. The quality of the image is poor, but now I'm looking with fresh eyes, I see them.

"It's Isaac and Monique," I say. I see the difference in height and Isaac's bulk. Monique's hood is quite high, resting on top of her tied-up hair. "It is, isn't it?"

He taps his pen against his hand. "Yup."

"You worked it out, but instead of telling the police you went to them. You blackmailed them."

He spins his chair round. "You make it sound ugly. It wasn't like that. I noticed Isaac's trainers." He points to a grey smear around the tallest person's feet. "That brand. It's hard to get hold of. I knew the police would catch up with them eventually. I … you wouldn't understand."

"Try me. Are you telling me you didn't ask them for money?"

Scott throws the pen on to his keyboard. "All right, I did ask for money." He holds his hands up. "Hear me out! I gave the money to the Justice for Jim campaign. It was never about the money, for me. It was about Khalid. I did it because Isaac made Khalid's life a misery for years. I knew if I went to the police they'd get away with a slap on the wrist and some community service. I wanted more. Happy?"

"No," I say slowly. "There's more to it."

He shrugs. "I was working on the identity of the third person, the one who just stood and watched the attack, then poured urine over Jim out of shot. Isaac and Monique wouldn't tell me who it was. You can see the bottle there…" He points to a blur by the third person. "You'd think it would be Dani or Jay, but they have confirmed alibis that night… Anyway, I've tried and tried but I can't figure it out. So I went and told the police I had two names."

"When?"

"A few days ago," he says quietly.

I'm incredulous. "You left it till then?"

"I thought I could solve it."

"You delayed going because you'd have rather gone with three names? It was about your *pride?*"

He looks away from me, and there's my answer.

311

"Why wouldn't Monique and Isaac tell you who the third person was?"

Scott seems grateful I've moved on. "Linesmen have a *code*, apparently. They never snitch."

"What about the fourth person?"

"I'm not sure there *was* a fourth person," says Scott. "The photo that's supposed to show the fourth person is inconclusive." He pulls it up, and he's right. It's like viewing a photo that someone thinks shows a ghost but is actually just the way the light's falling. I ask him to go back to the other image.

I look at the screen again. At the arm in a denim jacket. "So is the third person in danger, or is it them who murdered Isaac and Monique?"

"That, Ruby, is the million-dollar question."

"Can you enlarge it even more?"

He's more eager to help me now, keen to keep me onside and perhaps a bit pleased to have someone to show off to. "I've tried. It just becomes pixels." He shows me, then brings it back to the original size. "It's hard to discern any distinguishing features. Jacket's a bit big, stitching coming loose at the shoulder. Unisex. Judging from their arm, they're slim. Tesco own brand bottle of water. You can just about see where the urine comes up to."

A memory stirs in my brain as I look at the picture, and makes the faintest of connections, and then it fades.

"Can I trust you to be discreet about all this?" says Scott. "It's best for it to come out of the official channels.

There are enough rumours flying around."

"Of course," I murmur, trying not to roll my eyes at his self-importance.

"I'm still up for collaboration, by the way," he says. "If you ever needed some good PR, it's now."

"Do you ever give up?" I say.

He grins. "Nope."

I pause as a new thought comes to me. "Can I ask you something about Naz? I saw online that her house had been sold. Did her family lose their money or something? Was it anything to do with Isaac?"

He gives a heavy sigh. "It will become general knowledge when there's a court case, and I hope Naz will be better prepared for it when that happens. Her dad was involved in a fraud. Yes, they've lost their money and Isaac found out and thought it would be fun to tell everyone."

"Why didn't he?"

"Because I had a whole list of true things I could have easily published in Robinson Reveals about him. He was absolute scum. A total bully. He nearly broke Khalid. I'd help anyone who had a problem with Isaac, but they had to be open with me, tell me everything. They had to help me in return, too."

I nod. "But you enjoyed it too, right?"

He hesitates. There's a knock on the door and Amber pops her head round. "Can we come back in? I need to get that article finished."

"Sure," says Scott. "Ruby's just leaving."

# CHAPTER 43

I'm back in the focus room, thinking about the CCTV image. The teacher in charge is busy with a couple of boys who are still kicking off about some argument that happened in class. I draw spiky stars round the edge of my practice exam paper. The afternoon goes by slowly. I scroll through TikTok on my phone under a textbook, noting yet another stupid message from Dad telling me he wants to meet. I have an ache in my stomach which might be because I forgot to bring lunch and had no money on my lunch-card to buy any.

More people turn up in the focus room, and a few refuse to sit near me, presumably in case I murder them.

I ask to go to the toilet and make my way to the music

practice room instead. I sit with my back against the radiator, hoping not to be seen through the glass square in the door, but being in the same room as a silent piano is like looking at a loaded buffet table without being allowed to eat any of it, which is Grandma's method of torture every Boxing Day morning. I sit on the piano stool, hold down the quiet pedal so I don't draw attention to myself, and let my fingers choose the notes.

I play a piece I didn't know I could remember, played when I stole some music from my last school and brought it home. It feels as if I'm among crashing waves on the edge of a beach, the music crescendoing then receding, gentle then fierce again. I stall partway through, the notes neither in my brain nor my fingers. The room echoes with abrupt silence, and I return to the focus room.

When the bell rings for the end of the day, I leave slowly. I spend a while in the toilet, then walk the long way round by the recycling bins, watching for the gates to come into view so I can assess the reporter situation. Georgia comes out of a side exit as I'm going past. She's wearing running leggings and an oversized athletics-club hoodie, a tote bag over one shoulder, and her hair tied up.

"Hey," she says. She looks exhausted, and as if she's lost even more weight. "I've been to collect work from Mr Baldini."

"Hi! I saw your mum today. Are you OK?" I ask.

"My anxiety's bad," she says. "I can work better from home at the moment."

"I want to do that too," I say. "I'm not coping very well here any more."

"You're not?" she says blankly, as if she has no idea I'm being whispered about all day, every day. We walk towards the gate. There are a couple of reporters, or maybe photographers by the gate, having a smoke.

"I hate this," I say. "They know who I am."

"Oh, God," says Georgia. She looks nervous.

"I'll walk the other side of you," I say, taking charge of the situation. "You can block their view of me. I'll go whichever way you're going."

The two men who remain are too busy laughing about some sexist thing one of their colleagues said earlier in the day. So I happily tread on the collar of the puffy black coat that's fallen off a fence post as we walk quietly by.

"I've got athletics training," Georgia says, walking fast. "It's at my old primary school, Marchwood." I wonder if she wants to try and lose me. My bus stop is in sight of the reporters though, and I'm determined not to let her go.

"I'll walk with you a while," I say.

She gives me a resigned look. "OK. So what's been happening at school?"

I tell her the main bits — lots of people staying home despite letters home saying it'll be considered unauthorized, the library and surrounding areas still cordoned off, fewer police around but more hysteria, me being banished to the focus room.

A car draws up next to Georgia and I shrink back, expecting a camera lens. It's Mr Baldini – and Euan. I catch Euan's eye but I can't read his mood. With my own eyes, I attempt to communicate *Can we talk sometime?*

"Georgia, I was given this practice paper for you by the history department after you'd left," says Mr Baldini. He nods a quick hello to me and thrusts the wodge of stapled sheets of paper through the car window for Georgia, who takes them and puts them in her tote bag, nearly spilling the rest of its contents into the street.

"Where are you two going?" asks Euan, leaning over. He's frowning. He's looking at Georgia, not me.

"Marchwood," says Georgia. "Athletics club."

"Home," I say, though Mr Baldini is already closing his window and he probably didn't hear.

My phones rings and I answer Alice's call as the car drives off. "Good day, darling?" she trills, in the high-pitched voice of a fifties housewife. "Vegetarian sausage and mash, or three-bean chilli for dinner?"

"Sausage and mash, darling," I reply in the same tone, "and it was a rubbish day, thank you for asking."

"'Ladders'?" she says in her ordinary voice.

I snort. It still sounds like a swear word. "Yep, 'Ladders'," I reply. "See you later," and hang up on her before she has a chance to say anything else. "My sister," I say to Georgia, who's still fumbling with her bag. "Back for the weekend and basically thinks she's my second parent." I sigh. "Not sure I can face going back home just

317

yet. She'll have me peeling potatoes and carrots and setting me targets for sorting out our bedroom."

"Come to Marchwood with me, then," says Georgia. "I need someone to time me doing laps round the track. It's only ten minutes away."

I feel like it's probably more than ten minutes away, but there's nowhere else for me to go, so I agree.

We finally reach the sprawling one-storey primary school with its huge field. It looks as if the session is winding down. People are mucking about with water bottles and throwing a bruised banana around.

"What time d'you call this, Georgia?" says an older boy carrying several hurdles, which he places on the ground when he sees us.

"Hi, Brett. Couldn't get a lift," she says. She nods at me. "My friend's going to time me, though."

"You've missed hurdles, but you can get a few running laps in. You'll need to work on your times if you want a place on next weekend's squad," Brett says. He looks at me. "Don't distract her." He picks up the hurdles and walks off down a path and out of sight.

"That's Brett. Assistant coach," says Georgia. "I've missed a few practices lately, so I'm not his favourite these days." She sounds wistful, as if she misses being his favourite. She dumps her bag on the ground and pulls off her hoodie. "I'll stretch for a bit. Can you get the stopwatch up on your phone?"

I leave my own bag on a nearby bench, and sit on one

of the arms, my feet on the seat. The sun pulses gentle warmth. I remove my coat, taking out my phone and swiping up for the stopwatch. Behind the bench is a play park almost the size of the one where... My mind snaps down a shutter.

I shake my head, then turn my gaze at Georgia doing some deep lunges, and imagine what she was like as a pupil in primary school: competitive, good at everything, uniform neat. Not one of the popular kids, but liked by teachers. It's strange to think Isaac, Khalid, Amber and Euan were also here.

*Don't think about Euan.*

Georgia's waving at me now, and I shout, "I'm ready," and step down from the bench and jog slowly to the side of the track.

She runs a lap. She does it again, then again, each with a better time but, she tells me, way off her personal best. Her expression throughout is tense and anxious. The fourth time, she stops after a short distance and limps back across the grass towards me. "I've done something to my foot," she says, sounding irritated. I lead her to the bench. Two boys on the far side of the field are throwing sticks up into a tree. There's another girl on the track now. She's younger than Georgia but she's faster. I can tell that without my stopwatch.

Georgia is breathing hard.

"Are you OK?" I ask. "Is it really bad?"

"I'll be all right." She looks behind her at the school's

play park area. There's a big wooden climbing frame in the middle, a chunky see-saw, and a fitness trail round the edge.

"I loved this school," she says. "I was really happy here."

I think of my primary school and how few happy memories I have. "Yes, it looks nice," I say. But I know that's not what matters; a school is about the people in it.

"I loved that climbing frame," says Georgia. She stands up, testing her foot. "It doesn't hurt so much now." She limps over to her hoodie, wriggles into it, and gulps from her water bottle. She holds it out. "Want some?"

I'm thirsty and I almost reach for it, but it looks too similar to Monique's. I can't do it. "No, thanks. I've got a phobia about drinking from water bottles now."

"Understandable." Georgia screws the metal cap back on. "I'm going to text my dad to ask him to pick me up. He can give you a lift home, too, if you like?"

"OK, thanks." I'm curious to meet her dad.

Georgia texts, then brings her bag over to the bench to leave it next to mine, fussing about her water bottle having leaked over the practice paper Mr Baldini gave her.

The climbing frame looks as if it's seen better days, but the last of the sun is shining on it, like a spotlight. "Fancy it?" says Georgia.

I smile at her. "Sure. If you're up to it."

We pull ourselves up to the top at the same rate. It's fun, like being a kid again.

When we reach the top we sit side by side on the top bar, our feet resting on the jutting wooden plank below.

"Different year-groups had different days when we could play on here," she tells me. We're high up but we don't need to hold on. It's pretty cool. "This was the spot everyone wanted. When Amber and I got to sit here, we felt life couldn't get any better. I think we were right." She sounds sad.

"Did you know that Monique was living with Amber's dad?" I say. I figure Georgia deserves to know.

She pulls loose hair away from her face. "Not until the other day. Someone told my mum. It explains a lot. Amber should have told me. She shut me out." She squints against the sun. "Mum's glad we're not friends any more. She didn't think Amber was good enough for me."

"Really?" I say.

Georgia says, "My parents just want the best for me. They worked really hard so I could go to Barchester House. That's the best private school in the area, if you didn't know." Her eyes are glistening with tears. "I didn't get in. I wasn't clever enough, or sporty enough. So now I'm trying to get into their sixth form." Her skin is a greyish colour.

"You seem pretty clever to me," I say. "And sporty."

"The standard at Barchester House is unbelievably high." She pulls the sleeves of her hoodie down, so they half-hide her hands, and I stare at them, my heart faltering. "Don't look at my nails," she says. "I bite them. I'm trying not to, but I can't break the habit."

I hear Scott's voice in my head: *Jacket's a bit big.*

321

"I saw your mum today," I begin slowly. My brain is making connections, working up to something terrible. "I was waiting outside Miss Starling's office. I like how she dresses. That pink denim jacket – so much cooler than anything my mum would wear."

Georgia smiles faintly. "Yes, it's nice."

The black-and-white image on Scott's screen. The stitching on the shoulder seam coming loose. Just like on Georgia's mum's jacket. Had the jacket also been pink?

Nausea creeps up my throat. "D'you ever borrow your mum's clothes? I would."

Georgia nods. "Sometimes, when I don't think she'll notice."

My voice is shaky. "You're a bit smaller than her though."

"I like my clothes baggy." She's frowning at me now.

It was Georgia. She was the third person with Isaac and Monique on the night Jim Mason was attacked, and I don't know how it's related to anything that happened afterwards, but I know I have to get away from her fast. I ease myself off the top bar so I'm standing with my weight on the wooden ledge. "I should be going," I say, as casually as I can. "My sister will be waiting for me."

Georgia stands too. With shocking speed, she grabs my arm. "No," she says. She brings something out of her hoodie pocket with her other hand: a knife.

# CHAPTER 44

Georgia, who cries so easily, who looks like a strong breeze would knock her over, has a knife at my chest. Her grip is like steel. Fear closes my windpipe and makes my muscles weak.

"You can't go," she says.

I have my phone in my blazer pocket. That assistant coach Brett will turn up soon, I think, or a caretaker when it comes time for the school premises to be locked up. The boys by the fence have disappeared, but the girl is still doing laps on the track. I need to keep calm.

Georgia is crying, but the tip of her knife stays near my chest. "Isaac laughed at the pink jacket. He said I looked like my mum."

"What…" I swallow and try again, working hard to make my mouth move. "What were you doing with him and Monique?" I ask.

"Why didn't he fancy me, Ruby?" It sounds like a wail.

Cautiously I put my hand in my pocket.

"Give me your phone," says Georgia, more composed now, pushing the knife against my blazer lapel. "Do it."

"It's in my bag," I lie.

She makes an angry sound and slices at my blazer pocket so that my phone is exposed. I'm rigid with shock. She could have cut me.

"Throw it to the ground," she shouts. "Now."

I reach for my phone slowly. I need to try and call someone, Alice, but my hands are out of sync with my brain and liquid fear rushes through my veins. Georgia snatches my phone herself and hurls it on to the bark chippings below.

I find my voice. "Hey!" I scream to the girl on the track, and Georgia grabs me round my neck.

"Stop," she says. Her eyes frighten me. She's scared too, but she has a knife.

The girl on the track keeps running.

"I'm sorry," Georgia whispers. "It's gone too far. There's no other way."

"Let me go home," I say. "Please."

"I can't," says Georgia.

"I don't understand," I say. I need to reason with her, to remind her that when I started at Robinson she seemed to like me. "I'm your friend. Tell me what happened with Isaac."

"He asked me out," says Georgia, looking at the knife against my neck. "He said he'd always liked me. That he'd split up with Monique, but we had to take it slowly. She was going to overreact, he said, so we should keep it a secret, at first, in case she found out. He'd find the right moment and tell her."

My heart sinks. Isaac was playing a cruel game with her.

"He said we'd go for a burger. I didn't mind keeping it a secret – Amber hated him and would have been mad at me. He said he'd meet me at the Burger House," says Georgia. "But when I got there, I saw he'd already bought his food. He was looking at me with this weird expression, like he was trying not to laugh. I was confused but I said hi and then I went up to the counter and bought some chips. When I went to sit down with him, he asked me what I thought I was doing. I said … I said I thought we were having a date. And…" She swallows. "He said that he wouldn't date me in a million years. That he found me repulsive. And then I saw Monique. She was laughing and filming me. She said everyone in Robinson would find it funny."

"That's so mean," I say.

"I begged her not to," says Georgia, and the memory of the humiliation goes so deep she does an odd sort of gasp. She wipes both eyes with the back of the hand which isn't holding the knife. "I said I'd do anything if she didn't show anyone. Monique said I had to do a dare instead."

"So you helped attack a homeless person?" I can't keep the disgust from my voice.

"The dare was to pour a bottle of water over a stranger. That was what they told me." She looks at me, as if she's willing me to understand.

"But it wasn't water ... and it was a homeless person."

She screws up her face. "I swear I didn't know. I thought that was it. I didn't know they'd hurt him too. He was crying and pleading for them to stop. They thought it was funny."

I glance at the track; the girl who was running has gone. There's no one else around.

"I wasn't a violent person, Ruby." Georgia has moved even closer to me. I can smell her breath and it's horrible, chemical and sour. "But Isaac and Monique made me violent. I didn't want to do it, Ruby." Her voice is slow, slurred. She rests a hand on her stomach as if it hurts. "I had to. I couldn't let my parents find out what I'd done. It would kill them." She gives a whimper of pain and doubles over suddenly. "I decided this is the only way."

Blood pounding in my ears, I reach for the knife. As she releases it, it cuts her hand. She looks ready to faint, but as I hesitate, she catches me off guard, shoving me hard.

My stomach drops away and there's nothing around me except air and I'm falling. Screaming. I have one thought, which isn't words but a panic: *drop the knife*. I land on my shoulder and the pain is intense and excruciating. My ankles throb and there are bark chippings against my face. I lift my face and then, out of nowhere, a meteorite lands.

Pain. So. Much. Pain. *My body is broken*, I think as everything fades.

I have a hand which still moves. It hurts to lift my head, so I feel with my hand. I feel soft hoodie material around an arm. Georgia. She's fallen too. Landed next to me, partially on my leg.

From a distance, someone shouts. "Oh my god! I'll call an ambulance."

I know that voice. It's Mara. I attempt a wave, but it's more of a twitch of my hand. She must have discovered something about Georgia and tracked me down. She's too late to warn me, but she's in time to save me. Then her voice seems to slip away, or maybe I lose consciousness, and when I come back she's crouched next to me, stroking my hair, telling me it's going to be OK. She's talking to someone else now. "No, you go. Stand by the gate, so the ambulance knows where to come. I'll stay here with them. I know them both."

"If you're sure?" The voice is young, uncertain, male. It's Brett, less self-important now there's an emergency.

"Yes, I'm sure. Oh god, please hurry."

Footsteps leave at a run, soft crunches across the bark chippings.

There's pressure on my shoulder. It hurts.

"Ruby? Can you hear me? It's me, Mara."

Her voice is soft. I want to move to let her know I can hear her, that I'm grateful, but I'm so weak.

"Georgia's poisoned herself. The poison's in your bag, by the way." There's a pause. "With any luck, you'll be dead by the time the ambulance comes. If not, I'll use Georgia's knife over there to finish you off. I'd rather not. I've kept my hands clean so far. But I'll make it look like a struggle between you and Georgia. Don't worry."

I'm hallucinating. I must be.

"You killed Hannah. My sister. You think I'd want you to be alive for one second more than necessary?" Her breath is hot against my face. "I'm clever, so much cleverer than you could ever imagine. And you're so stupid."

Fear seeps into every one of my cells. I move a foot. The sharp pain almost makes me vomit. There's no way I can escape from her.

A shout across the field. Brett, coming closer. But not close enough.

"The coach has gone," he yells. "There's no one else here."

"The ambulance will be here soon," she calls back. "Go to the nearest house, tell them what's happened!"

He nods and leaves at a run. "The ambulance isn't coming," Mara whispers. "I gave them the wrong school. Easy mistake, in all the panic. And the nearest house is far enough away. I think we have plenty of time." She leans

328

closer. "When Nan heard from Jan Lipperton that you were coming to Robinson, she was horrified. But I was excited."

I hear a vibrating noise. My phone. It must be near.

"I hate it when people do the wrong thing and don't get what they deserve," says Mara. "Like you. It's not fair. They need to be punished. That's why I filmed the attack on Jim Mason. It would have been three against one. I couldn't stop them, but I could make sure everyone saw."

Mara was the fourth person, the witness.

"I was changing buses in Barchester that night, and I saw them. I was going to give the footage straight to the police. But as soon as I saw their faces, I knew I'd lucked out. Georgia had strict parents and I knew she'd be someone who would work with me. I could use her to take you down. I didn't know there was a CCTV camera, but it didn't matter. The footage was all blurry.

"I tested Georgia out ... got her to write that first note. I wanted to put the pressure on from day one. I wrote on the locker myself the next time and it was fun! Isaac played his part as I knew he would. I messaged him from my granddad's old phone and told him I was someone from your old school. He happily passed on information, didn't he? Some of it was from Jan Lipperton, who prides herself on her information gathering and some of it, well, I made up. You made it easy, Ruby. So unfriendly, so rude, so aggressive. Who *wouldn't* believe the worst of you?"

I'm getting sleepy. Every breath hurts. But I want to

live. I want to play the piano again. I want to go for hot chocolate with Mum and wind Alice up... I want to see Euan. I want to... My phone vibrates again, somewhere close. My leg is trapped. I can still move my hand slowly, though. I move it now, millimetre by millimetre, feeling for my phone.

"Georgia did well though, didn't she, Ruby?"

Immediately I stop moving my hand.

Mara continues. "She did exactly what I asked her to. I told her you'd killed Hannah. She understood. I've never met anyone who follows instructions so well. 'Do it right,' I told her, 'and you can still get into that school. No one need know it was you who did that disgusting thing to that homeless man.' She got rid of Isaac and Monique, and she made it look like you were responsible. She watched and waited for the right opportunity. Isaac let her into the gym to look for her green scrunchie because he wanted her to spot for him. He thought she'd do whatever he wanted. I couldn't have planned it better myself. And slipping poison into Monique's water bottle when there were so many people around was bold."

I conjure up the image of Georgia fidgeting nervously with the green scrunchie in the library. She'd already killed once and was waiting for a chance to do it again and frame me in the process.

"What she's done today is inspired. She was feeling guilty. I said she shouldn't – you're evil. But she couldn't stop worrying about it, and in the end I knew she would have to go. So we talked it through. She's been waiting for the right moment – to poison herself with the same rat poison that killed Monique, and make it look like you did it. I'd come in time to save her, of course. But will I, really? The poison came from my granddad's shed, by the way. He has so much stuff in there, he'd never notice it missing, and if he did, Nan would stop him from saying anything. Did you think Georgia was texting her dad? Poor, deluded Ruby. She was texting me. I hope you touched the water bottle. It doesn't matter if you didn't, I'll make sure you do, and your fingerprints will be on the knife. It'll look as if she went down with a fight. She deserves that. Bringing you here and pushing you off the climbing frame was inspired. Shame it wasn't a big slide, eh? But you can't have everything. I guess you could have had some poison too. We could have worked with that. Murder-suicide, perhaps?" She gives a little laugh noise. "You really thought I was trying to help you, didn't you?"

A moment's quiet, and when I open my eyes slowly, I see she's standing, scanning the horizon. She takes out her phone, calling 999, crying, saying in a high voice there's been a terrible accident. Giving the correct address, saying she might have been mistaken last time. I'll admit it: she's clever.

I'm sinking into the darkness, but I want to speak to Alice. The wanting becomes everything. I move my hand feverishly, patting the bark chips, searching. Something smooth. My phone. I know the weight of it so well. I'm scared to open my eyes but I have to. I can't see Mara, but I can hear her, acting hysterical. I see chips of wood, blood, and my keypad.

Quick. Be quicker. Fingers like carrot sticks.

The phone rings and I drag it closer to my mouth. My tongue is thick and sore.

"Where are you?" says Alice.

For a terrible moment, I think I'm not capable of speech, and then I rasp, "Marchwood primary. Ladders," before I sink under a wave of darkness.

# CHAPTER 45

When I surface into light again, Mum and Alice are there, hovering over me with anxious faces. I'm not sure where I am. I close my eyes and listen to them tell me I'm safe.

Later, I'm not sure how much later, I open them to see a different woman. A nurse, I realize. "Ruby," she says gently. "You're in hospital. You're going to be having a little operation on your leg this afternoon, OK?"

I close my eyes. Georgia, Mara, the knife, falling. Thoughts are mashed in my head, blended into each other, hard to extract and examine.

Another time I open my eyes and see a police officer and my heart squeezes with fear. Am I about to be arrested? I feel the wetness of tears leaking down my face.

*You're so stupid, Ruby. It was easy.* The police officer disappears. Somewhere in the background are Mum's and Alice's voices, but their words are fuzzy. Once I think I hear Dad's voice. "Ladders" is on loop in my head.

I hear someone say my leg was broken in two places, that I twisted both ankles, and sustained a concussion, extensive bruising and mild abrasions.

I wake again, and Mum is holding my hand. Her mouth is moving, and, slowly, I realize I can understand what she is saying.

"You're OK, Rubes. You're OK. The operation went really well."

"I didn't hurt her," I whisper. "Georgia..."

Mum squeezes my fingers gently. "Georgia told the police everything."

I'm confused, then elated. "She's alive?" I croak.

Mum nods. "She's doing well. When you're ready, the police want to talk to you." I stiffen. "Only when you're up to it," she says. "But let's not talk about that now."

It's a grey, rain-threatening day outside when I'm lifted into a wheelchair and moved to a side room for my meeting with Kath Ward. I look out of the window, down at all the different rooftops as I wait for her to arrive, and feel separated from the ordinary life going on in those houses. Mum and Alice wait with me, and so does Tamsin.

Kath's manner is just the same – formal and mostly unsmiling. She says, "I'm glad you're recovering well,

334

Ruby. I know this will be hard but I'd like you to tell me everything."

I start with pushing Hannah off the slide that spring day in my navy coat with the flowers. I end with the phone call to Alice. When I finish, I'm exhausted. But I've done it. I've told her everything.

After the formal bit is over, Kath says, "Thank you, Ruby. We always knew there was more to the murders than initially met the eye. It's been a shocking case. I realize Mara's grandmother and her friend Jan Lipperton have been behind a lot of unpleasantness where you used to live, and I'll be speaking to Ms Laurel at Robinson to ensure your teachers know the full extent of what you've been through." She looks at Mum. "You've got a strong daughter here."

"I know," says Mum. "I've always known that."

"She's the best," says Alice.

"That's enough!" I say, blushing, but they can tell I like hearing it.

Alice lies on my bed next to me eating ginger nuts.

Mum's gone to buy hot chocolates from the Costa Coffee at the main entrance. She's been talking to us about how much she likes her job and her co-workers, how her health has improved, and how we mustn't worry about her. When she's tired or stressed, it's normal tiredness and stress. Alice makes her promise that she'll tell us if that ever changes.

"Mum's boss has been genuinely fine about her taking time off," Alice says to me now. "She was talking to him on speaker phone and I heard him. They clearly all love her." She twists the top of the biscuit packet closed. "I'm sorry I gave you a hard time about that. So, in other news, I seem to be tasked with juggling your social diary. First off, Dad."

I pull a face.

"He left a live gig when he heard about you. He saw you briefly when you were out of it, but he wants to come back this evening." I scowl and she puts her hand on my arm. "Shhh. You should see him. Do it. Make your peace." She raises her eyebrow.

"Maybe."

"Tell you what, I'll pencil him in for a strict ten minutes-only this evening."

I roll my eyes, which gives me a headache. "The second thing?"

"Euan … Baldy?"

"Baldini," I say. "What about him?"

"He wants to visit you too. In fact, I'd say he's desperate to."

"Why?"

Alice looks at me. "You don't remember me telling you this?"

I shake my head.

"By the time Mum and I got to Marchwood, Euan was already there. He'd seen inside Georgia's bag when

336

his brother gave her some papers and saw a bottle with a picture of a rat on it. He couldn't get it out of his head. He persuaded his brother to give him a lift to Marchwood to see if everything was OK. They arrived just before the ambulance and saw Mara leaning over you with a knife. They asked her what the hell she was doing, and she leaped away with some stupid story of self-defence. Like you could actually move. They were the ones who called the police."

Her phone buzzes and she glances at it. "Speak of the devil. Euan would like another update. Shall we let him have a five-minute audience with you this afternoon?" She gives me a sly look. "He's keen. I'm going to say … yes." She's messaging back already, and I don't stop her.

"He's just being nice," I say.

"Yeah, absolutely," says Alice. "That's what I think too." She looks at her phone. "A couple more things on the agenda. Amber. She says she wishes she'd tried to get help for Georgia earlier, but Georgia kept pushing her away. She wants to come and visit you once you're home. I said that would be great."

"Poor Amber," I say. "Yes, I'd like to talk to her."

"Next, The Luffster. He's sending you a get-well soon card. He says he's sorry he's been pathetic at staying in touch."

I give her a look. "I'm sure he didn't say the word *pathetic*."

"Nope," says Alice readily. "That's my interpretation.

Apparently he's drawn a piano. If it's any good you could frame it and put it up in our room."

I'd like to have a reminder of Luffy. "*My* room," I say. "It'll be good. Art is his thing."

"You've got a hell of a lot of cards," says Alice. She's placed some of them on the windowsill and Blu-tacked others to the wall next to me. The card from Grandma and Grandpa had clump of mushrooms on the front, and inside it said *Happy Birthday to a Fun-ghi*, which Grandma had at least crossed out and put *Get Well Soon, Dear Ruby*. It's in the bin now.

"Mum's told Grandma she isn't allowed to visit until you're one hundred per cent better, and she promises to be more positive," says Alice.

"Go, Mum!" I say.

Euan turns up while Alice is still spraying dry shampoo into my hair, but I'm wearing clean clothes and I've brushed my teeth and applied mascara. Alice pulls up a chair for him. She and Mum make a thing of popping out for a walk.

"Hi," he says. "You look way better than the last time I saw you." He places a squashed bunch of flowers and a huge bar of chocolate on the locker next to my bed.

I smile. "Thanks." I must have looked a sight when he last saw me. "Thanks for what you did too. You and Mr Bal— your brother."

He shakes his head. "We should have got there sooner.

338

Frazer feels terrible. He says he's been a really bad form tutor as well. Felt he should have helped you more. It's made him question teaching."

"That's ridiculous," I say. "He's definitely one of the good ones."

"I'll tell him you said that. It'll make him feel better. I think he'll improve," says Euan. He looks embarrassed now. "And I'm, er, sorry about the cancelled date."

It's my turn to go red. "I'm sorry I blabbed all that private stuff to Mara. I'm so stupid."

Euan says, "No. No, you weren't. She was totally convincing. She always seemed so sweet."

I haven't properly got my head round how far Mara went for revenge, or how humiliated and panicked Georgia must have been to do what she did. "Let's not talk about her today," I say.

Euan moves his chair closer. "You are coming back to Robinson, aren't you?" he asks. "I know you've had a crap time there, but please don't change schools. You'll mess up your exams if you do."

"Are you worried about my exams?" I raise an eyebrow.

"Absolutely. Speaking of which, I only went and passed my flute exam!"

"Woo!" I squeal. "You star!"

He stands up to do a little victory dance. I brush away the ginger nut crumbs Alice left earlier, and pat the bed next to me.

"I'm going to get told off by a nurse or your mum, aren't I?" he says as he slips off his trainers.

"Most likely my sister," I say. "She's very protective of me."

He climbs up gently so not to knock against my leg. After lying still for a moment, he strokes my wrist as if he's scared touching me is going to hurt, and I take hold of his hand.

"It'll be OK when you come back to school, I promise," he says. "Scott swears he won't hound you for an interview. We'll probably have to keep reminding him he said that, though. His new campaign is about anabolic steroid abuse. Khalid's in trouble for selling steroids to a few people at school. He's been suspended and stripped of head-boy status."

I nod. I feel sleepy – the medication I took before Euan came is kicking in.

Euan's eyes shine. "I've got something to tell you. It's supposed to be a secret, but Mr Williams asked me if I thought you'd like to have piano lessons at school."

I blink. "What?"

"There's a school fund which can pay for them."

"That would be amazing."

Euan nods. He knows how badly I'd like that. I snuggle up against him.

"Music room's empty without you," he murmurs.

"I miss it," I murmur back, closing my eyes.

"You'll be back there soon," he says.

I squeeze his hand lightly, and hear beautiful, swelling music in my head as I drift towards sleep. The piece we played together in the Baldinis' Dance School. Flute and piano together.

Five months have passed since I was discharged from hospital. At first I didn't want to go over everything, remember the little details, think about the betrayal. It was Amber who said I should write it down. To think like a journalist, in charge of my own story. It began with rereading the notes I'd already jotted down in my notebook, and continued with random paragraphs in a new one Alice gave me for my birthday. Snippets of dialogue that came back to me with piercing clarity. How it felt at school to be the person everyone thought was getting away with murder, and to be hated so deeply by Mara.

One morning, I decided to type up my notes, putting them in order. I became obsessed with writing and rewriting whenever I wasn't at school or seeing Euan. I saw connections I hadn't noticed at the time, good things which happened, as well as the mistakes which were made, and I realized it was finally time to forgive myself for what happened with Hannah.

For better or worse, it's my story.

And I'm still here to keep telling it.

# ACKNOWLEDGEMENTS

Thank you to everyone who helped with this book. Becky Bagnell, for being an excellent agent. I can't believe this is Book Five. Genevieve Herr, you helped me draw so much more out of this book and I loved working with you. Linas Alsenas, one conversation with you at the very start made all the difference. Liam Drane, for another perfect cover. Pete Matthews, for keeping me on the straight and narrow. Harriet Dunlea, for all the PR skills.

Huge thanks to Jon Howe for helping me with the gym scenes, Frances Quinn for guiding me through some areas of the law and Max B for answering police procedure queries. Any errors are my own.

Thank you to everyone who walked with me in 2020 and 2021, either literally or figuratively. I appreciate you all.

Big love to my girls and lockdown-housemates, Phoebe, Maia and Sophie.

To my colleagues at Teddington School, thank you for your support. Victoria Wilson, you are still missed!

To students who have found life tough recently, keep going with your projects and dreams. Better times are ahead.

# ALSO BY
# SUE WALLMAN

Lying About Last Summer

See How They Lie

Your Turn to Die

Dead Popular